LOYALTY, LOVE
& VERMOUTH

Advance Praise for *Loyalty, Love & Vermouth*

"Eric Peterson's debut novel is a heartwarming and charming tale of love, loss, community, and self-discovery featuring man's best friends of the two- and four-legged kind. A delightful read."—Michael Nava, Lambda Literary Award–winning author of *Lies With Man*

"Eric Peterson's endearing debut novel shows us how one man's streak of bad luck can blossom into a big, beautiful, and rollicking queer family. *Loyalty, Love & Vermouth* is the toe-tapping, feel-good book of the season."—Ann McMan, Lambda Literary Award–winning author of *The Big Tow*

Visit us at www.boldstrokesbooks.com

LOYALTY, LOVE & VERMOUTH

Deb, Enjoy! Happy reading

by

Eric Peterson

BOLD
STROKES
BOOKS

2021

Credits
Editors: Jerry L. Wheeler and Stacia Seaman
Production Design: Stacia Seaman
Cover Design by Tammy Seidick

Acknowledgments

Writing my first novel in my late forties wasn't as easy as it sounds, and it doesn't even sound easy. So it should be no surprise that I didn't do it alone. Therefore, there are many, many people to thank. In a very real way, this book wouldn't exist without each of them.

First to the people at Bold Strokes Books, who read my manuscript and liked it enough to welcome me into the family. Much gratitude is due to Radclyffe, Carsen Taite, Sandy Lowe, and everyone else who keeps the lights on and the presses running: I'm so grateful for you and the community of writers that you have created.

Next, to the readers who read my rough drafts (very rough, for some of you), and told me where you were invested, where you were confused, and where you were disappointed: you made the story much stronger, and my writing so much better. Big thanks to Randle Robinson Bitnar, Rebecca Fuller, Justin Godwin, Stephanie Jenkins, Catherine Paul, Michael Reed, and Jeb Stenhouse. Also, I'm indebted to the trio of editors (Elizabeth Andersen, Fay Jacobs, and Jerry Wheeler) who gently took the book apart and helped me put it back together again—thank you.

And finally, to my families, both of origin and of choice, thank you for locking arms and supporting me when times are tough and refilling my martini glass with love and laughter (and the merest spritz of vermouth) when times are easy and breezy. I love you Mom, Dad, Amena, Bonnie, Brendan, Christian, Fay, John F., John J., Justin, Kyle, Matt G., Matt H., Nicole, Patrick, and Thom, so very much. This book wouldn't exist without you—because without you, there would have been no reason to write it.

This book is dedicated to my family of choice
(the humans and the canines), and especially to
the memory of Bobby T Boaz

CHAPTER ONE

Thursday, 5:52 p.m.

It had already been a bitch of a day. It was one of those days at work where nothing went spectacularly wrong, but nothing went particularly right, either. I was just spinning my wheels with this job, and perhaps it was time to get my résumé out there again. On the other hand, I should have felt lucky to be employed. As the nice lady on National Public Radio informed me, most of Washington had been out of work for nearly a month in the longest government shutdown in our history. Many of my friends hadn't seen a paycheck since before Christmas.

Neither the news nor the cold January mist were doing much to lift my spirits. After increasing the frequency of my windshield wipers, I pushed a button on my steering wheel and intoned, "Play. Broadway. Radio." Just like that, the nice NPR lady was silenced and replaced by Angela Lansbury and Bea Arthur. They sang a song about loyalty, love, and bosom buddies. Even on the grayest of days, I remembered, there was friendship and family. And, of course, show tunes.

Later, as I turned into my driveway, it occurred to me if Washington was going to be this cold, it should at least snow. Any city that wants to freeze my ass off should have the decency to put on a pretty dress. But instead, the temperature hovered slightly above freezing, and the drizzle was quickly becoming rain. Mamie wasn't going to want to walk around in this, and frankly I agreed with her. I watched the windshield wipers perform one last high kick, removed the keys from my ignition, and calculated the time it would take to exit the car, ascend the staircase to the back door, and enter my home. It wasn't long enough to require an umbrella, so off I went.

The holidays were over, but winter would linger for a long while. It was already dark outside this time of night. The house was quiet when I entered, which wasn't a big surprise. The house was usually quiet and dark—at least in January. I did notice a slight chill. Why the hell was it so cold in here?

The counter seemed bigger somehow. And the kitchen window—also bigger. Had I tidied up and forgotten I'd created more counter space? I'll confess it took me a moment to understand the television was not there. Old bills, paid but not yet thrown away, the novel recently praised by *The New York Times* I had purchased in a fit of pretentiousness but, let's be honest, I would never finish—those were still there. But the flat screen TV was gone, the one partly blocking the kitchen window, where I'd watch the news with my morning coffee and cereal. It was just gone. Looking back, there was one obvious conclusion to draw when a television disappears, but I was still moments away from reaching it.

Oh, shit. I've been robbed.

When the situation sank in, I went upstairs past my other, bigger television. It was still there, too big to carry around without being noticed. What else did they take? On the way to my bedroom, I passed my office. Laptop, gone. Tablet, gone.

And then I saw the crate. Mamie stayed in her crate whenever I left the house. I read from multiple sources that dogs who are crated from birth learn to love their crates. While they might seem like prisons to us, dogs who are used to them think of them as cozy, safe enclaves, far less scary than a big, empty, humanless house. Or at least this was the bullshit I said to myself every morning before I crated her, because I always felt a little guilty about it.

Now the crate stood on its side. And empty. It wasn't supposed to be empty. There was supposed to be a dog inside, wagging her tail and happy to see me. But she wasn't there.

I dropped to my knees, hoping to find a scared little dog under the bed. There was only empty space and a stray ball of lint, like an urban tumbleweed. I told myself not to panic, but it wasn't working. I felt my pulse pounding in my temples. I raced downstairs and checked under the couch, behind the bathroom door, scouring every corner. Eventually, I found myself in the basement, hoping Mamie—sweet, resilient, brave little Mamie—would have found a way to hide behind the box of vinyl records I refused to throw out, that she had escaped from whoever had stolen my television and computer and surely would have no need for a little dog, *my* dog. I didn't find her there, either.

And now I wasn't merely cold. It was freezing down there. I could see my breath. I looked at the door leading to the driveway out back. The thin pane of glass closest to the doorknob was broken. The door was closed but unlocked. The burglars had not bothered to lock up on their way out, and why should they?

Hoping Mamie had somehow escaped both the burglars and the house, I went to the front door to see if her leash was still there. If the burglars wanted to take a dog, I figured they would have needed a leash. If the leash was there, perhaps Mamie had escaped. Maybe she was somewhere in the neighborhood, lost but recoverable.

No leash, either.

I dialed 9-1-1, reporting a burglary.

"Are they still in your house?" asked the woman who picked up.

"No," I said. I hadn't even considered the possibility when I had charged up the staircase moments ago.

"Your name?"

"Vernon."

"Last name?"

"That is my last name. Sorry, um…Charlie Vernon. I mean—Charles."

"Charles Vernon," she repeated.

"Correct."

"What's the address?" I directed them to my little rowhome in the northeast quadrant of the city, east of Capitol Hill.

"And just to clarify," she said, "no one is in any physical danger."

"They took my dog," I said.

"Excuse me?"

"My dog. She's been taken. Kidnapped," I replied, trying to impress upon this person that someone *was* in physical danger, actually. Someone very important was gone, who knows where, hopefully still alive, very much in physical danger. So please and thank you, hurry the fuck up.

"Thirty to forty minutes," was the answer. And perhaps I should use the time to have a look around the house to see what else might have been taken.

"Thank you very much." I hung up the phone, immediately regretting my good manners.

I did not take the extra thirty to forty minutes to look around the house. Instead, I immediately called Jean and Irene, the rhyming lesbians.

"I've been robbed," I said, my voice remarkably clear and steady.

"Oh, shit," said Irene. "What's missing?"

"Mamie," I said. "They took Mamie."

"Oh, honey…" As I fought to utter another phrase, she repeated herself again, and again. "Oh, honey."

I should have been crying, but I wasn't. Even when I want to cry, I usually can't. I cry easily during movies and plays, but real life doesn't seem to activate my tear ducts in the same way. Like most little boys in America, I grew up stifling my tears, but I thought I'd left that bullshit behind when I became an adult, especially after telling the whole world I was gay. And I get it. A good cry can be very cathartic, and healthy, blah blah blah, but I probably hadn't cried real tears in twenty years.

I told Irene everything I knew, which wasn't much. She relayed the news to Jean. They lived three hours away, and they couldn't do much to help, but that wasn't why I had called. I needed to tell someone what had happened so the situation would be real. I needed to speak with someone who didn't know what to say so I could realize there was nothing *to* say. This was bad, and I couldn't pretend otherwise.

"We'll be there tomorrow," Irene said. "As soon as it's light out, we'll hit the road."

"No, you don't have to do that; that isn't why I'm—"

"Jean is insisting. We'll be there around ten. You hold tight. We're going to get her back from these assholes."

And I believed her. I believed her because the alternative was unacceptable, and because I knew better than to argue with an angry lesbian in her sixties.

After hanging up, I moved to my dining room table, pulled a chair out, and sat. I don't ever sit at the dining room table. I'm not even sure why I have a dining room. I don't cook, and I rarely entertain. I usually eat out of a paper box from the Chinese delivery place, upstairs in front of the television with Mamie curled up by my side—or on the floor if it's summer. I looked at a week's worth of mail dumped on the dining room table. I'd get to it eventually. Obviously not today.

Who would have wanted to steal my dog?

Could it have been Freddie? No, surely not. Except maybe? All I knew for sure was this felt personal somehow, and Freddie was one of the few people I could conjure who hated me enough to do something like this.

I shivered as the chilly basement air drifted upstairs, and I wondered what was taking the police so long.

I'm not a spiritual person. I generally call myself an atheist because it's a word people understand, and most religious people want to change the subject as soon as it passes my lips, which suits me. But almost every atheist I've ever met is agnostic at heart. We'll believe whatever you want, just give us some proof. And sometimes, even without evidence, it's tempting to send a few wishes up to whoever might be listening, to hedge your bets in case you're wrong. So, I considered a silent prayer for Mamie's return, but I couldn't carry it off. It felt like I was talking to myself. My mother always said I'd start believing in God when I needed God again, but I could tell he wasn't there. Still, I was desperate enough to defy objective reality, and just in case telepathy was real, I spent the next few minutes trying to establish a mental connection with my little yellow dog. I didn't expect a response, of course, but I told her to be brave. I told her I'd be looking for her. I told her I loved her.

Then I called Tucker and Jack.

A familiar Tennessee accent answered. "Hey, Charlie. What's kickin'?"

A few seconds went by before I remembered it's customary to respond when someone answers your call. "Tucker. Hi."

"Hey, pardner, is somethin' wrong? You okay?"

"No."

Tucker Pickett grew up in a tiny town in Tennessee called Sewanee—and according to him was one of the few who ever left, although his accent would never leave home. He lived with his husband Jack, not far away, in a neighborhood called Swampoodle, which Tucker thought was adorable but Jack thought was dumb. Jack often said if he'd known he would be living in a place called Swampoodle, he would never have agreed to buy the house.

"Jack! Jack, get down here, now." Having been filled in on the situation, and all the details I could provide, Tucker was now in full Southern church lady panic mode. "We'll be right there, honey."

"Take your time," I said as calmly as I could.

"Jack! Call Claude, grab Russ, and tell him we're all comin' over!"

"The police aren't even here yet."

"Charlie, honey, pour yourself a stiff drink, and we'll be there before you're ready for seconds."

"Really, just drive safe, okay?"

"I will, sugar. You sit tight."

"Bye."

And then I was alone again, with the quiet and chill overwhelming me. I considered that stiff drink, but decided to have my wits about me when the cops arrived. I sat in silence for I don't remember how long.

I often welcomed the quiet at the end of a long day, but now I hated it. I thought about turning on some music but wasn't sure how to craft the appropriate soundtrack for a burglary and dognapping. Looking back, I suppose the Sarah McLachlan tune that always plays when the sad menagerie of condemned kittens and puppies stare into a camera, imploring us to save them from certain death, was an obvious choice. But no matter. I didn't even hear a halting bus or a distant siren from the street. I usually love the sirens, even though they mean someone is either in danger, dead, or being rushed to a hospital. They are wonderful to me because, if the siren got close enough, Mamie would sometimes howl along, her little mouth creating a perfect "O," her nose pointed ninety degrees to the ceiling. I loved that.

Goddammit, where was she? My head pounded, and I felt like I'd swallowed a brick.

This was wrong in every way, so wrong it didn't feel real. I have a fairly morbid imagination and a unique ability to catastrophize any scenario, but I'd never even considered someone entering my home and taking Mamie away. This wasn't merely criminal. It felt evil. This wasn't part of the deal.

After Freddie left—or rather, cheated on me, stomped all over my heart, humiliated me, and *then* abandoned us both—Mamie offered me a deal. And the deal was we would soldier on together, the two of us, at least for a while. I would provide her with food and walks and belly rubs on demand, and she would reciprocate by always being happy to see me, always being a little sad when I left, and most importantly always being, just...there, a source of love and dependence and joy without any of the complications that come with romantic entanglements. After Freddie left, she wasn't a poor substitute for human beings; she had been elevated to a station far above them. The very best people, I decided, were dogs.

I needed to pee. My brain was a tangle, and my heart had never hurt so much in my life, but my bladder was fully operational. I had two toilets in the house. One was in the basement, next to the door with the broken window. I never used the basement toilet, and it probably hadn't been cleaned in months. The light in the basement was dim, and it was freezing cold down there. To get to the one upstairs, the clean one in a heated room, I'd have to pass by Mamie's upturned crate. I opted for the basement.

After relieving myself and zipping my pants, I regarded myself in the mirror. I was forty-three years old. My eyes were a pretty shade of blue, but they were too close together—and typically hidden behind a pair of eyeglasses because I told myself they made my face look thinner, but it was really because contact lenses are a pain in the ass, and I don't want anyone putting lasers in my eyeballs. My thick, brown hair was getting grayer by the day, although Irene assured me it looked very distinguished. I noticed one large black hair protruding from one of my nostrils. Charming. My face had always been round, even before putting on an extra ten pounds after Freddie left, so I didn't have any obvious wrinkles. If they appeared, Irene would no doubt proclaim them distinguished as well. I didn't feel very distinguished.

Suddenly, I heard a loud banging on the door upstairs. This would have been Mamie's cue to bark her head off until she was good and ready to stop. Though she was a small animal, she had the deep, gruff bark of an animal twice her size, which is a virtuous trait in an urban canine. Now there was no barking, just a moment of too-quiet calm before more loud banging.

I ran upstairs and opened the door. Two police officers, uniformed for a cold winter evening, greeted me.

"Are you Charles Vernon?" the female cop asked.

I nodded a yes. "Come on in."

And the interview began right away. "When did you arrive home?"

"Around six o'clock."

"When did you notice things were missing?"

"Almost immediately."

The male cop looked around the room. "Do you know where they entered?"

"The basement door. The glass is broken."

"Show us?"

And we headed downstairs, where the female cop examined

the brass doorknob. "We can send someone over to dust for prints tomorrow," she said. "So, if you could not touch that in the meantime."

I nodded.

"Do you know what time they were here?"

I did not.

"You have a security system. Was it on?"

"No," I said. "I forgot." I had been running late that morning, and it had slipped my mind and oh fuck, this is all my fault.

"You can look it up, though," the officer offered. "You have an app on your phone?"

"Yes."

"The times should be there even if the system wasn't on. Here, let me show you."

I opened the app and handed the cop my phone. He poked around for a moment.

"Looks like between 2:47 and 3:05 this afternoon."

The female cop wrote the times in her notebook. "Okay, great."

Four hours. Oh my God, she'd been gone for four hours.

She continued to ask me questions while he investigated the nooks and crannies of my basement. "What did they take?"

"My dog."

"Anything else?"

"She's a cockapoo. That's a mix between cocker spaniel and poodle—"

"Was anything else taken?"

"Her name is Mamie. She weighs twenty pounds, she's microchipped—"

"Anything *besides* the dog?"

"Um. I mean, the television. And a laptop, and a tablet."

"Got a picture? Of the dog?"

My phone was still in my hand, and an assortment of photos was quickly at the ready. I showed them to her. And to her credit, she gave me a little smile.

"Cute."

"Yeah, um…thanks."

She continued taking notes. "Female?"

"Yes," I answered. "Mamie, her name is Mamie. She's almost three years old—"

"And how much is the dog worth?"

Everything, I wanted to say, she's worth everything. "We paid twelve hundred dollars. For the dog."

"We?"

"Well, my ex," I said. "We're not together now. It's just me here. With the dog."

"How much for the TV?"

I wanted to say I didn't give a shit about the goddamn television, you pair of soulless fucking creeps, but I took a deep breath instead. These two were only doing their jobs. And they were helping me. "I don't remember. Seven hundred maybe?"

And on it went until it was over. "A lieutenant should be calling you tomorrow," she said, verifying my number.

As they were about to leave, I offered a glass of water. They politely refused, and I showed them out. Instinctively I positioned myself in such a way to prevent a little dog from running toward the open door, but of course this was not presently necessary.

As I said my good-byes, I looked across the street, where Tucker and Jack had managed to squeeze their giant SUV in between two unsuspecting little coupes. Tucker barely looked both ways before leaping from his driver's seat and darting in my direction while Jack, on the passenger side, struggled to affix a leash to Russell.

Tucker drew me close. "Oh, sugar. C'mere, give me a hug."

I obeyed because that's what you do when a distraught Tucker Pickett gives you an order, and because he sounded like *he* needed a hug. I was about to let go before I remembered I was the one needing the hug, but by then it was too late to ask for another.

"Russell, hold still!" Jack hollered, finally getting the leash on Russell's collar. Russell bounded out of the car and would have bolted across the street had Jack not been prepared for this very move, steadying his whole body to force Russell to heel.

"That boy is stronger'n two fingers of brown liquor. We had

no idea when we brought him home," Tucker said, tut-tutting and shaking his head.

Once Russell was inside the gate, Jack set him free, and into the house he ran, directly up the stairs looking for Mamie. Of all the dogs in our little makeshift family, Mamie was Russell's favorite, and he was hers. I could hear him upstairs, trotting through the office into my bedroom, where he would find only the upended crate. Then he ran back around to the room in front where I sat and watched television most nights, and finally back to the top of the stairs, where he stood waiting for an explanation.

"She's not here," I told him. Russell cocked his head, refusing my answer and waiting for another.

Tucker turned to Jack. Jack looked at me. I took them both in. I had nothing else to say. *She's not here.*

"C'mon, Russ," beckoned Jack, and the dog came lumbering down the stairs.

Russell was a hound of indeterminate breed, with a brindle coat except for a spot of bright white in front between the elbows. We didn't know how old Russell was. He couldn't have been more than six, probably closer to three and a half, a little older than Mamie. He was a handsome beast, but now looked doleful and sad. Or was I simply projecting my emotions on to the nearest animal, which I was frequently wont to do.

"You doing okay?" Jack asked.

No, I wanted to say, I'm not doing okay. Jack was probably the best-looking man I knew, with his square jaw and perfect, tousled hair and more abdominal muscles than I thought existed in the human species. And he wasn't stupid. He was a scientist of some sort who spent his days surrounded by beakers and test tubes. In the realm of emotional intelligence, however, he was often lacking. But I forgave him as I always did—and was struck, once again, by how unreasonably handsome he was. I must have looked like hell, and here was this Greek god standing around my kitchen, looking as if he'd just stepped out of a magazine, asking if I was doing okay. I thought it was extremely impolite.

"Thanks," I said. I could have responded with something more authentic, I suppose. But I didn't feel like it.

"Go upstairs and pack a bag," Tucker said. "You're not staying here tonight."

"I have to. The cops will be calling, and—"

"And you don't have a landline anyway. You'll take your phone with you. Go."

"Goddamn, it's cold in here," Jack observed. "Did they break a window or something?"

"Basement door."

"Okay," he said. "If I were a heavy-duty trash bag and a roll of duct tape, where would I be?"

"Under the sink," I said. "And the duct tape is in the cabinet by the basement door. I'll go with you—"

"I've got it. You go pack, and we'll be all set by the time you're ready to go."

"No, really, I—"

"You know better than to argue with Tucker," said Jack. "Just look at him."

I looked. Tucker's face was nearly as red as his Irish-on-his-mother's-side hair. His lips were pursed, and his hands were balled into little fists, like he was Popeye after swallowing a can of spinach. Jack was right. And Tucker was right. I didn't want to spend the night in this house without Mamie.

"Don't touch the doorknob," I said. "They might dust it for prints."

Ten minutes later, bag packed and basement window at least covered, I found myself in the back seat of Tucker and Jack's SUV. I sat next to Russell, who was still confused by Mamie's absence. Tucker drove, and Jack sat in the passenger seat, scrolling through something on his phone.

Occasionally, Tucker would try to make conversation, asking me what the police had said or generally wondering what would motivate someone to steal a dog. I appreciated the sentiment, but it wasn't helping me, practically or emotionally—so I quietly focused most of my attention on Russell, who comforted me by being too genuinely upset to worry about comforting me. Perhaps I was projecting? *OH MY GOD OF COURSE I WAS PROJECTING* but I didn't care because it made me feel better. Russell seemed to be the only one in the car who knew exactly what to say by saying nothing at all.

CHAPTER TWO

I met Freddie Babcock four and a half years earlier, and I figured he was the love of my life.

I'd joined the Gay Men's Chorus of Washington that year because all my friends were straight people. Nice people, but it was time to branch out, and I might even meet somebody worth dating. So, I auditioned and made it in even though my voice shook a little.

New Member Orientation happened on a late summer afternoon, upstairs at a gay bar the chorus rented for the occasion. I arrived early, because I was eager, slightly nervous, didn't want to walk in late, and was, okay, I admit it, irrationally nervous.

I had been to Pansy's before, but only late at night when it was so crowded it took fifteen minutes to travel the thirty steps from the bar to the patio door. Now, I was surprised how cavernous it was, how cheap and tacky the floors looked, and how small the stage was without a big drag queen on it. One could, however, still smell the Axe body spray from the night before. Don't judge. It's tough to be a young gay paying DC rents with an entry-level job.

Freddie was the only person there. He was taller than me, dressed in a bright pink polo shirt, which he filled out magnificently, and a pair of seersucker shorts, which displayed two very skinny legs. Apart from the legs, I thought he looked a bit like Superman—black hair with a hint of curl, square jaw, icy blue eyes, even the dimple. And so I behaved the way I always do when confronted with perfect specimens of male beauty. I became my five-year-old self, refusing to make eye contact, so—in the unlikely event he might meet my gaze—the blood rushing to my cheeks wouldn't cause my head to spontaneously combust.

"You here for GMCW?" he asked.

I nodded.

"Name?"

"Charlie Vernon," I replied, extending a hand.

Freddie chuckled, opened his arms, and said, "We hug a lot in the chorus. Welcome." He would tell me later he didn't hug new members as a rule, but he thought I was kind of cute. "I recognize the name," he said, still in my embrace. "Gary thought you gave a wonderful audition." *That* was a lie, but I appreciated it.

"I didn't catch your name," I stammered when he finally let me go.

"Oh. Sorry. I'm Freddie Babcock, president of the chorus."

As I remember this day, there's always a fleeting freeze frame at this moment, and I can hear Barbra Streisand as Fanny Brice belting "Freddie Babcock! Freddie Babcock!" in appreciation of his form and manner. Then again, Fanny was always a sucker for a pretty face.

"Nice to meet you, Freddie, um…how early am I?"

"About ninety minutes?"

I made my awkward face, and we both laughed as I backed away. "Let me get out of your hair." Your luscious, curly, black-as-night hair.

"No, it's okay. The bar opens soon. You're more than welcome to—"

But I was too embarrassed to stay. "You probably have to set up or something, right?"

"Yeah, but you don't have to go. Feel free to hang out, or—"

"No. There's a coffee place across the street, where I can study my music or something."

"You sure?"

"Yeah, yeah. Positive. I don't want to be in the way."

On my way down the stairs, it occurred to me this was why I didn't have many gay friends. Gay people, especially handsome ones, scare me to death. Hopefully, this chorus would contain lots of ugly people I could be friends with. Otherwise, I had no hope.

When I returned to the bar, I was only ten minutes early, and there were a lot more people there, including a freckle-faced redhead holding a clipboard, greeting people.

"GMCW?" he asked.

I nodded.

"Name?"

"Charlie Vernon."

"Nice to meet you, Charlie. I'm Tucker Pickett, vice president of membership. Welcome."

"Thanks," I said, both relieved and disappointed that Superman in a hot pink polo was, for the time being, nowhere to be found.

"Your chorus buddy is…oh, fiddlesticks."

"Excuse me?"

"Oh, I'm sorry. Roger isn't here yet. They were all supposed to be here early. Dammit, there are folks behind you too. Will you be all right on your own for a bit?"

I smiled. "I'm a Navy brat. I'm used to being the new kid in school."

"You're sweet," he said, pointing to a lone gentleman leaning against one end of the enormous bar, scrolling through his phone. "That's my fiancée, Jack. Tell him I said to buy you a drink. Roger should be here soon."

I took one look at Jack, whose tight T-shirt revealed every abdominal muscle an adult male could possibly acquire, and I knew I'd *not* be casually sauntering up to him and requesting a drink. Instead, I made my way to the other end of the bar, started a tab in exchange for a plastic cup of pinot grigio, and just observed. As people began to fill the place, it felt less like a cavern and more like a sardine can. It still smelled like Axe.

"You're back," said a soft voice in my ear.

"I'm back." I smiled, turning to face him. What Freddie Babcock didn't know was I never made it to that coffee shop. I opted instead for a wine bar, and this was now my fourth glass of fermented grape juice in ninety minutes. But hey, what Freddie didn't know wouldn't hurt him.

"Don't you have a buddy?"

"I've been stood up. Like Lucille Bremer in *Meet Me in St. Louis*. They're going to make me go to the Christmas Ball with my brother."

His spacious, masculine, gorgeous forehead furrowed in confusion. "I've never seen it," he said, sitting on the empty barstool next to mine.

"I'm afraid I'll need to confiscate your gay card immediately."

"You'll have to wrestle me for it," he said, leaning in. "Listen, I have to go up there and give a little speech in a minute. And if you don't have a buddy when I get back, maybe I can fill in."

I might have had a seductive, witty retort at the ready, but I made the mistake of looking directly at him, powerless to do anything but stare into his magnificent blue eyes for five awkward seconds.

"Y-you're very polite," I finally said. It made him smile. He had perfect teeth. Goddammit.

"I try."

And with that, he was gone...for the moment.

Roger Lindsey, who was meant to be my "chorus buddy," never did show up, and for years afterward, I didn't know whether I should have thanked him or slashed his tires. For his part, Freddie played the role beautifully: introducing me around, fetching my fifth serving of wine, placing his hand on the small of my back whenever we moved through a particularly congested area, and then letting it linger there a little too long when crowd management was no longer an issue.

The next night, at our first Sunday rehearsal, Freddie—also in the second tenor section—sat next to me and complimented my singing voice. The next week, at our second rehearsal, he invited me for a drink afterward where he asked me about my life and revealed little about his own. The next week, after our third rehearsal, he kissed me for the first time and held my hand as he walked me to my car.

The following Friday evening, I cooked dinner for the two of us at my place, and Freddie spent the night. It had been a while since my bedroom had seen any action at all, much less an overnight visitor. The sex was fantastic and repetitive, but what I remember most was waking up the next morning. He was already awake, staring at me lovingly, smiling. We didn't trade I-love-yous at that moment, but we didn't have to. I was only too aware I was falling for Freddie, and I chose to believe his big, goofy, oblivious smile meant he felt the same.

The following day, I attended Tucker and Jack's wedding as Freddie's plus-one. When Tucker visited our table during the reception, Freddie introduced me as his boyfriend. Tucker seemed surprised, but I wasn't. Delighted, naturally, but not surprised.

A dream had never come true with so little effort. Had I been a little more skeptical, I might have given this matter more thought, but I was too busy enjoying my happily ever after to worry about how easily it had been acquired. This is how it happens, I thought. You try, and try, and just when you're about to give up, he appears. The One. I could practically hear an orchestra playing when he said that word: boyfriend. Moments later, I realized I actually *was* hearing an orchestra, or at least a string quartet, hired by Tucker and Jack for their swanky reception.

As we spent more time together, I learned a little more about Freddie. He was raised on the outskirts of Chicago by a single mom and a revolving door of her boyfriends, each one becoming an instant father figure to him until they reliably and predictably disappeared. His mom used a lot of drugs, he said, but she was better now. He came out early and was sneaking into gay bars in the city by the time he was sixteen. His first boyfriend was a college professor for whom even the undergraduate co-eds were a little too old, and Freddie had three other "boyfriends" before his seventeenth birthday, all of them in their thirties.

With too much freedom and not much direction, his grades

were good enough for a high school diploma but bad enough to keep him from applying to college, not that he would have known how to pay for it. For years, his lack of a degree embarrassed him, and he was thinking about going back to school at some point.

In response, I tried to strike a balance between encouraging his ambition and letting him know I thought he was just swell, with or without a degree. He'd dated lots of people, he said, but no one all that seriously until his last partner, a man named Arthur.

To hear Freddie tell it, the first two years were wonderful, before Arthur began experiencing bouts of severe depression. Freddie didn't know how to help and often took the dark moods personally, even as he was being assured he was not to blame. When Arthur proposed, Freddie thought this was finally something he could do to make them both happy again, but *quelle surprise*, it didn't work. Arthur's depression still came and went without warning, but he wouldn't seek treatment. Freddie began to feel hopeless. A week before the wedding was to take place, Freddie called it off and moved out. It was a minor scandal among his friends in GMCW, he said, and he wanted me to know about it before I heard the gossip.

"You did the right thing," I told him.

"I don't know about that, but it was the only thing I could do."

"You could have gone through with it, which would have been bad for everyone involved. No, you did the brave thing."

"Thanks." He kissed me, and when we parted, I could see his eyes glistening. He was embarrassed and tried to wipe the tears away, but I caught his hand in mine. I fixed my eyes on his until he couldn't look away. I kissed him again. He kissed me back.

By January, we decided Freddie should request a cancellation of his lease and move in with me even though it would cost him two months' rent. Freddie was a bit gun-shy when it came to weddings, but I assured him I was in no rush to march down the aisle. I convinced him cohabitation was a financial decision more than a romantic one. Even though we'd known each other less than six months, we rarely spent a night apart. It made no logical sense for him to throw his money away on rent. Had he refused, I might have cried real tears. Luckily, or not, he didn't.

In mid-February, a single snowflake touched the pavement outside the Office of Management and Budget, which predictably led to every workplace in Washington being closed the next day. It was as if the universe conspired to make our first Valentine's Day a true holiday. On the morning of the fourteenth, a Wednesday, Freddie woke me up by placing a freshly brewed mug of coffee beneath my nose. I smiled as I quickly drifted into consciousness and opened my eyes a moment later. There Freddie stood, holding two steaming coffees, wearing nothing but a smile.

The year before, I had spent Valentine's Day by myself, with a bottle of Chianti and a private screening of an old movie or three. This Valentine's Day, I was Lois Lane, and Superman was naked in bed beside me in our very own secluded ice fortress.

In the spring, the Gay Men's Chorus of Washington staged an all-male production of *Gypsy*. It was obvious from the outset that Claude Williams would play the coveted role of Papa Rose as he was a founding member of GMCW and a warm, bigger-than-life presence onstage.

I was content to sing along with the rest of the chorus, but Freddie encouraged me to audition for a more substantial part. He was cast as Tulsa and had a lovely romantic ballad in Act One. I won the role of Mr. Mazeppa, a cranky old stripper who wore the breastplate and plumed helmet of a Roman centurion, and who played the trumpet—badly. I sang a comic song in the middle of Act Two with two other boys who wore a lot less clothing than I did. Jack played Electra with twinkling Christmas lights adorning his nearly naked body, while a young man named Leonardo García Dorsett played Tessie Tura, who wore butterfly wings and lots of see-through gauze. Leonardo was Lee to his close friends, and so far it seemed like pretty much everyone was his close friend.

Our part of the show was silly and fun, but initially I was disappointed Freddie and I hardly ever rehearsed at the same time. I had been used to him being my guide as I mixed and mingled with my two hundred new best friends. Soon, however, I began to appreciate that doing this show with him but also away from him gave me a chance to create some friendships where I could simply be Charlie, as opposed to Freddie's boyfriend Charlie. And for the most part, it was working. Nearly everyone I met was warm, friendly, and encouraging, with only a few notable exceptions. When I finally met Roger Lindsey, the man who was meant to be my chorus buddy at new member orientation, he was noticeably frosty.

Jack told me not to worry about it. "He's jealous," he said. "But you're doing great, and everyone who matters says so."

Normally, that kind of thing would have gnawed at me, but I was having too much fun to notice. I grew especially fond of Lee, who was quickly becoming the little sister I never had. He was young, he was fabulous, and his wit was razor-sharp. His hazel eyes were offset by copper brown skin, and he wore his dark curls in a perpetual mop. He thought he was too skinny, but I envied both his zero percent body fat and the way his wish for a different kind of body in no way dimmed his confidence, sass, or *joie de vivre*. About three weeks into rehearsals for *Gypsy*, Lee gave me a little poke on the shoulder.

"My husband thinks you're really great, by the way."

"Really?" I said. "Wait—who's your husband?"

At that, Lee pointed across the room to Claude Williams, who was in deep conversation about the nuances of Papa Rose's inner dialogue with our director. "El gordo, con el gran ego."

"Papa Rose is your husband? I had no idea."

"Don't look so shocked," he said. But I was shocked, a little. Lee was probably ten years younger than I was, and if I had to guess, Claude probably had twenty years on me. Thirty pounds as well. Claude was the last person I'd have expected Lee to be married to, and I hoped Lee was enjoying the surprise I was clearly terrible at hiding.

"He wants to invite you over for dinner. And he wants to know if you're single." I gave my eyebrow a cynical arch. "Oh, nothing like that. We're super boring and monogamous. But Claude likes to play matchmaker. Él piensa que eres lindo."

"I'm actually not single, but tell Claude I said thanks anyway."

"You can still come to dinner. And bring your guy. Is he cute?"

"I think so." I must have immediately blushed.

"Ooooh, girl, he must be cute. Look at you! And hung, am I right?"

"I have no complaints."

"Well, I want to meet him. You're coming over sometime this week, for sure."

"You probably already know him. Freddie? Babcock?"

And Lee's face fell. Suddenly, something very interesting about his ballet shoes demanded his immediate attention. "Oh. Oh, yeah. I know him."

"We moved in together a few months ago." I could feel my shoulders tense up a bit.

"Claude and I were a little closer to Arthur."

Oh shit, they knew Arthur. Well, what did I expect? I was new here, and almost everyone but me probably knew Arthur.

"Yeah. He told me all about that. That was an unfortunate situation."

"Okay! Well, you know what? You should come to dinner. Dios mío, I'm such a bitch. And you should bring Freddie with you." I believe Lee was trying to defuse the awkwardness of the moment, but he was only making it more uncomfortable. "I don't know him that well. It's just that Claude—it doesn't matter. Shut up, Lee, shut up, shut up. You like him, we like you, we should make you some food, and you should eat it. Okay?"

The difference between Lee being free and easy and Lee pretending to be free and easy was palpable. It never occurred to me to doubt Freddie's version of events; after all, he was my Superman, and I was his intrepid girl reporter. But it was clear this intrepid girl reporter had failed to interview multiple sources. Maybe Freddie did the right thing leaving Arthur, but Arthur could also have had a point of view.

My silence worried Lee. "Okay?"

"Okay, that sounds nice."

Lee turned to Jack who, unsurprisingly, was looking at his phone, and gave him a small poke. "You too."

"Huh?" Jack looked up. "Me too what?"

"Tell Tucker to come to dinner at our place next Friday. Bring the wine I like."

"I'll ask," Jack said, turning back to his phone.

"We'll see," Lee said to me, as Jack had already floated back into the ether.

❖

Either Jack remembered or Lee called Tucker himself and arranged everything, because the next Friday Lee and Claude hosted the four of us for dinner in their enormous home in Silver Spring, Maryland, just outside the city. It featured a kitchen straight out of *Architectural Digest*, all granite countertops and stainless steel, and a palatial dining room complete with a chandelier and high-backed chairs.

"You realize," Freddie whispered to me as we first walked inside, "that I shall expect to be kept in a home at least twice this size by the time you're Claude's age."

"Then I suppose you'd better find yourself a rich lawyer on K Street," I whispered back.

As we entered the formal living room, we were assaulted by the furious yapping of two minuscule Maltese. They were "more accessories than animals," Claude would say, but Lee loved them dearly and, in truth, so did Claude. The first was born with some sort of vitamin deficiency, and during her first three months she had little capsules ground into her food. Claude named her Peggy Lee and would cradle her in bed singing "Is That All There Is?" until she fell asleep in his arms.

The second puppy came six months later, and unlike Peggy Lee, who sometimes needed to be fed by hand to ensure she'd eat, would clean her bowl twice a day and then attempt to eat Peggy's food while no one was looking. Claude named her Mama Cass, which Lee thought was adorable until he searched for Mama Cass on the internet and realized Claude's joke. But by then, it was too late. She was already answering to the name and all its variations: Cass, Mama, Cassie, Mamita Casita.

The evening began with a round of cocktails, followed by a second round of cocktails, a pre-dinner glass of wine, wine with dinner, and then a dessert wine Claude insisted on. It was an intoxicating evening in every sense.

To top it all off, we adjourned to the back patio where we shared a joint under the stars. Well, all of us except for Tucker, who is a government contractor with a top secret clearance, so he stayed indoors with Peggy Lee and Mama Cass while we sat under the stars getting stoned.

By the time we moseyed back inside on a literal and figurative cloud, Tucker was asleep on the couch, with Mama Cass curled in the crook of his arm and Peggy Lee keeping watch on the armrest above Tucker's head.

"C'mon, Goody Two Shoes," Jack said as he kicked the couch, waking both Tucker and Cass, who growled her disapproval. "It's time to drive me home."

As we were both too full of substances to drive, Freddie and I spent the night in one of Lee and Claude's many spare rooms. By the time I ambled downstairs the next morning, wearing my clothes from the night before, Lee was in the kitchen, slicing bagels and placing them in a bowl next to generous piles of lox and cream cheese. "Buenos días."

"Oh my God. This is amazing. How are you so awake right now?"

"A good hostess always pours twice as much as she consumes."

"You are a wonderful hostess," I said, already reaching for the coffeepot.

"Yeah, about that," Lee said, more quietly, as he handed me a handmade ceramic mug. "I owe you an apology."

"I'm sure you don't, but I'm curious, so go ahead."

"I feel really bad about how I acted last week. About Freddie."

"What? Oh, don't worry about th—"

"No, no. People give me shit all the time about Claude, like he's some kind of sugar daddy and I'm, I don't know, a gold digger, I guess. I should know better. I was way out of line. Besides which, Freddie's great. We really like him."

"Me too."

"Cream and sugar by the fridge," Lee said, going to the door. "*El Gordo* insists on being served his first cup of coffee in bed every morning. It makes me feel like the goddamn maid."

"But secretly you love it? Be honest."

"I don't. Love stinks like un pez muerto, but what's the alternative?"

I laughed as he dramatically wheeled around and marched toward his bedroom. "*Claude,*" he bellowed, and Peggy Lee started to yip-yip-yip furiously in response.

❖

And from then on, the six of us became a little family: Freddie, me, Claude, Lee, Jack, and Tucker. And even though Lee was the youngest, he quickly became the matriarch of our little clan, arranging the outings, planning Thanksgivings, remembering everyone's birthday, and eventually pulling together theater trips to New York or little vacations to the beach.

Freddie popped the question on one of those beach trips.

We were walking along the boardwalk in Rehoboth Beach, a small seaside resort in southern Delaware. Lee and Claude walked in front of us, pushing Peggy Lee and Mama Cass in a covered stroller, receiving oohs and aahs from every little girl who walked by. Tucker and Jack strolled behind us, probably fighting about something—Jack had been sullen the whole weekend if I recall.

Meanwhile, Freddie and I were walking hand in hand, covered in greasy sunblock, listening to the sounds of waves caressing the beach and kids playing in the surf when suddenly he turned to me and casually made his proposal.

"What if we got ourselves a dog?"

CHAPTER THREE

Thursday, 10:44 p.m.

It was my fourth martini, so clear it looked a liquid diamond. Maybe my fifth. You could always count on Claude to pour the good stuff even if your guest of honor had been robbed, his precious dog violently stolen, and he'd just as soon drink bathtub gin directly from the bathtub.

The conversation hovered around Mamie without ever landing for long. Occasionally someone would ask a question we already knew the answer to. Do you know what time she was taken, what else did they steal, something like that. I would answer, everyone would nod, and someone would change the subject. Sometimes I would listen, but most of the time I sat silently at the head of the table like a turd in everyone else's punch bowl, sipping my drink, staring at my hands, sick with worry, and simultaneously loving my friends for gathering around me and resenting the hell out of them for not being able to do a damn thing to help.

Lee sat to my right and was unusually chatty, even for him. But while he was blathering on about why it was permissible to mix your neutrals or why disco is an underrated musical genre, he would occasionally put his hand on mine and give a little squeeze, as if to say I'm here with you even if you're not exactly here with me.

Jack sat next to Lee and was characteristically quiet, throwing in a word here or a word there. Russell's head was on his lap, and

Jack was gently scratching behind his ears, occasionally chiming in but mostly focused on his dog, who I still imagined was reeling from Mamie's absence.

Tucker sat across from Jack. His eyeballs frequently glistened with tears, which threatened to flow but never quite appeared. I remember wishing he would have wept, openly and loudly. It would have been a relief of sorts, as it would have offered a catharsis, whereas I could only offer a lead weight in my gut and long, depressing silences. Peggy Lee sat in Tucker's lap while he spent most of his time tapping his smartphone. "I've started a hashtag," he said at one point. "It's 'hashtag Find Mamie.' And I'm sending her cutest pictures around. Charlie, send me all the Mamie photos you have." And I did.

Finally, Claude sat at my left, ready to pour out another martini the moment I should empty my current glass.

"Barbra was a wonderful Dolly," Lee said. "If she'd been twenty years older, she would have been better, sure. And yes, Carol was upset, but her performance would not have transferred to film, and she toured it for sixty fucking years anyway, so what's there to complain about?"

"It's not fair," I said.

"Life isn't fair, darling. But I will die on this hill. Gene did the right thing."

"Gene who?" asked Tucker.

Lee was incredulous. "Gene Kelly. He directed the film."

"I don't think that's right." Tucker's face registered skepticism, Lee's face answered with defiance. Lee was right, of course, and normally I would have relished this conversation, but not this night.

"Dogs are supposed to be easy," I said, and the room fell silent. Suddenly, the subject of whether Gene Kelly had done Carol Channing wrong was moot. "You don't have to work for their approval, and you never let them down."

"You were robbed, sugar. This is not your fault," Tucker assured me.

"I know we outlive our dogs," I continued. "I mean, we have to say goodbye eventually, right?" Mamie was only the third dog I'd ever had in my life, but I knew what it was like to watch a member of your family grow old, slow down, collect a dusting of gray in their coat, grow blind or deaf or both, and breathe their last. This was not that. "But I have no idea where she is. I don't know if she's alive or dead. If she's alive, she could be in terrible pain, she could be sad. God, I hope she's sad."

"She wants to come home, of course she does," Lee offered, again squeezing my hand. In response, I exhaled a sharp but exasperated chortle. Lee, to his credit, didn't let go.

"If I wanted to," I said, "I could tap my phone three times and some stranger would show up at the door in twenty minutes with a bag of General Tso's Chicken. How is it possible I don't know where she is? How, in the twenty-first century, can someone just take the thing you love, and you have no fucking idea why or where?"

The room fell silent, with no answers to these questions. I emptied my glass and looked around at Lee, then Jack, then Tucker. Finally, my eyes met Claude's, and he intuitively responded by prepping another martini.

Claude owned a sterling silver atomizer he filled with dry vermouth. Held at the perfect distance from an empty martini glass, one spray supplied a perfect coating of vermouth before adding the ice-cold gin or vodka, but Claude would be the first to tell you that a martini made with vodka was a vodka martini, while a martini made with gin was simply a martini. He was very particular about it.

"I don't know why you use that thing," Lee said. "You can't even taste it."

"Nobody likes vermouth, it's true," Claude said as he sprayed. "But without it, it's just not a martini, and Charlie here is swilling straight gin like an overgrown Toby Ragg. I don't make the rules." And he lovingly stirred the gin with some ice using a long metal spoon made expressly for this one task, then strained it into my glass. "Voilà," he said, presenting it to me.

These were my best friends in the world, the "family of choice" our people are always talking about. My wonderful, imperfect, affectionate, snarky, comforting, maddening, married friends. Their presence at this table touched me in a way that was both surprising and completely predictable. Where would they be at this moment if their friend's dog hadn't been taken? Did they have plans? If so, they were canceled. And as awful and drunk and angry as I felt, I was also grateful. I was even a little guilty, because all too often I couldn't help but resent these seemingly perfect pairs whose very existence sometimes made me feel like an onerous fifth wheel.

But being single wasn't the worst thing. It certainly beat the last few months I had spent with Freddie Babcock when I went to bed angry more often than not and was twice as lonely as I'd ever been since. Well, maybe not on this specific evening, but in general.

Besides, I wasn't the lonely type. Sure, there were moments first thing in the morning or late at night, when it would have been nice to share a wry observation or a good snog with someone who loved me, but I didn't suffer for it long. The worst times were the Friday and Saturday evenings when I had forgotten to make any plans, only to discover Claude and Lee had tickets to the theater, and Jack was dragging Tucker away for another weekend of clothing-optional gay camping, where Tucker would always avail himself of the option for clothing while Jack availed himself of every possible option, as was his way.

On those evenings, I typically looked at Mamie and sighed. "It's just us tonight, girlie girl," I'd say, and Mamie would curl up beside me on the couch while I watched *All About Eve* for the fiftieth time. And I'd momentarily wonder why a boyfriend wasn't sitting next to me, passing a single bowl of popcorn back and forth. But by the time we fastened our seat belts, Mamie was snuggled close while Bette Davis misbehaved terribly, and all things considered, I figured I was okay.

"—and what the hell is a pansexual, anyway?"

I had drifted away, and the conversation had continued without me. Now Claude was railing on about new, progressive vocabularies he couldn't or didn't want to comprehend. "Bisexual was a perfectly good word. Even though bisexuals don't exist in real life."

Lee rolled his eyes. "Oh, Claude, c'mon."

"Have you ever met a bisexual? I mean really?"

"My office mate is a bisexual," Tucker said, "and she's very nice."

Unhelpfully, Jack began to sing the chorus to NSYNC's "Bye Bye Bye" just under his breath. That he and I were the only ones not dancing along seemed to irritate Claude even further.

"A bisexual is attracted to both men and women," Lee continued. "Pansexuals are attracted to people regardless of gender."

Claude then prepped a martini for himself, only his second. "That's the same goddamn thing," he said, vigorously shaking his sterling silver atomizer.

"There are more than two genders, dear."

"Oh, goddammit," Claude said. "How many? Three? Four?"

"It's a continuum."

The specific way Claude rolled his eyes let us know he knew he would never win this argument, but please don't continue to explain it to him because he would never understand. Lee gave him a smile. Claude was a narrow-minded curmudgeon, but he was *his* narrow-minded curmudgeon, the Archie Bunker to his Edith.

The conversation about the infinite number of specific genders was momentarily interrupted by three distinct notes on an ascending scale, recognizable to everyone in the room as a Grindr notification.

"Sorry," Jack said, muting his phone.

Tucker cleared his throat, and all eyes in the room traveled from Jack to his husband. "I'm getting some action on this hashtag." He held up his phone, which was full of tweets.

Jack looked up from his phone. "What are they saying?"

"Nothin' yet, just retweeting."

Claude huffed. "What the hell does that mean?"

"It's a good thing, honey," Lee said. "I think."

Tucker poured himself a glass of red wine, his second. "Are you on the Nextdoor app, Charlie?"

"I don't think so."

"It's like a Facebook but for neighborhoods. You should get on that and spread the word."

"Go ahead," I said, taking another sip. "Post away. Whatever helps."

"I've already got it," Tucker explained, "but I can't post in your neighborhood. That's the whole point."

I couldn't spend the mental energy necessary to fathom a new social media platform, but what I could do was unlock my phone and pass it to Claude, who handed it to Tucker, who proceeded to do whatever needed to be done.

"Would you mind?" I asked. "I appreciate it."

And Tucker smiled—happy, I assumed, to be useful. "Sure thing, sugar."

I took a swig of gin, feeling it burn the length of my esophagus until meeting the pit in the bottom of my stomach. Claude whipped out his sterling silver atomizer, but I shook my head in polite refusal. Even in my miserable state of mind, I could tell I'd had too much already. I got up and meandered to the adjoining living room where I sat on their giant blue couch. I gingerly kicked off my shoes, rested my head against the armrest, and put my feet up. I folded my hands across my belly like someone who was dead or in therapy, both of which seemed like ideas worth considering.

"If you're going to sleep, drink some water first," Lee shouted from the dining room. "Your head is going to hurt like hell en la mañana."

"It's your husband's fault," I replied.

"Hold tight. I'll get you some," Lee said, moving to the kitchen. Soon, I could hear the faucet running.

Tucker and Jack were talking about something in the dining room I couldn't quite make out. But when Claude joined me in the living room, he rolled his eyes and shot me a warning glance. They were clearly having an argument. When Lee entered a moment later with a tall glass of water, he was humming some show tune or other, which only partly obscured the quarrel next door.

I took the water from Lee without getting up, doing my best not to spill. "What's going on in there?"

Lee held my head as if he were my nurse while I took my first sip. "Jack says he's leaving."

I was surprised and not surprised. It wasn't unlike Jack to pick inopportune times to make an exit without saying why, although the metallic strumming noise emanating from his phone was an obvious clue he'd found his next hookup.

Sometimes I wondered how we became friends with Jack. In the social hierarchy of the gay culture, he was a certified A-Gay, one of the rarified beautiful ones, and his mixing it up with such imperfect specimens must have been baffling to onlookers. But beyond the gorgeous exterior, he could be selfish and sullen, and was probably a sex addict, so perhaps it evened out. And if I was being generous, he could also be funny, warm, and kind, so long as you were prepared for him to disappear whenever an amorous mood struck.

The voices around the dining room table were getting louder.

"You can't just leave," said Tucker.

Lee tried humming a little louder. It didn't work.

"Actually," said Jack. "I can. And I'm about to."

Let him go, I thought. It's not like Mamie's any closer to home because your husband is sitting at this particular dining room table, sad and useless and horny to boot.

"What about Russell? And how am I supposed to get home?"

"You can have the car if you want it."

I was upset, however, about the way his behavior affected Tucker. It obviously stung a little bit every time Jack pulled something like this. Whatever the A-gays thought about the relationship, Tucker was the one who deserved better.

And then the voices got a little quieter. I lifted my head. Lee stopped humming. "Maybe he's not going."

Claude and I answered quietly but simultaneously: "He's going."

A few tense moments later, Tucker walked into the living room and crouched beside the sofa. I felt like Greta Garbo in *Camille*, a pale French whore with a Swedish accent dying of consumption while Robert Taylor bravely watches her slip away. Or maybe it doesn't happen that way exactly. In point of fact, I've never seen *Camille*. Moreover, I'm not quite sure what consumption is, only that death by consumption is tragic, but beautifully so.

"We're going," Tucker said.

"Okay," I said. Bravery with a hint of pathos, exactly like Greta if she'd been a gay man in his forties after too many martinis.

"I'm sorry," he continued. "It's just that—"

Having had enough of the Garbo imitation, I pulled myself upright. "It's okay," I said. "Really. I appreciate you coming to collect me, but the truth is, sitting around a table and getting drunk and feeling hopeless isn't accomplishing anything."

Jack appeared in the doorway, hovering.

"Anyone who can feel good tonight should do so," I said. It occurred to me Jack was the only person in the room for whom this was possible, and I pondered whether I was right to judge him as he sought his own pleasure while I soaked in a bathtub of pain. Tucker, meanwhile, was clenching his jaw and a little red in the face. Probably embarrassed, I thought. Whatever he was thinking, he didn't want to discuss their sudden exit any further. "And tomorrow," I said, "I'll talk to the cops and figure out what to do next."

"Listen," Tucker said. "I'm going to go home and post a bunch of photos on Instagram with the hashtag." He handed me my phone. "You're on Nextdoor now. It's right next to your Facebook app. There's a post up, so keep checking it for any leads. I'll make a flyer we can start hanging up tomorrow."

A flyer was a good idea. I hadn't even thought of that. "You're the best," I said.

"I'll call you first thing."

I must have made a face indicating I might not be conscious or coherent first thing in the morning because Lee jumped in. "Call the house. I'll be up."

Tucker put his hand on my knee. "Hey," he said. "We're going to get her back. You know that, right?"

"Yeah," I said. "I know."

Except I didn't know. She had been plucked from the only place I'd know to look for her, and she was somewhere in the city—maybe, if we were lucky—but I had no earthly idea where. Or who took her. Or what they planned to do with her. Or why they wanted her to begin with. Or if she was still alive. I had a million questions and absolutely no answers. In the corner of the room, Lee was praying again. Which I appreciated, though it seemed even less useful than retweeting cute doggie photos and hanging a bunch of flyers.

"This sucks," said Jack. "Maybe you'll get some good news tomorrow."

I applied a plastic smile. "Thanks. Get outta here."

And they did.

As soon as they were gone, Lee tut-tutted like an old biddy. "Poor Tucker."

"He made his bed," said Claude. "You don't settle down with a man as good-looking as Jack unless you're asking for trouble."

Lee rolled his eyes in response. "Must be why I'm so happy," he said, prompting Claude to chuckle.

"So, what, Jack is going to drop Tucker and Russell off at the house, and then say, 'See you in fifteen minutes'?" I asked.

"Be nice," Lee said. "I'd give him at least a half an hour."

Claude chuckled. "I'd settle for five."

Lee laughed. "You couldn't get your socks off in five, you big orangutan."

"Ah, romance," said Claude. "See what you're missing out on, Charlie?"

"I wouldn't say I'm missing it, Claude."

"Speaking of things we don't miss," said Lee. "I hate to even bring this up, but..." And his provocation hung in the air for a moment.

"Go on," I said, "you can't stop now."

Lee sat and made eye contact with each of us, a preemptive plea for forgiveness before he spoke. "I've just been wondering. Do you think Freddie might have had anything to do with this?"

"No," I said, a little too quickly. "I mean...I don't know. Maybe."

"I shouldn't have said anything," he said, going into the dining room to clear away the stemware. "Shut up, Lee, shut up, shut up."

"It's all right," I said. "I wondered the same thing."

A split second later, Lee reappeared in the doorway, wine and martini glasses in hand. "I mean, okay, he was my friend before he started treating you like hot garbage, and I'd like to think he wouldn't, but he's got motive, you know?"

"You watch too much *Law & Order*," said Claude.

"Mamie is adorable, don't get me wrong, but if you want a cute dog to keep you company, you can go to the shelter." He went back to the kitchen but kept on talking. Loudly. "Why would some stranger commit second degree burglary—"

"Third degree," Claude chimed in, ever the lawyer.

"Whatever degree. You see what I'm saying."

"But why would Freddie take my television?"

"To throw you off! Because you're sitting there, asking that very question right now. Besides, it's a beautiful television," he said, reappearing in the doorway. "He doesn't have a TV like that. And he took your laptop just to piss you off. I hate him."

"He moved to New York," said Claude.

"You can drive here from New York easy," Lee said. "If he left at nine this morning, he would have been here in plenty of time."

"He doesn't have a car," I said.

"So he joined a gang full of gay burglars, one of whom has a car, and they all did it together, and while Freddie was stealing your dog, they picked up some electronics. Eso fue lo que pasó. I'm telling you, it was him. It's like, what's his name's razor."

"Occam's razor," Claude said.

Lying back down, I became Garbo again. "Who has a razor?"

"The simplest solution is probably the right one," Lee explained. "That's Freddie."

"The simplest solution," Claude argued, "is some random kid we've never heard of broke into your house, stole some stuff, thought the dog was cute, and grabbed her."

Lee picked up the glass of water, still half-full, and held it in front of my face until I took it. "I still think it was Freddie. Drink up, then go to bed. Guest room's all made up. Tomorrow is a big day."

"What are we doing tomorrow?"

"We're getting your dog back. Bébelo."

CHAPTER FOUR

Friday, 7:47 a.m.

My head hurt.

At least four times the night before, I had woken with a start, unsure of where I was. When I realized I was in Lee and Claude's guest room, I remembered why. And I tried to go back to sleep while wondering where Mamie was sleeping. On someone's bed? A floor? The back seat of a car? Outside in the freezing cold and wet? Even in the best-case scenario, I knew she was confused and scared. I didn't want to think about the worst case.

And it was now light, so bright and sunny outside you could almost believe it was no longer winter. A good night's sleep was now a lost cause, so I thought it best to put my two feet on the floor and face the day. I felt like a list of side effects in an ad for prescription medication: nausea, headache, anxiety, increased likelihood of death. I wanted coffee. And maybe a shower.

First things first. I checked my phone, now fully charged, which was more than I could say for me. I did a search for #FindMamie on Twitter, Facebook, Instagram, and this new app Tucker had signed me up for, Nextdoor. Lots of well wishes and teary-eyed emojis, but nothing helpful. I did see a text message from the rhyming lesbians. *Got an early start. Leaving Rehoboth now. ETA 9 a.m.*

I wrote a quick reply. *Come to Lee's house*, and sent them the address.

I quietly made my way to the kitchen, careful not to wake anyone. I needn't have bothered. Claude could have slept through Armageddon, and Lee was naturally already awake.

"Good morning," he said, scooping grounds into the coffee machine.

"Is it?"

"No, it's actually not, but it will be. Coffee will be ready soon."

The little television was on, but muted. I saw the words *Top Story* appear on the screen, and out of habit grabbed the remote and turned the volume up. It was the story of a school shooting from the day before, this time a middle school in the suburbs of Baltimore. The police had discovered another body, bringing the death toll to seven.

"Ugh," said Lee. "Change the channel."

I clicked the button to CNN. There, the Baltimore shooting was noted in the crawl below the anchors, but the topic at hand was the California homes and small businesses that still hadn't recovered from the spate of wildfires the summer before.

"I'm sorry," Lee said. "I just can't with this." He picked up the remote where I had left it on the counter and muted the television again. I couldn't hear about the struggle any longer, but I could still see video of trees engulfed in flames and clouds of black smoke billowing above them.

"It's such a shitty world," I said.

Lee shot me a skeptical look. "It can be."

"Look at these people. Their lives are completely destroyed."

"I'd rather not. We've got problems of our own."

"I didn't get much sleep last night."

"Me neither."

"Meanwhile, this was happening," I said, referencing the images on the television. "Look at the size of that fire."

Lee inserted himself between the television and me, obscuring my view. "Okay, you can cut that shit out right now."

"What?"

"You want to know who cried himself to sleep last night?"

"So what? You cry watching *The Real Housewives of Beverly Hills*."

He gently slapped my arm. "For your information, there are times when Lisa Vanderpump's story arc is very moving."

"I'll take your word for it."

"Anyway. Not me. My husband."

"He cried himself to sleep?" I was stunned. "Claude the Clod?"

Lee nodded. "After he got into bed last night, Mama Cass climbed onto his chest and did her little staring thing. He started talking about how he would feel if one of our little munchkins was lost somewhere and he didn't know where, and he started sniffling and shaking all of a sudden. Now, listen to me. Someone broke into your house and stole something you love, and you are allowed to feel like shit. If you want to cry your eyes out or scream or break things, it's all good. Just don't sit around acting like this is not a big fucking deal, because it is."

"Okay."

"Don't tell Claude I told you he cried."

"Why, because you made it up?"

"Huh! I wish. I was motion sick until he finally fell asleep."

I chuckled, and then the television caught my eye again. A handsome television anchor was solemnly saying something I couldn't hear about some random tragedy befalling someone else somewhere in the world. "How are we going to find her, Lee?"

"I don't know. But the coffee's ready, and Tucker's coming over. Pour yourself a cup, take a hot shower, and we'll figure it out when he gets here."

Friday, 8:24 a.m.

When Tucker arrived at the house, he knocked loud and long on the front door, sending Peggy Lee and Mama Cass into a panic.

Lee opened the door, and Russell came bounding up the stairs. "That was fast."

"Traffic was light." Tucker turned to me. "Have y'all looked at Twitter this morning?"

"About a half hour ago," I said. "Why? Has someone found her?"

"Next best thing," he said. He noticed my face fall. "Sorry."

"No no. What is it?"

"Angela Woolsey wants to interview you."

Russell climbed into my lap and was trying to lick my face. "Angela who?"

"She's the news anchor on Channel Two," Lee said. "You know, Black woman, mid-forties, nice suits, cute little bob."

"You've just described half the anchors in Washington."

"Every week, she talks about some dog who's about to die if somebody doesn't adopt it," Lee said. "She makes everyone cry."

"That's the one. Here, look what she wrote."

Tucker handed his phone to me. At the top of the screen was a tweet from @AWoolseyWDMV. "Let's get to the bottom of this," I read aloud. "Hashtag Find Mamie, and there's a photo."

"It's got over five hundred replies in less than an hour," Tucker said.

"Yeah, but this doesn't mean she wants to interview me."

"Keep reading. Look at the replies."

And immediately below Woolsey's tweet was a reply from @TuckerPickettTN. *Thanks for spreading the word, @AWoolseyWDMV. We're worried sick. If we can't #FindMamie here on Twitter, would you be willing to put the story on tonight's news?* And below that, from Woolsey: *Send me a DM.*

I looked up at Tucker. He was very proud of himself. I will admit I was also very proud of him, and a little chagrined he was a better dog-uncle than I was a dog-dad, and also annoyed with myself for being annoyed with someone who only wanted to help me and was really good at it. "Did you send her a message? What did you say?"

"I was fixin' to. Wanted to talk to you first. I assume you want to do it?"

Lee reached for Tucker's phone. I handed it to him. "I mean, of course, yeah."

After reading the tweets for himself, Lee looked up. "Can I do your makeup?"

"Only if you give me really large bags under my bloodshot eyes."

Tucker agreed. "He's right. The worse he looks, the better."

"So like an Elsa Lanchester *Bride of Frankenstein* look? With the hair?"

"I'll do my own makeup, thanks."

"I was only trying to help. Coffee's in the kitchen."

"I'm fine, thanks," Tucker replied. "Oh, and I also made a flyer." He dug a folded piece of paper out of his pocket and handed it to me.

"Did you also remember to pick up my dry cleaning?"

Tucker looked a little confused.

"I'm kidding. This looks great. Really great. You were busy last night. And I appreciate it. I just feel extra useless now."

"I'm sorry. I only—"

"No. God, no. Thank you. Thank God one of us is competent."

My phone started to buzz. I fished it out of my pocket.

"It's Mamie's vet."

Tucker lit up. "Maybe someone found her. Scanned the microchip?"

I answered as Lee took a seat next to me. "Hello?"

"Mr. Vernon. This is Bea from Beekman Animal Hospital. Hi."

"Um, hello."

"Is it true?"

"Excuse me?"

"Oh, I'm sorry," she said. "I just opened my email, and I've got a message here from Tucker Pickett? Is that name familiar to you?"

"Yes," I said, and the disappointment in my voice told Lee and Tucker all they needed to know.

"He sent us a flyer about Mamie. Is she really missing?"

"Yes, um…she was taken last night."

"Taken? Oh my God."

"Yeah, the, house was broken into. They took the dog."

"Oh my God."

"So. It's true."

"Oh my God."

"We're talking to the police soon. But also trying to spread the word."

"Well, we'll definitely put these flyers up. And leave a stack for people to take with them. And if anyone says they might have seen her, I'll call you right away."

"Thanks, Bea."

"I really hope you find her."

Yeah, I thought, no shit. "Yeah," I said, "me too."

"Don't tell anyone, but she's one of my favorite patients."

"I won't tell a soul."

"Good-bye, Mr. Vernon."

And I hung up the phone. "They got your flyer," I said.

"I'm sorry," Tucker said as Lee slipped back into the kitchen. "I should have let you look at it first. I wanted them to hang it up as soon as possible, and—"

"And they are. And leaving a stack for their patients to take with them. It was a good thought. Thank you."

"I get a little carried away when bad things happen."

"I wonder if we should send some to the groomer we use," I said. "They love Mamie, and Friday is usually pretty busy for them."

"I'm on it," Tucker said, reaching for the laptop in his shoulder bag.

"And sometimes we use a dog walking service. Maybe they could help us paper the neighborhood as long as they're walking around everywhere?"

"I bet they will," Tucker said. "That's brilliant."

"I'm going to send Angela Woolsey a message, see if I can set something up." I picked up my phone just as it started buzzing again.

"Well!" said Tucker. "Ain't you as popular as a preacher on a Sunday mornin'."

I didn't know the number, but I answered. "Hello?"

"Am I speaking to Mr. Vernon?" The voice was deep and quiet, but dripping with authority.

"That's right," I said.

"Mr. Vernon, my name is Lt. Herman with the Washington Metropolitan Police. I'm calling about a burglary that took place yesterday at your home."

"Y-yes," I said. I've never committed a crime worse than removing a mattress tag in my life, but I was suddenly nervous being interviewed by a police lieutenant.

He verified my address and some of the details filed by the cops I'd met the night before.

"Says here they took your dog."

"That's correct."

"Can you tell me about the dog," he said, more a command than a question. The more I'd get to know him, the more I'd notice this was the rule, not the exception.

"Um, her name is Mamie. She's a cockapoo. Mom was a cocker spaniel, dad was a poodle. Yellow, about twenty pounds. I can send you a picture if you like."

"Could you please," he commanded, giving me his number, which I jotted down.

"She has a microchip, so if anyone finds her and brings her to a vet, they'll be able to scan it and get in touch with me. She had a red and white collar and tags, but they're probably gone by now. They also stole her leash, which is black, one of those retractable leashes. That's all I can think of right now."

"It's very helpful, Mr. Vernon, but I do want to caution you about something."

"Yes?"

"Most robberies go unsolved. Whoever broke into your place knew what they were doing. It wasn't a very sophisticated hit. It doesn't take a genius to break a window. But they were efficient, and my gut tells me they've done this before. Which means your television, your laptop, other property they took is probably long gone by now. Fenced."

"I understand."

"I see a lot of cases like this," he said. "And what I know is if we don't find these guys within twenty-four hours, we're probably not going to find them."

"That doesn't give us much time."

"No, it doesn't. Now," he continued, "what makes this case a little different was they stole a live animal, who you say is a mixed breed. Is she fixed?"

"Spayed, yes."

"Okay, then. They're not going to get a lot of money for this dog, which gives us three possible scenarios. One, these are kids who know how to steal things but otherwise aren't too bright. Two, they thought the dog was cute and figured they'd keep it. Or three, someone wanted your dog, and the other stuff was just a bonus. Do you know of anyone who might have wanted your dog specifically?"

"No, not really."

"You sure about that," he said. Another command. I looked up. Lee was in the kitchen, but within earshot. Tucker was looking at his laptop, but I could tell he was also paying attention to my conversation with the police.

"Well," I said, "I adopted the dog with an ex. When we broke up, we fought a lot. Over the dog. Which I ended up keeping, so…"

"So, you're wondering if your ex took your dog."

"It has occurred to me."

"Your ex, does she still live in town?"

"Uh, no. *He* moved to New York City last year with *his* new boyfriend."

"Okay," he said. "And you really think he did it?"

"I don't know. He's the only person I know who might've."

"Does your ex have a habit of breaking into people's homes?"

"Not that I know of, no. But…"

"But what." Not a question.

"Well, let's just say there's a lot about him I didn't know."

"Mr. Vernon, my guess is it's not him. But let me take down his name and a description. In the meantime, we'll continue to investigate all other possibilities."

I gave him Freddie's full name and a brief physical description, consciously avoiding eye contact with Tucker during this part of the conversation. They all knew about Freddie, and how it ended, and they all agreed he had been rotten to me. All the same, he was once their friend too.

"One last thing, Mr. Vernon. You haven't offered any kind of reward for the return of your dog, have you?"

"No, I haven't."

"Good. If I could ask you a favor, it would help us out a lot if you didn't."

"Can I ask why?"

"Well, rewards tend to result in a lot of false leads. Suddenly, everyone in DC has a dog meeting your description and wants to talk to the police about it. It really slows us down and makes some of the more credible leads less noticeable. There's nothing illegal about posting a reward, but it muddies the waters. You understand."

"I do."

"Mr. Vernon, thank you for speaking with me this morning."

"Of course. I mean, thank you."

"I want to temper your expectations," he said. "But I also want you to know we're going to do everything we can to get your dog back."

"Thank you."

"You know," he said, "I got a dog too. Pit mix. I named him Killer, 'cuz I thought he was a mean ugly motherfucker. Turns out he's just ugly. He might kill you by licking you to death, but I guess what I'm saying is I know how important this is."

"I appreciate that."

"Call if you have any questions, and I'll be in touch if I get anything. This your cell phone?"

"Yes."

"And this is mine. Keep your phone handy, and call me if you have any questions. We'll talk soon."

"Okay." And I hung up the phone. The room was silent, except for Tucker's clickety-clack on his laptop. And eventually that stopped too.

"You think Freddie did it?" he asked.

"I don't know. Not really. But maybe?"

Lee got up. "Well, I think he did it. I think Mamie is in his stupid little one-room apartment in the Bronx right now while Freddie watches his brand-new TV."

"The police don't think it was him," I said. "They said whoever did it has broken into houses before."

"Okay, but be honest," Tucker said, "do you know for a fact Freddie has never broken into a house before?"

"Do *you* think he did it?"

"The thought has occurred to me," he said.

"Aha!" Lee was victorious. "You see?"

"Okay, I'm going to message Angela Woolsey now," I said.

"The groomers have the flyer," Tucker reported. "What's the name of your dog walker?"

"Paws on the Pavement."

"Clever," he said, tip-tapping away. "Found 'em."

Lee looked at Tucker buried in his laptop and me in my phone. "What can I do?"

"Just sit," I said. "You can keep us company."

"I want to do something important."

"Tell us again how Bette Midler should have won an Oscar for *Beaches*."

"Don't make fun of me. I'm serious."

"So am I." I looked him in the eye. "This is the worst fucking day in my whole life. I'm sad and angry and hopeless and scared, and the one other thing I cannot feel right now is alone. Sit down. Please."

"Okay," he said, sitting. "So first of all, bitch wasn't even nominated, and she was flawless. And if Sigourney Weaver—love her—is going to get nominated for literally acting opposite a bunch of monkeys, Bette deserves *at least* a nod for being able to emote next to Barbara Hershey's fucking vaca gigantesca lips."

❖

Friday, 9:02 a.m.

After two cups of coffee and a shower, I was feeling slightly more human.

Lee cooked an enormous breakfast for the four of us, but only Claude had the stomach to eat his share. He may have cried himself to sleep the night before, but his appetite was unaffected. Still, he seemed genuinely apologetic about leaving for work. "Big client meeting at ten."

As soon as he left, I turned to Lee. "Oh shit," I said. "It's Friday."

"You are *not* going into work today," Lee said. "I forbid it."

"No, but I need to call in. We have a new HR person. Her name is Muriel, and she really *is* terrible. Give me a minute."

Luckily, I had a fantastic relationship with my boss. Agnes Roche was warm, smart, and funny. More importantly, she lived alone with a bichon mix named Morton and harbored a vague notion that all straight men were either idiots or assholes. So, when we found ourselves alone, we spent a lot of time sharing dog photos and extolling the virtues of the canine, especially as they compared with the male variety of the human species. She would understand.

Unfortunately, when I dialed her office, she didn't pick up.

"Applewhite Learning Solutions, may I help you?"

"Um…hi. Is Agnes around?"

"Who am I speaking to?"

"This is Charlie Vernon."

"If I'm not mistaken, Mr. Vernon, it's past time you should be at your desk."

I didn't have to ask who I was speaking to. I recognized the condescending attitude, if not the voice, of Muriel Ball, our brand-new director of human resources.

"Muriel, hi. I need to speak with Agnes."

"I'm afraid *Miz Roche* is unavailable at the moment."

"Could I get her voicemail, then?"

"Mr. Vernon, why don't you just tell me what's going on?" When Lt. Herman asked a question that wasn't really a question, it seemed authoritative, and a little badass. When Muriel did it, it was just annoying.

"I won't be in today, Muriel."

"I see," she said. She was sitting up taller in her chair now, I could tell. "Have you requested time off on the intranet, and has your request been approved by your manager or myself?"

"No, that's why I'm—"

"Are you ill? Will you be visiting a doctor, and are you prepared to bring written verification of a doctor's visit if away for more than three business days—"

"I'm not sick, Muriel. Please, if I could just leave Agnes a m—"

"I'm afraid this is in direct violation of our policy, Mr. Vernon."

"I'm dealing with a personal emergency today, Muriel. If you could please pass my message along to Agnes, I'm sure we can sort it all out when I'm back in the office."

"And when will this be, Mr. Vernon?"

"Well, Monday. I hope."

"And what is the nature of your personal emergency?"

"Well, Muriel, it's of a *personal* nature, and—"

"No need to get snippy, Mr. Vernon. I adhere to a strict confidentiality policy when discussing HR issues with staff, and besides I'll find out anyway."

"Well," I replied, "my home was broken into last night."

"And?"

"And that's my emergency."

"Mr. Vernon, I fail to see how a break-in yesterday prevents you from being at work today."

"Well, my home is still vulnerable. The robbers entered through a window, which needs to be repaired. Until that happens, I really shouldn't leave the house." I neglected to tell Muriel I left the house last night and hadn't been back, but I wasn't feeling especially chatty.

"So, you'll be working from home today while your window is repaired?"

"No, there's more to it. Look, my dog was stolen yesterday. So, I'm going to be spending the day working with the police and looking for my dog in the hopes I can get her back. That's my personal emergency. It's a *family* emergency."

"Mr. Vernon, our policies are very clear as to the definition of dependents. That term applies only to spouses and children. So, I'm afraid our family leave policy won't apply here, and I suspect you already knew that. I'm disappointed you would attempt to—"

"Yeah, well, I'm disappointed we hired you to do a job with the word 'human' in it."

"Mr. Vernon! There's no need to take a hostile tone with me. I'm simply—"

"You're a replicant. After the apocalypse, there will be cockroaches, piles of nuclear waste, and you, citing policies and procedures to anyone who will listen."

"I will certainly be speaking to *Miz Roche* about this."

"You know what? Please do. Please relay the entirety of this conversation to *Miz Roche*, and in the meantime please take your employee handbook and shove it all the way up your ass." And I hung up.

Tucker and Lee stared at me, mouths agape. "Well," Lee said. "That escalated quickly."

"Fucking Muriel. So, on top of everything else, I'll probably lose my job today."

"You hate your job anyway." Which wasn't exactly true. Lee hated my job, only because he thought they made me work too hard. I liked Agnes a lot. I'd miss her when I was fired. "And besides," Lee said, "this 'fuck you' energy is exactly what we need if we're going to get Mamie back."

Then, suddenly, a knock at the door, followed by a howl of protest from Peggy, Russell, and Cass. Another knock, and then the unmistakable voice of Irene. "Hey! Let me in!"

"It's Jean and Irene," I said. "They're here."

CHAPTER FIVE

I first met the rhyming lesbians two decades ago, back when I still dreamed of a career in the theater. I had graduated from college four years before with an utterly useless BA in Theatre Arts, and I figured I'd come to Washington where I knew a few people, get some professional experience, and move to New York by my twenty-fifth birthday or as soon I earned my Equity card, whichever came first.

But work was hard to come by. I didn't have the right look, I got too nervous at auditions, I was unlucky, or maybe I just wasn't very good. In any event, by the time my quarter century came and went with no hope of gaining entrance into Actors' Equity anytime soon, I decided the dream was not to be. So, I resolved to figure out what I wanted to be when I grew up. I put some of those theater skills to work in a corporate training gig, and I enjoyed it. Or at least I was good at it, and it paid well. And I did a little community theatre in the meantime because I still loved it.

I met Jean and Irene that year. One of the community theaters in suburban Maryland was holding auditions for *The Heidi Chronicles* by Wendy Wasserstein. I had read the play in college and loved it. I told some theater friends I planned on auditioning for it, and the responses to this news ranged from "that's nice" to "I'd sooner die." When I asked why everyone was so down on Wendy Wasserstein, I was told, "Oh, it's not that. It's Irene."

Irene Epstein, I was told, was the meanest, toughest director in the history of theater dating back to Aeschylus. She had directed

Barefoot in the Park the year before, they said, and had made the talented young actress playing Corie cry during almost every rehearsal. The poor thing never did learn all her lines, and after the show closed, she was never heard from again. There were whispers of a lonely suicide, but nothing had been confirmed. Irene Epstein was a monster, an authoritarian, and her—and this part must be whispered—*lesbian lover* was her stage manager. Who, they said begrudgingly, was very nice.

Frankly, I found words like "tough" and "demanding" appealing. Far from discouraging me, they made me even more determined to audition. In fact, I was not just going to audition, I was going to get this part.

Predictably, I was the first person to show up on the first night of auditions. I was met by a forty-ish woman with a shock of red hair. She had a warm smile and said I could have a seat anywhere in the lobby while they finished setting up inside. She doesn't seem so bad, I thought. "Are you, by any chance, Irene?"

"No, sorry," she said. "I'm Jean Muldoon. I'm helping Irene stay organized tonight."

"Charlie Vernon," I said, offering my hand. Smiling, she shook it. Can't hurt to get in good with the girlfriend, I thought. She likes me. Also, how very open-minded of me.

When the auditions were scheduled to begin, the lobby was crowded with actors, most of whom I hadn't met before, which was odd, as I'd already done three shows with this company. These must be the serious actors, I thought, the ones who aren't afraid of being challenged. I was clearly where I belonged.

Jean appeared at the top of the hour and invited us into the main theater where we all filed in and sat down in the audience. Irene, a forty-ish woman with a shock of white hair, stood onstage. Everyone knew better than to speak in the presence of such a commanding personality. When everyone was settled, she told us about the play, why it was important, both theatrically and to her personally, and the high expectations she had of any actor who dared approach this monumental work. And then she began. I was asked to read twice, both times as Scoop, Heidi's on-again off-again boyfriend and an early adopter of what we now call toxic masculinity. The way Irene thanked me and conferred with Jean after each of my reads made me optimistic about my chances. They both seemed to like me.

After ninety minutes of readings, she asked if anyone had any final questions for her. I raised my hand.

"Who are you again?"

Jean whispered to her.

"Vernon, is it? Go ahead."

I asked if I might read for Peter, Heidi's onetime Plan B who dashed her dreams by coming out of the closet. Irene's expression became pinched.

"I don't really see you as a Peter," she said, with some finality. But Jean whispered something to her, something which made her reconsider me. "If you don't mind," she said, "I'd like to ask you a personal question."

"Okay."

"Why do you want to read for this role? Is there something about Peter's story that's important to you personally?"

She's asking if I'm gay, I thought. "N-no," I answered. And I thought I was telling the truth, at the time. "I just think Peter is a better role."

"And why is that?"

"He changes the most from the beginning to the end," I said. "Probably more than any other character in the play."

"More than Susan?"

"Well, if you don't see me as a Peter, I really doubt you see me as a Susan," I said, and there was a smattering of laughter that died down as soon as it was apparent Irene was not similarly amused. "But, um…I don't think Susan really changes much. She tries on different costumes every time the culture changes, but Peter turns into his, y'know, authentic self."

And this satisfied her for the moment. "Okay, then. Let's see what you've got. Act Two, Scene Five. The monologue."

I walked up onstage with the script in my hand. I had been looking at this monologue all day, the one about how friends are just as important as lovers and just as easily betrayed, and had practically memorized it. I gave it my all, and when I was done, I looked at Irene, who regarded me very coolly. Jean, on the other hand, was beaming—until Irene shot her a look, at which point her face took on a more businesslike air.

I was called back on a Wednesday, and I read only for Peter. On Thursday, I returned to my apartment and heard the message on the machine. The part was mine.

❖

Those early rehearsals were great. Irene was demanding, but not the monster she'd been made out to be. Her vision for the play was clear and her direction precise. She wasn't afraid of telling you what you were doing was wrong, but neither was she stingy with praise. And when she was pleased, you felt as if you'd earned it.

On Thursday nights, we'd typically adjourn to a nearby pub for beer and greasy food. Those nights were especially fun, as Irene would let her hair down. This was a metaphor if ever there was one, as she sports the short, spiky hairdo that says "I'm a dyke" in seventeen languages. One night, when it was clear Jean would be driving them home, Irene sidled up next to me at the long table we always occupied on Thursdays and said, "I really have to ask you something."

"Shoot."

She moved closer, with a conspiratorial look around. "Are you sure you're not gay?"

"I'm sure." And I thought I was.

"Why did you want this part so badly?"

"It's a great role." I eyed Jean, who was eyeing Irene nervously.

Irene narrowed her eyes, but what she was looking for I couldn't tell. "Well. You're doing a lovely job."

"Thank you."

"Tell me," she said as she leaned back, surveying me. "Are you offended by my question?"

"No."

"Because most men would be. Most straight men, I mean."

"Okay, Irene, that's enough," Jean said, taking a seat between us. "Leave the poor boy alone. Charlie, tell us about where you grew up."

The next week, we were off-book for the first time. Jean would call out our lines if we needed them, but I never had much of a problem with memorization, and it was good to get the books out of our hands. On Tuesday, we were running the second half of Act One, including Peter's first big moment, coming out to Heidi in the middle of a protest in front of the Chicago Museum of Art. The scene ends with Peter introducing Heidi to his new boyfriend, who was being played by an actor named Brian.

Brian was openly gay and had lobbied to play Peter himself. Therefore, acting alongside him always felt a bit awkward. But, as I would find out years later, Irene thought he was "pretty, but dumb as a box of hammers" and "couldn't be onstage for more than five minutes before he started farting rainbows all over the front row." Also, he had "too many opinions," one of which was Peter and his boyfriend should kiss each other at the end of the scene.

Irene was against it. "Brian, no."

"It would be a stronger statement," he argued.

"I understand what you're saying. I really do. But this scene takes place in 1976. It was a different time."

"I also don't think Peter would kiss a man in front of Heidi," I said. "I mean, he's just come out to her, and she was kind of maybe sort of in love with him? It's fraught."

"Okay," Brian said, "what if...hold on, what if...Mark is the one who kisses Peter, like that's their usual thing, because he doesn't know Heidi or doesn't think it's a big deal. That could work."

Irene wasn't happy, but she backed down. "Let's see what it looks like. You okay with this, Charlie?"

"Fine," I said. My heart was beating so hard I thought it might escape my rib cage.

"Are you sure?"

"We can try it." I was short of breath. My mouth was dry.

"Okay, take it from your entrance, Brian."

I gave Brian his cue. The erection in my pants wasn't just rising up, it was waving a flag over the battlements like an extra in *Les Misérables*.

Brian, smiling and affable, ran onstage and gently placed his hand under my chin, but the kiss he planted on my lips was a little showy, a little too long for Irene's taste.

"No, no, no," she interjected from the audience. The sky was opening above me. Angels were singing hymns in the distance.

"Brian, if we're going to do this, it has to be quick and casual. He's not showing off for anyone." I thought I was going to have an orgasm on the spot. "Try it one more time," she instructed us. I was dizzy, almost faint.

❖

The show opened three weeks later. The kiss never made it into the show as Brian simply couldn't master quick and casual. Every time he'd kiss me, it had the weight of a political statement. It was always ardent and a little sloppy, with lots of tongue. I didn't really mind while it lasted. Brian wasn't an unattractive fellow. Sadly, neither was his boyfriend.

Even without the spectacle of men kissing onstage, the show was a big hit.

By then, of course, my identity as a gay man who'd been in the closet my entire life had sunk in. It was liberating, of course. Also awkward. I wasn't embarrassed to be gay, but it was humbling to admit I'd been clueless about myself for so long.

At the opening night party, held at the Epstein-Muldoon home, I deposited wine from a box into a red plastic cup and wandered aimlessly by myself through throngs of well-wishers and congratulations, politely accepting their praise. "Thank you," I'd say, in a heartfelt way. Suddenly, I felt the urge to smoke a cigarette, and headed for the back porch where I hoped someone might be kind enough to spare one, but halfway through the kitchen I was intercepted by Irene Epstein holding a martini glass that contained only two gin-soaked olives on a spear.

"I want you to know how good you were tonight," she said.

"Thank you," I replied. Very heartfelt.

"You're really not what I had in mind for Peter, and I had my doubts about you at first. But you proved me wrong." I wasn't sure how to respond, so I simply nodded. Then, not wanting to appear arrogant, I abruptly stopped nodding and just stood there, mute. "If you knew how rarely I said those words, you'd know I'm offering you a very serious compliment."

"I appreciate it. I do," I assured her. "But listen, can we talk about something?"

"Of course."

"Maybe in private?"

Her eyes narrowed for a moment. Then a slight nod. "Meet me on the front stoop in five." And then, like a lesbian secret agent, she spirited away without a trace.

Exactly five minutes later, I stepped outside the front door where Jean and Irene were waiting for me. "So," Irene said, "what's this all about? It couldn't have been anything I said."

I don't remember how exactly I made my confession, but it all came pouring out. About the rehearsal, about the kiss, about how I had lied to her before at the pub but it wasn't really a lie because I hadn't known I was lying, about growing up in a Navy family and going to a Catholic college, about how free I felt but how humiliating it was to be finally coming out in my mid-twenties. When I finally stopped to breathe, I looked at them, waiting for a response.

"I knew it," Irene said. "I'm never wrong."

"Don't gloat, honey." Jean placed her hands on my shoulders. "Are you okay?"

I nodded. Tears were hovering on my eyeballs, obscuring my view. "Are we the first people you've told?" As I nodded again, the first tear fell, and she hugged me. "Honey," she said. "It's going to be okay. In fact, it all gets better from here. Believe me."

"What are you doing three weeks from now?" Irene asked. "Memorial Day weekend after the show closes?"

"N-nothing," I stammered, still cocooned in Jean's embrace.

"Because if you have any plans, cancel them," Irene said. "You're going to the beach with us."

And there, on the spot, plans were made and tears were dried. I marveled at the people who had tried to warn me away from Irene Epstein and her *lesbian lover*. Indeed, I thought these two women were the most wonderful people on earth. I thanked them, and Irene, the callous monster who made poor little Corie cry, gave me a hug. I think she was a little choked up herself, although she'll deny it if you ask her.

Soon, Jean and Irene returned to the house and their houseful of guests, and I remained on the porch, looking up at the stars, or as many stars as you could see from the suburbs of Washington, DC. The noise of the party, muted for the moment, was more poignant than raucous. It was the sound of people living their lives to the absolute fullest, I thought. It was a sound I'd perhaps one day be a lot more comfortable with.

I heard neither the door opening behind me nor Brian walking toward me until he spoke. "Hey," he said. "Really good show tonight. You nailed it."

I faced him. He had wanted my role, and we both knew it. His compliment, therefore, took on a resonance it otherwise wouldn't have carried. I looked into his eyes. His gaze was sincere.

I gently placed my hand under his chin, and I kissed him— deeply, ardently, with lots of tongue.

❖

Three weeks later, I was nestled in the back seat of Jean and Irene's Subaru Outback, which I shared with their miniature schnauzer, Beau. I was a little surprised to note Jean was driving. Of course, now that I know them better, it makes perfect sense.

We were headed for Rehoboth Beach, where they kept a little boat. On weekends during the summer, they would sleep on the boat and spend their days on the boardwalk or the beach and their nights in any number of bars and restaurants or the weekend estates of friends and wealthy acquaintances who made a living in Washington, Baltimore, or Philadelphia but made a life in Rehoboth.

Tallulah Bankhead brought her female lovers to Rehoboth in the 1940s, and while it was never the gay mecca Provincetown or Fire Island were, it's as close as the Mid-Atlantic gets. Weekending in Rehoboth is sort of like moving to San Francisco. It doesn't make you gay, although it does mean there's a good chance of it. At the very least it makes you gay-friendly. This was to be my first visit. I'd been looking forward to it and also dreading it for weeks. Three weeks, to be exact.

When we arrived at the boat slip, Irene fastened a leash to Beau, who darted toward the water, pulling Irene along. Jean and I followed behind, and they showed me where I'd be sleeping in the hull of the boat.

From there, we went for drinks at the Blue Moon, followed by dinner at Confucius. It's not particularly gay, but it's got the best goddamn Peking duck you've ever tasted. Then, more drinks and dancing at the Renegade.

The next day Irene took me to Lambda Rising, the town's gay bookstore, where she purchased a tome of first-person gay history with instructions to read the entire thing. She also took great delight in finding a copy of *The New Joy of Gay Sex* and loudly plunking it down on the counter, announcing to everyone in the store, "I am buying *this* for *him*." I wanted to melt into the floor. Within the next month, I'd read them both cover to cover, sometimes pausing to appreciate the pencil drawings in the latter.

That night we attended a garden party hosted by friends of Jean and Irene, where I met more gay baby boomers in one enormous beach house than I'd dreamed existed on the entire planet. If I squinted, it looked like the kind of gathering my parents might have attended, with lots of khakis and Hawaiian shirts. Only on closer inspection did I notice all the men were arriving with other men, and the women with other women.

At one point, one of the men I met, after hearing my story, adopted an arch accent and told me to take note of any words I didn't comprehend. This was clearly a reference to something, but I wasn't yet versed in the homosexual lexicon. Everyone laughed uproariously, but I didn't get the joke. My cheeks began to flush with embarrassment, but a smile from Jean let me know no one was laughing at my expense.

On Sunday, we went to Poodle Beach, where the gay people sunbathe and frolic in the ocean. I don't remember much, other than being too self-conscious to take my shirt off while surrounded by all the perfect, bronzed bodies—not knowing twenty years later I'd look back on photos from my coming out weekend and marvel at how skinny I was. After an exhausting day of lying in the sand and doing nothing, we were ready for a quick shower, more drinks at the Blue Moon, dinner at the Back Porch, and more drinks at Cloud 9, where we floated away until morning.

I got up early on Monday morning. My head throbbed slightly, but nothing too terrible, considering the number of cosmopolitans we had consumed the night before.

Beau noticed me stirring. He figured as long as I was up I might as well take him for a walk. I didn't have a counterargument, so I rummaged around, found his leash, slipped my sandals on, and we quietly walked down to the pier.

I surveyed the scene around me—boats, water, seagulls, a clear blue sky, and a schnauzer who desperately needed to pee—with a sense of…not joy, exactly, but wonder. I had spent most of my life denying such a crucial part of myself. And for what? Fear of something, I suppose, but now that I could see up close how fun and wonderful this world was, I kicked myself for taking so long.

And, to be fair, being a homosexual in the mid-nineties wasn't all glitter and rainbows. The AIDS crisis wasn't a distant memory in those days. The cocktail was helping, but the diagnosis still felt like a death sentence, and Jean would spend hours over the next few years asking me if I had a supply of condoms on my person at all times. People still got fired for being gay, and the thought of attending legally sanctioned same-sex weddings in my lifetime seemed like a childish fantasy.

Still, my life opened up before me on that magical weekend. I would meet a nice man. We would settle down. We would keep a home in the city and a home, not a boat, at the beach. I had already decided having friends with boats was infinitely preferable to the boat itself. And we would have a long, happy life filled with laughter, love, good friends, garden parties, mimosas over brunch, and martinis before dinner, like civilized people. And dogs, naturally. We would always have at least one dog. I knew it was possible for my life to be rich and happy. Jean and Irene, the rhyming lesbians, gave that to me.

"Ready to go back, Beau?"

He wasn't.

Neither was I.

CHAPTER SIX

Friday, 9:06 a.m.

Irene Epstein banged on the door. "Hey! Let me in!" As soon as she heard the chorus of canine protest inside, she returned to her car where she held open the passenger door for her wife, Jean Muldoon.

As Tucker gripped Russell's collar and Lee expertly scooped up both Mama Cass and Peggy Lee in one sweeping motion, I opened the door in time to see Jean emerge from the car. I caught her eye too. She gave me a smile—not an *isn't it a wonderful day* smile, but an *I know it sucks that's why I'm here* smile.

She required a little support from Irene to stand, but once she found her balance, she was fine. Although I tried to prepare for it, it was always a shock to see Jean without her bright red hair, once a product of her Irish heritage, and later I suspected a product manufactured by L'Oréal and applied routinely. These days, there was just a bandana. Today's was sky blue. The last time I saw her, she wore a bandana sporting blue, pink, and ivory stripes, like the flag for Trans Pride. When I asked her if there was something she ought to tell me, she said, "Hell, if I have to be bald, I might as well go all the way. Maybe they'll pay me more."

Jean easily lifted her arms in the universal sign for *give me a hug*. This looked to be a good day for her. I was glad. I was already feeling guilty for putting her through a three-hour drive to and from Rehoboth Beach, where she and Irene now lived full-time.

As I held her gingerly in my arms, she whispered in my ear, "Tighter. I won't break."

"Yeah," I whispered back, "but Irene might. She's got that line between her eyes just looking at us." This made Jean laugh, and I was relieved.

She let me go and stared into my eyes. "How are you holding up?"

"Fine," I lied. "Y'know, under the circumstances."

"That's my boy."

Irene approached us and took Jean's arm. "Be a dear," she said, "and get Windsor. He's in the back seat."

Windsor was Jean and Irene's fourth miniature schnauzer since I had known them. When Beau was on his last legs, they adopted Radclyffe to be a little sister. After Beau died, Raddie was lonely, so they adopted another schnauzer, Halston. They died within six months of each other, and Jean swore there would be no more dogs. But it didn't surprise anyone when they eventually adopted a new puppy. They named him for Edie Windsor, the lesbian whose victory at the Supreme Court secured marriage rights for same-sex couples, and he bore the name with great pride and dignity.

I unfastened Windsor's seat belt, scooped him up, and carried him into the house. He allowed it.

"Can you have coffee?" Lee asked Jean after she sat down on the big blue couch.

Jean made a face. "Better not. Tastes like shit ever since they started poisoning me. Water would be lovely."

"Coming right up," Lee said. "Irene?"

"Oh, coffee, please."

"How do you take it?"

"As black as Dick Cheney's soul."

"Let me help you," I said as soon as I was sure Jean was comfortable.

Lee and I entered the kitchen. He headed to the coffeepot while I grabbed a tall glass from the cabinet.

"She looks better than I expected her to," Lee whispered. "Last time you went to visit, you said she looked like death."

"She's having a good day," I said, grabbing a pitcher of water from the fridge. "Leave it to me to fuck it all up."

"Oh, stop it," Lee said. "She's here because she wants to be." He poured Irene's coffee into a mug emblazoned with Bette Davis's face and the caption *I Detest Cheap Sentiment*. "Let's go."

We walked back into the sitting room to find Jean besotted with Russell, and I tried to remember if they'd ever met. I held her water in front of her. She smiled and gently took it from me. "Looked like death, how dare you," she whispered, winking.

Irene took her coffee from Lee. "Thank you," she said. "Now. Tell me everything, starting with last night."

With occasional interjections from Tucker and Lee, I got through as much of the story as I knew: the time Mamie was stolen, all of Tucker's work on social media, and my conversation with Lt. Herman. I intentionally left out the part where I forgot to turn the security system on. It remained too horrible to say out loud.

"I still think it was Freddie," Lee said.

"Oh, I doubt it," Irene said. "I've met his type before. He's a serial predator, but he only deals with one conquest at a time. No offense, Charlie, but he disappeared a long time ago. He doesn't think about you anymore."

"You're probably right," I said. "The police don't think it's Freddie, either. But they have his name, just in case."

"Probably smart," Irene said. "I never liked him, you know."

This wasn't exactly true. When Freddie appeared on the scene, Jean and Irene had fallen under his spell like everyone else. When we adopted Mamie together, they referred to her as their "grand-dog." We took trips to New York and New Orleans together, and everywhere we went Irene loved introducing us as "her boys." When Freddie left, however, her familial feeling turned into a raging inferno almost instantaneously. History was rewritten to reflect Irene mistrusting him from the beginning, only putting up with him to appease Jean and me, and believing I was besotted only because Freddie was so handsome and honestly who could blame me.

"So, what's our strategy?" Irene asked.

We told her about the possibility of a televised interview with Angela Woolsey on Channel Two.

"Excellent. And what else?"

Tucker showed her the flyer we'd sent out to the vet, the groomers, and the dog walking service. It would be all over my Capitol Hill neighborhood in a matter of hours.

"Good, good," she said. "Wait, there's nothing here about a reward."

"The police don't want us to offer a reward," I said.

Tucker looked my way. "They don't? You didn't tell us that."

"They said offering a reward results in lots of false leads. People who don't have Mamie call in tips in hopes of getting the money. Makes their job a lot harder."

"With all due respect to the boys in blue," Irene countered, "we're not here to make the cops' job easier. We're here to get your dog back. A reward captures people's interest. It puts them on the lookout. They'll pay a little bit more attention to every little yellow dog they see on the street, and it might get someone to call in who wouldn't even have noticed before."

"But Lt. Herman said—"

"Look," Irene said. "I didn't spend thirty years in corporate PR for nothing. And what I know is it doesn't matter why people buy your brand of toothpaste. What matters is they buy yours and not the other guy's."

Tucker saw my confusion. "But what does that have to do with—"

"It doesn't matter why whoever finds Mamie picks up the phone and calls the police," she said, "just so long as they do it. 'Too many leads' is only a problem if you're lazy or an idiot. I have no patience with lazy idiots."

"But what if we're making it harder for them to do their job?"

Irene was unfazed. "What if we're forcing them to do their job?"

"But the lieutenant said—"

"Charlie, listen to me. No one is going to save Mamie unless they first know there's a dog to be saved and unless they're excited about saving her. Did your friend the lieutenant happen to say anything about the likelihood he could get her back for you?"

"He said he would do everything he could, but…"

"But what?"

That did it. I was convinced.

"Okay," I said. "So, how much of a reward are we talking here? Like a thousand?"

"More like ten."

"Ten dollars doesn't seem like a lot."

"Ten *thousand* dollars, you big schlemiel. If you want this Woolsey person to call you back, trust me on this one." She handed the flyer back to Tucker. "Ten thousand," she repeated.

"Whoa, whoa, whoa. I don't have ten thousand dollars."

Irene looked at me, disappointed. She looked to Jean, who regarded me with a sympathetic shrug.

"Let's get your dog back," Jean said. "We'll worry about the rest afterward."

"But—"

Irene stood up. "Charlie," she said, "we'll figure it out. We'll all figure it out together, and no one will hang you out to dry. Trust us. But Jean's right. We need to get Mamie home where she belongs, and we don't have much time."

Friday, 10:11 a.m.

After the flyers were changed to include the ten thousand dollar figure and re-sent to the veterinarian, the pet grooming salon, and, most importantly, the dog-walking service, Jean requested a moment to rest.

Tending to Jean gave Lee a task for which he was grateful and perfectly suited. Tucker took the morning off so he could monitor our progress on social media. I called Lt. Herman back to let him know my friends had convinced me to post a reward.

"Well, shit," he said.

"I'm sorry."

"How much?"

"Ten thousand."

"Well, shit," he concluded. "At least I tried." And then he hung up the phone.

I looked up at Irene.

"It's the right thing to do," she said. "I'm never wrong."

Russell looked doubtful. Or maybe he just wanted to go outside.

"Tucker, Russell looks like he wants a walk. Should I take him?"

"That'd be great, sugar, thanks!"

"Does Windsor want to join us?" I asked.

Irene pursed her lips. "Should Hillary Clinton have won?"

We walked in silence for the length of the block. When we reached the corner, I pointed. "There's a little park up this way." We crossed the street and continued for another minute or so in silence. Finally, it seemed safe to ask the question that had been on everyone's mind since the rhyming lesbians arrived. "How's Jean?"

Irene gave me a wide smile, but the rest of her face was impossible to read behind her enormous sunglasses. "She looks good, doesn't she?"

"That's not an answer," I said.

Irene shot me a look.

"Hi, I'm Charlie. I've known you for a while."

Irene exhaled. "We don't know. There's no reason to believe the chemo isn't working, but there's no proof that it is. Yet."

"Are you scared?"

"No."

I might have rolled my eyes when I thought she wasn't looking. "Because if you were, you could always talk about it—"

"I'm not scared, Charlie." She took off her sunglasses so I could see her entire face. "Jean and I have been together for almost forty years. They weren't perfect, but I wouldn't give them up for anything. She's the very best person I know, and I really don't want her to die."

"But."

"The only thing that scares me, young man, is worrying I'll get to the end of my life and have regrets. And with apologies to Frank Sinatra, I've had a few."

"Such as?"

"I always said I should have moved back to New York after college. Convinced my father to leave the restaurant to his dyke daughter instead of his idiot son. But if I'd done that, I never would have met Jean. I would have had a different adventure. Maybe not as good, who knows? I have no regrets where Jean is concerned. None. Don't tell her this, but I almost said no when she asked me to move in with her."

"What? Why?"

"We'd only been dating about four months. I thought it was too soon. Jean knew better. She convinced me. So, I did. I have no regrets about that. I could have been kinder to her sometimes. Otherwise I've behaved perfectly, as you know."

I chuckled. She smiled and put her sunglasses back on.

"If our time is almost up…" Here she paused, I assumed to stop the catch in her voice and perhaps the tears that might follow. We walked for a moment in silence. I pointed to indicate we needed to cross the street again to get to the park around the corner. When we reached the other side, she stopped and faced me. "If she dies, my heart will break. And I'll get over it. Or not. But heartbreak is part of the deal, and the time we've already spent makes it worth it."

"And she might get better."

"And she might get better. We caught it relatively early, or so they tell us. We have every reason to be hopeful."

When we reached the park, I opened the gate to the little enclosure that would allow us to let the dogs roam around without a leash. As soon as he was free, Russell bounded away toward a much bigger dog. Little Windsor began straining at his own leash, incensed by the injustice of his being restrained. Irene struggled a bit with his leash, but eventually released him. Immediately he scampered after Russell, hoping to get in on the fun.

Irene found a bench and sat down. I joined her. "And what about you?" she asked.

"What about me?"

"When you're on your deathbed, what will you wish you'd had the guts to do, but didn't?"

"A lot, probably. Right now I just want my dog back."

"Fair enough." As if on cue, Windsor appeared in front of us and stood up against the bench, wanting a kind word or a scratch behind the ears.

As Irene supplied Windsor with the affection he required, I looked around for Russell, eventually spotting him darting across the park. He was playing a game of fetch with another dog and its human guardian. Not a care in the world, I thought to myself. But what about Mamie? Were they feeding her? Where was she sleeping? Was she wondering what I'm doing? Did she know we were trying to get her back? Did she miss me? Yes, I was sure she missed me terribly.

My phone buzzed in my pants. It was Tucker. I put him on speaker so Irene could hear.

"Hey, Tucker. What's up?"

"Check your Twitter messages right now."

"Just tell me."

"Angela Woolsey is interviewing you at noon at your place, and we have to move. Faster than green grass through a goose."

Irene peered at me over her sunglasses. "What a charming notion."

"We'll be back in five," I replied, and he hung up.

I called out to Russell, and Irene was already fastening Windsor's leash to his collar.

Friday, 10:57 a.m.

We returned to Lee's house to find my bag already packed for me, and Tucker's laptop and all his various cords and chargers put away. Lee was throwing powders and cremes into a backpack, presumably to doll me up before my big close-up.

Irene looked around. "Where's Jean?"

"Still sleeping," Lee said. "We didn't want to wake her. Listen, if you want to stay here with her, I can leave you a key."

"Not on your life. We're not about to miss this."

Lee pointed in the general direction of the guest room, and Irene darted down the hall.

Moments later, we were seat-belted into two cars. Lee hitched a ride with Tucker and Russell, and I climbed into the back seat of Jean and Irene's Subaru with Windsor. Irene drove, which seemed odd but entirely appropriate, given the circumstances.

I rode with the rhyming lesbians because they had never taken this particular route to my home, and I figured they could use some direction. Irene apparently felt the same about me.

"Don't look at the camera. Just focus all of your attention on Andrea Whoever."

"Angela," I said. "Woolsey."

"Her. You're having an intimate conversation with her. She's your new best friend."

"Got it."

"But don't let her steer the conversation. She'll probably want to talk about the crime angle, but you need to figure out a way to put the focus back on Mamie and implore people to be on the lookout for her. Don't forget to mention the reward *and* the amount at least three times."

"You'll want to take a right up here."

"Sad, but not too sad. If you do nothing but blubber, it's completely forgettable. Let the audience feel sad."

"Oh, I already have that all planned out. I'm going to let my eyes water up ever so slightly throughout, and then as soon as I'm done I'll blink so one single tear falls down my left cheek right at the very end. And then I thought maybe I'd try fainting, but it seemed a bit much. Left turn at the light."

Irene took the turn as directed. "Is he making fun of me? I think he's making fun of me."

"I think you're right," Jean answered, turning back to me. "Listen, kid. The best director I ever worked with used to give the same advice over and over. 'Don't act,' she said. 'Just get out there and tell the truth.'" She gave me a smile, then turned to face the front, adjusting her bandana.

It was good advice. And if it wasn't, it would have to do because I didn't have time to prepare anything else.

"That was me," Irene said. "I said that."

"Do you know where you are now?" I asked.

"Yeah, I think I got it."

Jean placed her hand on Irene's knee, and we drove the rest of the way in silence.

Friday, 11:42 a.m.

When we got to the house, Lee—who knew where I kept my key and had his own code to the security system—was already inside, dusting every horizontal surface he could find.

"That's really not necessary," I said.

"The camera picks up everything."

"He's right," Irene said. "Get me a dust cloth, and I'll help. Charlie, do something with all of this clutter."

I picked up last week's mail and moved it to the kitchen counter, sorting envelopes either into a pile for things to consider later or into the trash. I noticed a large brochure from the University of Maryland addressed to Freddie. Trash.

When I finished, I left the kitchen to find Tucker and Lee moving my furniture around under Irene's direction.

"What are you doing?"

"There was no place in here to put the camera," Irene said, pointing to the opposite corner of the room. "A little more to the left," she instructed Tucker.

I was about to object when I felt Jean's hand on mine.

"Let her be," she whispered to me. "She's doing this out of love, which you know already. But more importantly, she's good at all this stuff. Just breathe, okay?"

She gently squeezed my hand, and I squeezed back. "Okay."

Windsor, who was sitting in Jean's lap, began to growl at

some movement outside. Acting from pure instinct, Tucker grabbed Russell's collar, and the onslaught of barking commenced seconds before the knock.

Russell and Windsor were guarding the castle in the absence of its maiden, and suddenly I felt a rush of affection for these animals so intense that it didn't immediately occur to me to answer the door.

"We'll be right there," Irene shouted, then silently urged me on. Taking direction well and remembering to breathe, I opened the door to a renewed chorus of disapproval from the hounds.

Angela Woolsey, someone I had only ever seen on television, stood on my front porch. She wore a burgundy suit matching her lipstick perfectly, and her smile was warm but not too broad, suitable for the occasion. She was flanked by two men, one carrying a camera and the other a microphone on the end of a boom. She extended her hand.

"Mr. Vernon, is it?"

I took her hand, and she held it in both of hers.

"It's good to meet you. I'm here to talk about Mamie. May I come in?"

CHAPTER SEVEN

Knickerbocker Farms bred cockapoos and miniature goldendoodles in Virginia's Shenandoah Valley, about two hours away from Washington by car. The bitches were either cocker spaniels or golden retrievers, and the studs were all miniature poodles. I had filled out the online application, including detailed histories of every dog, cat, or gerbil I'd ever met, and had been granted the honor of a telephone interview.

"How do you get a miniature poodle to impregnate a golden retriever?" I asked the nice woman on the phone, after our initial pleasantries.

"Well, we have stepladders for that."

"You're kidding."

"Listen, when a bitch is in heat, she'll take it wherever she can get it. They manage. Now how can I help you today?"

"I'd like to reserve a cockapoo from your next litter."

"Very good," she said. "I just have a few questions to get us started."

"I'm ready." I could hear pages rustling. This was going to be official.

"Name?"

"Charlie Vernon."

"I'm Norah. It's nice to meet you. Any preference on gender?"

"I'd like a female."

"Any preference on color?"

"People do that?"

"Some people have a very particular idea of what they want their new puppy to be. We're happy to accommodate those requests, but it might mean a longer wait."

"Any color is fine," I said.

"Very good. How many people live in your household?"

"Two," I said, and it felt good to say it. Freddie and me. Two.

"Any children?"

"No."

"Tell me a little about your home. Is it a house? Apartment? Do you have a yard?"

I already wrote all this down on my application, I thought. Are they looking for holes in my story? I told her all about the Capitol Hill neighborhood of Washington, DC, and the blocks and blocks of little row houses built here just before the crash of 1929. "We have a little bit of yard in front," I said, "about the size of a postage stamp."

"Fence?"

"No, but we're thinking of putting one in." Oh shit, I thought, I'm going to fail the test and be denied a dog. "The neighborhood is very walkable."

"Very good. Puppies can be taken home at eight weeks. Do you promise to spay your puppy between six and eight months at your own expense?"

"Yes, that's fine."

"You're doing great. One final question."

"I'm feeling confident," I said, with all the bravado I could muster.

"Are you sure you want a cockapoo?"

"Excuse me?"

"Have you considered a goldendoodle?"

I was looking at the Knickerbocker website while on the phone, and I could see the goldendoodles were slightly more expensive. Holy crap, I thought, she's *upselling* me.

"Is there something wrong with the cockapoos?"

"No, nothing like that," she assured me. "It's just that poodles are very smart dogs."

"Yes, I understand."

"And golden retrievers are very sweet. Cocker spaniels, we've learned, can be awfully stubborn. So, I guess what I'm asking you is do you want smart and sweet, or smart and stubborn?"

"It's a little house," I said, "and a tiny yard. I think we were looking for a smaller dog."

"Our goldendoodles only reach about forty pounds," she said, "and the females are even a little smaller."

"It's okay," I said. "I'll take one smart-and-stubborn, please."

"Coming right up in about two and a half months. Go to the website and enter your credit card. When a litter is born, you can choose a puppy in the order your deposit was received. It looks like you'll be, let's see here, fifth in line for our next litter of cockapoos."

"Thanks very much, Norah."

"You're very welcome, Charlie. And don't say I didn't warn you."

I had tried to convince Freddie to try a shelter where we could adopt a puppy who needed a home, perhaps even save a life, but he wasn't interested. A few weeks after he proposed adopting a dog, I went online to find the shelters closest to us, but Freddie was hesitant.

"We should know what we're getting," he said.

"A dog, Freddie. We're getting a dog. Why don't we visit a shelter and look around. No pressure."

Freddie laughed. "Oh no. You'll fall in love with some random one-eyed mongrel and insist we bring it home."

"I promise I won't make that kind of decision without you. But they say the dog often chooses you, and that wouldn't be the worst thing."

"We should get the dog we really want. Lee and Claude didn't go to a shelter. It's not like we can't afford it." I suppose what he really meant was that I could afford it. "Cass and Peggy don't shed all over the house, for starters."

"You want a Maltese? You'll need a Birkin bag to carry her around in."

"No, I don't, but lots of dogs don't shed."

"We can tell the shelter we want a non-shedding dog."

"I wouldn't trust them, would you? There are a million dogs in there. How can you tell which ones shed and which ones don't?"

I blamed Freddie's reluctance on a combination of growing up poor and moving to a city surrounded by status seekers. He had spent his entire life trying to convince people he wasn't a poor kid from the wrong side of Chicago with a single mother who probably would have repeated the eighth grade if anyone had been paying the least bit of attention. I tried to foster some sympathy for his predicament, but I'll admit it was difficult.

I hadn't ever been wealthy, but growing up in a Navy family certainly meant we never worried about whether we'd have food on the table. Being the son of an officer meant I had always enjoyed some level of status. But in my case, I spent my childhood learning to downplay my privilege to fit in with the kids around me, most of whom weren't allowed to swim at the Officers' Club pool in the summertime. Bragging about your father's rank typically didn't win you many popularity contests on base.

I could understand Freddie not wanting "some random one-eyed mongrel," but I didn't want a dog that cost a million dollars. Obviously, I didn't have a million dollars, but more importantly, that wasn't why I wanted a dog. I wanted a member of the family, not a possession we would wear like an expensive watch or a fancy cologne.

My compromise was a "designer mutt," although I learned quickly never to use that phrase around Freddie. He was a bit more receptive to the idea of a "doodle," a mix between a non-shedding poodle and some other breed of pure and untouched lineage. There were lots of doodles to choose from: schnoodles, doxie-doos, cavapoos, labradoodles, yorkipoos, and the smart-and-sweet goldendoodles. But when I searched for "cockapoo puppies" on the internet and showed him the resulting photos, I finally saw his heart melt.

"That's it," he said. "That's our dog."

Secretly I searched for "cockapoo rescues," but there wasn't much there. By all accounts you could end up waiting the better part of a year for a dog and would also have to be ready to take one home at a moment's notice. I was too planful for that, and Freddie was too impatient. And if I was honest, I was eager to have a dog sooner than later myself.

I found Knickerbocker Farms through a simple internet search and thoroughly browsed the website before filling out their application, which took the better part of two hours. Only when everything met with Freddie's approval did I accept Norah's invitation for an official interview. After learning more than I wanted to about stepladders and the breeding of mini-goldendoodles, I paid the deposit and waited.

Mamie's litter was born in the second week of July. The evening of the birth, we were told that photos of the pups were available on the Knickerbocker Farms website for viewing. They didn't look like much, to be honest. To a puppy they all looked like someone struggling to wake up on a cold Monday morning after too much wine the night before. So, we relied on the descriptions, which really told us only weight and color. There was one yellow dog in the litter, and I resigned myself to the fact that someone else would probably choose her before it was our turn to decide. Another female was described as "sable," which I thought was sort of glamourous. And yet, I really wanted that blonde. But I could do nothing about it. We weren't about to wait another six months, and I had told Norah I didn't care about color, and had sneered at those who might. Dammit.

I noticed customers were naming the puppies upon claiming them in order of payment as soon as they were born. I mentioned this to Freddie, and for whatever reason he left the naming of the dog completely up to me. Not having an actual puppy to inspire me, I thought about the kind of dog I hoped to have. Smart and stubborn were qualities I knew to expect, but I also hoped the dog would be loyal, loving, adventurous, and full of personality. I went so far as to make a list of these qualities and stare at them, hoping for some inspiration. And suddenly she appeared, on the top of a staircase, bugle in hand, announcing the imminent arrival of the bootleggers. It was Mame Dennis.

If you're not familiar with the story, *Auntie Mame* is about a young boy named Patrick Dennis who, in the late 1920s when his father dies, is sent to live with Mame, his madcap, eccentric aunt. When they first meet at a wild party in her penthouse, she tells him to take a piece of paper and write down all the words he doesn't understand. From that auspicious beginning, they weather the Great Depression and the joys and sorrows of marriage, widowhood, adolescence, courtship, and riding an insane horse. She teaches him how to live courageously, and he gives her purpose. It was a book, then a play, a movie in the 1950s, and a Broadway musical in 1966.

When I was twenty-nine years old, Irene directed the musical version of *Mame* and asked me to audition for the role of Older Patrick. Since a young boy plays Patrick during Act One, I got to watch from the wings a lot, and I memorized everyone else's lines and nearly every note of the score. It's a zany, funny tale, but I was always profoundly moved by it. Above all else, it's a story about a woman who loves unconditionally, and it seemed only right that our new puppy would take her name because, really, why else does anyone bring a dog home? It's not because we relish the idea of putting a plastic bag on our hands and collecting steaming piles of poop from the side of the road.

One day I turned to Freddie and asked, "What do you think about Mame Dennis Babcock Vernon?"

"Fine," he said. "Can we call her Mamie?"

And that, as they say, was that.

It occurred to me this was also a perfect name for a dog described as sable. Auntie Mame came from a time when women still loved their fur coats. But three days later, the sable puppy was already spoken for. Our little blonde, however, was still available. We didn't hesitate, immediately claiming her with the click of a mouse and proudly informing Norah of her new name so the website could be updated. We fantasized a lot about what wonderful parents we'd be, and I kidded Freddie he should enjoy sleeping in while he still had the chance. Soon enough we'd have a puppy who desperately needed to pee first thing in the morning. "We can make that your job," he said, which I knew was probably correct. Freddie could barely get *himself* up to pee and out to work on time most days.

Mamie would be ready to come home eight weeks later, right before Labor Day weekend. Freddie and I did our research and lots of shopping. High quality protein-rich puppy food, house training pads for the front and back doors, a leash that ended up being too long, a collar that ended up being too large, a crate, a rhinestone-encrusted set of bowls for food and water Freddie insisted on, many training treats, and environmentally friendly poop bags. Lots and lots of poop bags.

When September finally arrived, we were ecstatic. We both arranged to take the Friday before Labor Day off as this was the first day puppies would be released to their homes. We were on the road by seven a.m., with absolutely no complaints from Freddie.

The three-hour drive to Knickerbocker Farms was easy and without incident. We arrived twenty minutes before scheduled pickups would begin. Even so, we weren't the first ones there. Two other families showed up before us, both with daughters who I guessed were in the fifth or sixth grade. We got out of the car, and I introduced myself to the mothers in line. The daughters were literally bouncing up and down with excitement and therefore a little too distracted to partake in interactions with adult strangers, but I found they could concentrate when I started asking them about their dogs. Boys or girls? What color? Had they already picked out a name? For both, the answer was yes. Buster and Max.

From the corner of my eye, I could see one of their fathers' eyes go wide at the sight of me and Freddie, two adult men, holding hands in the farmlands of Virginia, a three-hour drive from our liberal enclave. Looking suddenly nauseous, he almost said something to us, but his wife shot him a warning look before he was able. I was inclined to simply take my hand back, not wanting to cause a scene, but Freddie gripped it tightly and wouldn't let go. We were having a moment, and a no petty bigot was going to take that away.

I turned my attention to these young girls as they met their new best friends. It was the sweetest sight, enough to make me happy we were third in line. Freddie was as impatient to meet Mamie, but my heart swelled watching as Norah gingerly placed a puppy into each girl's waiting arms. In fact, I was so focused on them I didn't even notice when it was our turn.

"Charlie," Freddie whispered, nudging me, "there she is!"

Norah appeared, holding a little yellow ball of fluff smaller than the two hands that held her. She remembered me well. When she gently set Mamie in my arms, she whispered, "One smart-and-stubborn, sir."

I held Mamie while Freddie hovered. She looked up at us, her big brown eyes registering a moment of doubt before she closed them completely and buried her head against my chest, a gesture that seemed simultaneously full of love and trust but also an act of utter denial about the life-changing event now occurring for all of us.

Another family stood behind us, eager to meet their new puppy, so I shuffled backward, allowing Freddie to move with us as a unit. Everyone around us faded into the background, and there was only the three of us: Freddie, Mamie, and me, a new little pack. "You want to hold her?"

Freddie shook his head. "I just want to look at her."

I looked at him, looking at her. The feeling of family was overwhelming. It was one thing to be a couple, and don't misunderstand—it was a wonderful thing. But somehow the addition of this little furball who was completely dependent upon us made us a little tribe. I was never one of those gays who wanted to procreate. I always suspected that homosexuality was not only a natural phenomenon, but evolution's preferred method of population control. And as methods go, I figured it beat the hell out of natural disasters and communicable diseases, and I had long ago decided to cooperate. So, for me this little puppy represented the extent to which I'd have a family, and the feeling was surprisingly poignant and precious.

Freddie must have felt the weight of my stare because soon enough our eyes locked. He wrapped his arms around the both of us, not caring who in rural Virginia might take notice.

❖

Mamie's first day home was guarded and hesitant. We returned from Knickerbocker Farms by mid-afternoon. She was old enough for puppy kibble, but she was unsure about eating from a bowl, probably more accustomed to nursing at her mother's teats. The doggie beds and blankets were comfy, but she was hesitant about nestling in them alone without her nine littermates. She probably missed them, I thought. And her mother. Most of all, though, we tried to show her how much we loved and adored her with every coo, caress, and embrace. She was also unsure of Freddie and me, these two enormous humans who were very strange and not at all respectful of a puppy's personal space.

But it wasn't long—Monday afternoon, in fact—when she decided Freddie and I were hers. Lee and Claude cut their holiday weekend short specifically to come see her, and when they knocked on the door, she bayed in protest of these evil invaders. And at that moment, I knew we belonged to her. The more she growled at Lee's attempts to rub his nose against hers, the more I loved her.

Norah from Knickerbocker Farms was right. She was a stubborn dog, but I found her tenacity both adorable and admirable. More importantly, Mamie was easily the most intelligent puppy I'd ever met. Housetraining wasn't immediate, but she understood the distinction between inside and outside almost instantly. The only impediments to her progress were the size of her tiny bladder and the sheer amount of poop she generated. "I swear to God she shits her entire weight every damn day," Freddie said, soon learning never to take Mamie for a walk with only one environmentally friendly poop bag.

Very quickly, she learned to hide a toy under a piece of furniture while we weren't looking, then bark and carry on until one of us rescued it. It was a traditional game of fetch, but the humans were the ones who were retrieving upon command.

If she was randomly barking at a friend's couch, there was always a tennis ball or a plushy toy underneath. Much like Irene

Epstein, she was never wrong. When out for a walk, if she seemed interested in sniffing another dog's butt from fifty paces away, the other dog would turn out to be friendly and sweet. If she started walking behind me, the other dog would always be menacing and mean.

Speaking of which, walking the dog typically fell to me. Freddie was not a morning person, and I usually made it home from work before he did. By the time Mamie was about six months old, he was rarely home before seven p.m., and he was usually so exhausted he went to bed before me, leaving me with the late night walk as well. I didn't mind. Even when I felt sluggish or put-upon, her enthusiasm for a good sniff around the block never wavered, which buoyed my spirits every time.

One night, when Mamie was about eight months old, Freddie texted to say he wouldn't be home until eight thirty. When he finally appeared, Mamie barked angrily at the door until he opened it, then the barking was replaced with an excited whine of anticipation.

"Is that you, hon?" I yelled.

"Home at last. Hey, Mamie! Hi, girl! You happy to see me?"

I walked halfway down the stairs to greet him. "How was work?"

"Work was shit," he said, though he seemed happy to be home. "C'mon, Mamie! Go for a walk?"

Hearing the magic words, she sprang from the floor and began her dance of joy.

"She's been out."

"This one's for me," he said, flashing me a smile. "I need some Mamie time. I missed you, silly girl, yes I did!" He looked up at me. "Want to come?"

"No, I'm settled in. Have fun." He smiled again, blew me a kiss, and then he and Mamie were out the door.

They were gone a while, longer than a simple walk around the block. When I heard the door open again, it was followed by the sound of Mamie's paws against the wood as she bounded upstairs, happily spent. Freddie followed more slowly, heading straight after her into the bedroom. I picked up my glass of wine and followed.

"Hey. What's the matter?"

"I hate my job," he said, flopping on the bed dramatically. "These late nights are getting out of hand."

Mamie hopped on the bed, licking his face and causing him to giggle. I surveyed the scene happily and figured this would be a good time to follow up on a conversation I'd been meaning to have for a while.

"You don't seem very happy there. Want to look for something else? I'd be happy to help polish up your résumé."

"It won't help. I'll never get anything that pays this well without a degree. As it is, I don't make half of what you do."

"You know I don't care about that," I said, which was met with silence. "But if you want to get a degree, working adults do it all the time. The University of Maryland has a great program."

"School was never really my thing."

"That was a long time ago, and you didn't give a shit back then." He sat up, giving Mamie scratches behind her ear. She happily accepted them. "You're a smart man, Freddie. If Donald Trump and his menagerie of trust fund idiot babies can earn college degrees, you could too. If you wanted. And if you don't, that's fine. But it would make you feel better about your job if you knew it was temporary."

He kissed Mamie on the head and stood up. Walking over to me slowly, he put his arms around me and kissed me. He grinned, though I wasn't sure why. "How about I just be your housewife?"

"You're going to cook my meals and clean this house every day?"

"No."

"Then forget it." I curled up my nose. "Why do you smell like cigarettes?"

"My work wife smokes. I took a break with her tonight so I could stretch my legs."

"That's disgusting."

He kissed my neck. "I know it's gross," he said, kissing me on the mouth sloppily the way Brian used to. He tasted like an ashtray. And it *was* gross, but also kind of sexy. "You really think I could do it? Go to college?"

"Of course, if it's something you want to do."

He kissed my forehead, then went back to the bed and sat down next to Mamie, who was joyfully assaulting a squeaky toy. "You can't pay for it," he said.

"You can get a loan if that's what you want."

Freddie scratched Mamie behind her ears, which momentarily halted the squeaking. "Would you be proud of your dad if he graduated from college?" he asked her.

But it wasn't her job to be proud of Freddie, just to love him. And the look on her face said she already did.

Freddie acquired a loan with only nominal assistance from me on the application. While he appreciated the support, he seemed bound and determined to do this himself. To be honest, I was pleased. I loved many things about Freddie Babcock, but until then *ambitious* would never have been a word I would use to describe him.

He submitted his student application on the last possible day to be admitted for the semester. He worried his dismal high school grade point average would be held against him, but I assured him lots of adults getting their first bachelor's degrees were in the same boat.

When he called on a random Tuesday, I was concerned because he never called in the middle of a workday.

"Charlie! I got in! They took me!"

"Slow down, Freddie. What happened?"

"College! I'm going to college! I can't believe it."

I was pleased for him, and I tried to sound as excited as he was. But honestly, the acceptance letter was not a surprise to me at all. It had all happened so fast, I hadn't had time to register any suspense. At the same time, I was determined not to be a rain cloud on a sunny day, so I forced myself to squeal with delight as he was doing.

"That's great, honey. That's amazing. I'm so proud of you!"

I was so effusive, Agnes poked her head out of her office to see what kind of gay racket was happening outside. I pointed to the phone and mouthed the word *Freddie.* She rolled her eyes and disappeared back into her office. As I stuck out my tongue in response, I chuckled and hoped Freddie would take the spontaneous laughter as simply an indication of my joy at his success.

And from then on, as I predicted, I saw less of Freddie. Of course, he was still mine on the weekends, apart from the occasional study group before a big test or when he'd hole himself up in the office on a Sunday to work on a paper. It was quieter there, he said, and he could print as many copies as he wanted while he was editing.

But because Mamie was at home, she and I spent a lot of quality time together. Lincoln Park was a favorite destination where she happily fetched and returned her bouncy ball until she was almost too exhausted to walk home. There were lots of movies on the couch, things I could never get Freddie to watch because his tastes veered more toward the Kardashian, but Mamie enjoyed them without complaint.

Sometimes I'd sneak over to Lee and Claude's house for what we called a "wine and puppies" gathering where Peggy Lee would try to get Mamie to play while Mamie would studiously avoid her, and Mama Cass observed haughtily from atop the big blue couch. But I always made sure to leave by nine p.m. so I'd beat Freddie home. I didn't want him to think we were having a grand old time while he was hard at work. It almost felt like we were cheating on him.

"Oh come on," Claude once said. "He doesn't expect you to be some kind of shut-in, does he? He wanted to go to school."

"I know, I know," I said, gathering Mamie's leash and toys. "He hasn't said I'm not allowed to have any fun. I'm just being weird."

Lee opened the door for me. "And a little in love."

"That too. C'mon, Mamie, let's go!" And she came running. "There's a good girl."

❖

I became so used to finding Mamie home alone on Tuesdays and Thursdays when Freddie had class that, about eight months into his degree program, I was shocked to find he'd beaten me home on a Thursday. As I walked in the back door through the kitchen, I could see him sitting on the couch, staring out the front window.

He barely noticed my entrance, but Mamie came running. She was now full grown, so whenever I'd arrive, she'd stand against me, her little paws reaching up to my belt buckle. It was something all the training articles told us never to allow, but I indulged her. Plus it was adorable.

"Hey, girl," I said, leaning down so Mamie could give me a little kiss on the cheek. "Freddie? Is that you?"

He didn't answer, so I gave Mamie a little pat on the side of her chest, which was her cue to run upstairs and find the nearest, noisiest toy she could. I walked into the living room.

"Hon? You okay? Don't you have class tonight?"

No answer. He was being tragic for some reason. It was unlike him, so I probably should have been concerned, but I was annoyed. It had been a bitch of a day at work, and if he didn't want to tell me what was wrong, that was his problem.

"Has Mamie been walked?"

He now deigned to look at me with great big sad eyes. Big, sad, silent eyes. The only noise was Mamie's squeaky toy directly above us.

"Has she been out?"

He shook his head no.

"Fine," I said, trying to sound pleasant but likely failing miserably. "I assume she hasn't been fed either?"

Freddie turned away without a word and looked at whatever was so interesting outside.

"Mamie! C'mere, girl. Go for a walk?"

She abandoned her toy and came racing downstairs. As I grabbed her leash from the little hook by the door, I mumbled. "Nice to see you too, Charlie. How was your day, Charlie?"

I opened the door so Mamie could hit the landing and run

directly outside without even slowing down. I loved that. I fastened her leash to her collar on the front porch inside our newly fenced-in, postage stamp-sized front yard and took her for a walk around the block.

When we walked into the house again, Freddie hadn't moved. Mamie ran directly to her food and water bowls in the kitchen, which were both empty. He hadn't even bothered to give her any water. I filled them both. While she lapped at the water, I joined Freddie in the living room, sat down, and pretended to read a magazine, waiting for him to talk. He didn't.

When Mamie was full, she joined us in the living room and hopped up on the couch next to Freddie. At first I thought it tremendously disloyal. After all, I was the one who had just walked and fed her, but soon I saw what our little diplomat was doing.

Freddie and I rarely fought in those days, it's true, but even the mildest disagreement over emptying the dishwasher, or what television show we should binge next, would routinely be interrupted by a little yellow dog in desperate need of a treat, walk, or a snuggle. Suddenly, taking care of her took priority and our squabbles seemed unnecessary and petty. This didn't work as well a year later when things became much more acrimonious, but in those early, happy, look-at-our-beautiful-new-family days, it was charming and precious. I could never figure out if she interrupted our quarrels because she was averse to conflict or because she was more likely to acquire the treat, walk, or snuggle she craved. Either way, she ruled the home and we lived to serve.

She badgered Freddie for affection until he couldn't refuse. She couldn't eke out his famous smile. But she managed a belly rub, and in doing so, she brought him out of himself for a moment.

After an eternity, he finally spoke. "I have something to tell you," he said. "It's about Arthur."

Arthur? His ex? "What about him?"

"He called me today." And now he turned to me for maximum dramatic effect. "He said he's HIV-positive."

I wasn't sure what to say. I didn't hate Arthur. In fact, I rarely thought of him. He was Freddie's ex and a troubled man, but I didn't want bad things to happen to him. Or did I? Was I jealous or just annoyed at Freddie's sudden theatrics over the whole thing? Eventually, I cleared my throat and said, "That's too bad."

"Is that all you can say?"

"It's awful news, Freddie, but I've never met Arthur and I'm not sure how to react. I'm sure he's scared, but I don't know. It's a manageable illness for most people these days. I'm sure he'll be f—"

"He doesn't know when he got it."

I put my magazine down. "What are you saying exactly?"

"We got tested together when I moved in, and we were both negative. But we were together for three years, and when he called me today, he told me he'd cheated on me twice. And never got tested again until last week." Freddie looked at me. "I could be positive too." He was getting a little choked up. "And so could—"

You. The word he'd been unable to say was *you*. I could be HIV-positive too. He was now staring out the window again, tears streaming down his face.

"I'm so sorry," he said.

"It's not your fault." My mind reeled, and I was suddenly imagining a raft of pills I'd have to take every morning and whether or not I'd tell my mother right away. "It's not your fault," I repeated, and he began crying harder. I got up from my chair to sit beside him on the sofa, gently nudging Mamie back to the floor. "We don't know anything yet. We could both be fine." I put my hand on his shoulder, now shaking violently with his sobs. "Tomorrow we'll call in sick, and we'll go to Whitman-Walker. We'll get tested. Maybe we're fine." He caught his breathing and sniffed hard. He wiped a tear from his cheek. "It's not your fault," I said. "It's not your fault." And suddenly I hated Arthur.

The next day we both called in sick. I wanted to go to the clinic first thing in the morning, but Freddie kept putting me off. Let's have a real breakfast, he said, or let's take Mamie to the park since it's such a beautiful day. And it was.

Finally, around two in the afternoon I put my foot down. "We're going," I said. "After we get our results, we're going to be either happy or sad, but either way it's better than walking on eggshells until we know. Put your shoes on." I snapped my fingers to get Mamie's attention. "Kennel," I said, and she dutifully hopped into her crate, waiting for the obligatory treat.

At the clinic, after our blood had been drawn, we held hands in the waiting room, only letting go when it was time for me to have a private consultation with the attending physician. Right away I learned I was negative, but was forced to sit and listen to the doctor's song-and-dance about condoms and being tested every six months. When she told me I could go, I went back to the waiting room to find Freddie's seat empty.

When he finally reappeared, his cheeks were wet with tears, and he was smiling. He was okay. We hugged. The little gay clinician behind him smiled and shut the door. When we parted, I could feel all the eyes in the place on us. Some of these people were living with HIV, and suddenly I felt a little guilty for celebrating in the middle of an AIDS clinic. "Let's get out of here."

Walking back to the car, Freddie was giddy. Apparently, around three in the morning he'd resigned himself to an early death and still couldn't quite believe his good luck.

"Let's stop for a drink," he said. "I feel like celebrating. Let's call Lee and Claude and Tucker and Jack and buy them a really expensive dinner."

"One drink," I said. "I have to drive home. Besides, it's almost four thirty, and Mamie will be crossing her legs in her crate if we don't go home for the next four hours."

"We were just home," he argued. "She'll be fine."

I peered at him disapprovingly over my glasses. "Did you let her out before we left?"

"No, but—"

"Neither did I."

We walked a little while in silence. Freddie didn't like it when I was right, and while I didn't want to ruin the festive mood, I also didn't want Mamie to pay for our poor planning. After all, when we left the house, we didn't dare hope we'd have reason for celebration before returning.

Freddie stopped and turned to me, picking up the argument exactly where we had left off. "It's just that—"

"It's just that what?"

"Charlie, we're not going to die!"

"Not yet anyway." I smiled, and held his hand, pulling him slightly until we were both walking toward the car again. "Tell you what. As long as we're on this side of town, let's go to the wine store and pick up some Zinfandel and stinky cheese. After taking Mamie out, we'll order in. Anything you want. We can have a private celebration tonight. Just the family."

And when we got home, Mamie was there waiting, as joyful as we were but for a much simpler reason. She belonged with us, and we with her. And that was reason enough for all of us to jump for joy.

CHAPTER EIGHT

Friday, 11:57 a.m.

"Please, Ms. Woolsey," I said. "Come on in."

Angela Woolsey still held my hand in both of hers, giving it a little squeeze and offering a sympathetic smile before releasing it. She was wearing very expensive leather gloves, making her hands exceptionally soft and warm. "Call me Angela," she said. "We're friends now."

I moved out of the way, and she immediately greeted everyone in the room—Tucker, then Irene, then Lee—with the same solemn and graceful smile, a little wrinkle in the forehead, careful not to show any teeth. It was a smile that said she was happy to meet you, happy to be of service, but not at all happy about the situation bringing us all together. I'll admit I liked her immediately.

She noticed Jean sitting in the other room and gracefully made her way to meet her. "I'm Angela," she said. "I'm a reporter with Channel Two."

"Oh, I know who you are," Jean said, opting to stay in her chair but gratefully taking Angela's hand. "When Irene and I lived in Washington, we watched you every night. Thank you so much for being here."

"It's my pleasure," Angela said. "Where do you two live now?"

Jean began to tell her all about moving to Rehoboth Beach, where the local news usually focused on traffic accidents and the mysterious deaths of livestock. Angela didn't blink when Jean referred to Irene as her wife and never mentioned the bandana on her head nor the apparent lack of hair underneath. She's seen it all, I thought. Plus, she's a class act.

"The makeup is flawless," Lee whispered to me, inserting himself between Tucker and me. "It looks a little heavy in the daylight, but you have to really lay on the blush if it's going to show up on camera, especially on dark skin like hers."

The man holding the boom mic, himself African American, overheard Lee's dissection of Angela's face, seeming more amused than offended. Lee was oblivious as he continued to whisper the secrets behind Angela Woolsey's expert contouring.

"It was lovely to meet you, Jean," she said. "I'd better get back."

Jean beamed as Angela came back into the living room. She checked in with her crew. "Everything okay in here?"

"We'll be ready in five minutes," said the cameraman.

"We moved the furniture for you," Tucker said. "We figured it would be easier for you to shoot this way."

"That's perfect," Angela said. "Thank you, Tucker."

I think we were all struck by the fact she remembered his name. I think Tucker even blushed a little.

"Charlie," she said, looking at me. "Would you mind giving me a little tour?"

"Uh, sure. I mean, what would you like to see?"

"Can you show me where the burglars broke in?"

"Of course," I said. "I'll warn you, the basement is a bit of a nightmare."

"It's fine."

I led her downstairs and showed her the back door with the makeshift duct tape and garbage bag seal over the window.

"Is there broken glass behind that?"

"Yes."

"Do you think we could remove the seal, just for now? A shot of the broken window will be more impactful for my viewers."

"I understand. I mean, of course. Whatever helps."

"I assume we shouldn't touch the doorknob," she said, noticing the black powder left by the police.

"No, not until the cops come back."

She pulled her expensive leather gloves from her purse and put one on. She approached the door, turning the knob at the base with her gloved hand, careful not to disturb the police's work. Opening the door, she surveyed the broken pane behind the garbage bag.

"This will work," she said. "We'll place the camera where you're standing, and I can approach from the outside. I'll stick my hand through the window as if I'm reaching for the knob, and then I'll open the door from the outside with my other hand."

She looked to me for approval, so I nodded. Honestly, this was so far out of my realm of expertise, I felt unworthy of an opinion even if she was telling my story. None of her suggestions seemed to be stretching the truth past any reasonable boundary I could think of. And either way I wasn't a journalist. I was just a guy wanting my dog back, and whatever Angela Woolsey felt like doing to help Mamie come home was fine with me.

"Did Mamie have the run of the house while you were gone?"

"No," I said. "I kept her in a crate upstairs. When I got home yesterday, it was sort of turned on its side. I haven't moved it."

"I see," she said. "Can you take me there?"

Friday, 12:28 p.m.

I was told I didn't have to watch this part if I didn't want to. But I figured it was my story being told, and, besides, the house was too quiet and I hated that.

The plan was for Angela to walk down my street past my neighbors' yards, introduce the story, and stop in front of my yard so she could point to my house when she got to the headline: Mamie had been stolen.

As the cameraman consulted with the boom mic operator about where to stand so he'd not be seen or cast a shadow but still pick up Angela's voice, she was pacing up and down the sidewalk, practicing her lines. I was prepared at any moment to grab Irene's hand if she tried to give Angela direction, but she was on her best behavior.

"Wallet, phone, car," Angela kept repeating to herself, "wallet, phone, car," as she marked her movements down the street.

"Ready when you are," the cameraman noted with a deft hand gesture that indicated where we'd need to stand during all of this if we were to remain outside.

"Ready," Angela said, taking her mark.

Standing in front of her, ready to move backward once she began to walk, the cameraman pointed his lens toward her, counting down, "Three...two..." The "one" was silent as he pointed her way.

"You can steal a man's wallet," she said, slowly but confidently walking toward the camera, which was backing away. "You can steal a man's phone." She sounded stern, but caring. "You can even steal a man's car." She shook her head slightly as if unable to control the senseless inhumanity of the act she was about to describe. "But to steal a man's dog?"

At this point, she stopped directly in front of my house. "It happened to the man who lives here," she said, gently gesturing to my front door, "and he's devastated. When you hear the story and meet the dog, you'll know why."

And then she froze. I didn't know whether she had forgotten her speech, or whether something was wrong on the technical end, but it seemed like she just stood there for an insane length of time, though it was probably only five seconds.

"Got it," the cameraman finally said. "I'm good with this. Do you want another take?"

"No, it felt good."

And it did. I wanted to hear more about this story until I remembered I already knew the story and hated it.

"I'll meet you around back," she said to them, approaching me. "Walk with me?"

"Sure," I said, as she put her gloved hand around my elbow. Automatically I bent my arm, and as we walked to the corner and around the block it we looked as if we were posing for a prom picture. It was oddly formal, but weirdly comforting.

"So, the next segment will feature the photos you've sent us. I want people to see Mamie's face, to really connect with her."

"Okay," I said. "Will you tell people we're looking for her? And offering a reward?"

"We'll cover that in the interview portion," she said. "I assume you're willing to go on camera."

"Of course. I mean, if it helps."

"Oh, I think it's vital," she said. "While people are looking at the photos, I'll relay what we know about how she was stolen. What we're about to shoot is me coming through the alley to the basement door to show people how they entered. I want to communicate a real sense of violation. You don't have to be there if you don't want to."

"I don't mind," I said. "Unless we're in your way. I mean, I could ask everyone to wait inside if you—"

"No, no, it's fine," she said, smiling her sad smile as we turned into the alley. "Perhaps it would be best if you stood over there?"

From our assigned vantage point in the alley, we couldn't see or hear much. It was a bright, chilly day, and we huddled close together, bouncing up and down for a little warmth. The cameraman was inside the basement, and Angela spoke into a handheld microphone. She approached the door, reached in through the window with her left hand, and—unseen by the camera inside—opened the door with her right.

"We can't see much from here," Tucker complained.

"It's okay," Irene said. "She's a pro. This is great."

I felt my phone vibrating in my coat pocket. It was a text from Agnes. With all the hubbub, I almost forgot about the job I was certainly going to lose.

The odious Muriel Ball just left my office, the message read. *What on earth did you say to her??!!*

As I mentally crafted my response, wondering if my job was even salvageable at this point, I saw another undulating word balloon on my screen. Agnes had more to say.

Whatever it was, you're my hero. See you Monday?

Monday. I hadn't thought that far. If Mamie was found soon, of course I'd be at work on Monday. If not... I recalled Lt. Herman's words. "If we don't find the dog within twenty-four hours, she probably won't be found." My stomach dropped. I thought I might throw up. We had roughly three hours left.

I looked at Angela Woolsey, hitting her mark so she could demonstrate how my house had been broken into—twenty-two hours ago. She'd been gone for twenty-two hours, and hadn't been found. This time tomorrow it would be forty-six hours, and this time Sunday a total of seventy. If we didn't have her back by this time on Sunday, we weren't going to get her back. I looked at my phone.

Yes, I'll be back on Monday. Send.

"When are they going to air this story?" I asked.

"It'll be on the six o'clock broadcast," said the man beside me, holding the boom and microphone. "And the five o'clock too if Woolsey has anything to say about it. She's got that look."

"What look?"

"Look at her," he said. "What do you see?"

As if on cue she faced us. Her jaw was set, her eyes narrow. There was no longer any hint of a smile.

"Frankly," I responded, "she looks pissed off."

"That's the look. She's taking it personally. She wants your dog back as bad as you do."

She made a cursory gesture, and the man picked up his boom and walked toward her. The rest of us followed quietly.

Friday, 12:52 p.m.

Angela Woolsey's smile was back. "Are you comfortable?"

I wasn't. "Fine," I said.

I sat on one of my dining room chairs, oddly placed in the middle of the living room. My new friend with the microphone stood to my right, the camera set slightly to the left.

Angela faced me so we could talk about how Mamie was stolen.

Tucker, Lee, Jean, and Irene sat in the next room out of sight but within earshot, I hoped. It would seem like a private conversation, with the entire metropolitan area watching in about four hours.

"I won't ask any questions," Angela said. "I'll be saying things like 'Tell me about this' or 'say more about that.' And you can say as much or as little as you want to. Do you have any questions before we get started?"

"No, but I want to make sure we mention the reward. I'm offering a substantial reward for Mamie's safe return. I want people to know that."

"Of course," she said. "Let's get started. If you could begin by telling me a little about yourself. We won't use this for the piece, but I want you to get comfortable, and we can make sure the sound levels are good. Okay?"

"Uh, sure. Let's see, my name is Charlie Vernon, I'm forty-three years old. I've lived in the Washington area since my early twenties."

"Tell me about where you grew up," she said.

"I'm a Navy brat. I was born in California and have traveled all over the world. I graduated from high school in Scotland. I went to college in Washington State, but my folks were living in the DC area when I graduated, so I spent time in their basement while I looked for my first job. About four years later, I was all settled, my dad retired from the Navy, and my parents moved back to the Northwest. He and my mom both grew up in Idaho, so...is that good?"

"You're doing wonderfully. Charlie. Now. Tell me about when you discovered Mamie was gone."

"I, um..." I paused, brow furrowed. This was harder than I thought it would be. I cleared my throat and started again. "I came home from work last night and noticed my television had been stolen. When I went upstairs, I saw Mamie's empty crate. It was on its side. I looked for her everywhere, and when I got to the basement, it was really cold. They got in through the door leading from my basement to the alley out back. They broke the window and unlocked the handle from the inside."

"Tell me about what they took."

"They took a television, a tablet, a laptop, just stuff. Replaceable stuff. The only thing they took that I care about is my dog. She's not replaceable."

"Tell me about Mamie. Give me a sense of her."

"She's my family," I said. "I mean, sure, she's a dog. But I'm a single man at the moment. I don't have any kids. She's who I come home to. She's really smart. She knows what I'm about to do before I do it. When we go visiting, she can't wait to get into the car, but when we're going to the vet or something she hates, I try to fool her by smiling and acting all happy, but she always knows. And she won't come to the door. She sits and stares at me, like 'who are you kidding?' She can see right through me. And she's a terrible beggar. I shouldn't have fed her scraps from the table when she was a puppy, but she was so cute, and now if I'm eating, especially something that smells good, she whines like she hasn't eaten in months. But she's also sweet, you know? When I come home at the end of the day, she literally hops up and down, she's so happy. That's my favorite moment every day."

"Tell me how it's been for you since she's been gone."

"I feel sick. I'm so worried, I feel sick all the time. Dog people know we'll have to say good-bye someday. People live longer than dogs, I get that. But that's not what this is. I hope she's still alive, but I don't know what she's doing, if she's being walked or fed or taken care of. I'm pretty sure she's scared." My voice started to rise, and I was talking faster now. "I know she wants to come home if… she's…still alive. I'm her family."

From the adjoining room, I heard a sniffle. So I guessed my friends could hear. Angela heard it too, but didn't seem upset. She took a deep breath, encouraging me to do the same before she spoke again.

"Tell me about the reward you're offering, Charlie."

"I'm offering a ten thousand dollar reward to anyone who brings her home unharmed, no questions asked. If whoever took her brings her back, I'll give them the money. You know where I live. And if anyone watching this sees my dog anywhere, please call the police. If your tip results in her coming home to me, you'll get the reward. Follow 'hashtag Find Mamie' on Instagram or Twitter to get in touch with me."

"Is there anything else you'd like to say?"

"Um, Paws on the Pavement is a dog walking service here in Capitol Hill. They're hanging up flyers all over the neighborhood while on their walks. They've been great. If you don't see a flyer and you want one, go to Beekman Animal Hospital or Betty's Dog and Cat Grooming. Everyone who knows Mamie is trying to get her back."

After a moment of silence, Angela reached over and placed her hands on mine. "You did great," she said.

"That was it?"

The cameraman removed the camera from his shoulder and gave us a thumbs-up. It was over.

"Listen," Angela said. "I have a good feeling about this."

"Good," I said, not sounding so sure.

"What I mean is I think you're going to get your dog back. And when you do—not if, but when—I want you to call me so I can get it on camera. My viewers are going to want to see the two of you reunited." She smiled, broadly this time. "Promise?"

"Sure thing."

"All right," she called, "you can all come out now."

And suddenly my four friends appeared, Lee blowing his nose. He must have been the sniffler. Jean's eyes were moist. Tucker smiled and nodded, and Irene looked satisfied with my performance. I'm sure she had notes she was itching to give me but knew it would have been pointless. This had been a limited engagement, and the show was already closed. I might have done better, but this would have to do.

Friday, 2:06 p.m.

As quickly as the News Two crew swept into the house, they cleared away, leaving the five of us in the living room. Tucker continued to monitor his laptop, and I stayed glued to my phone in case something popped up. We'd occasionally share what we'd found with each other, then go right back to scrolling.

Meanwhile, Lee and Irene were quickly cementing a friendship based on showbiz. Lee had a new gig at Pansy's Bar & Grill. He was performing in drag on the third Friday of every month, hosting Bingo Night and occasionally lip-syncing Celine Dion. Irene had long ago directed a production of *La Cage aux Folles*, and she cautioned him not to alter his voice too much. "Women don't necessarily have those high, screechy voices," she said. "Hell, just listen to me."

Jean would bounce between conversations but never stayed with either one for long. She wasn't very sure how social media worked. She had a Facebook account but never logged on to a computer if she could possibly help it, and she simply didn't have the energy to keep up with Lee and Irene once they got going.

When I looked up from my phone, I could see Jean was exhausted, despite trying her very best. "Should you be getting back?" I asked Irene. "As it is, it'll be dark by the time you get home."

Irene nodded. "I wish we could stay," she said. "I'd love to be here when you get her back."

"I know. But I'll worry if you don't hit the road soon."

"I'm sorry," Jean said.

"I know. Your chemo is such an imposition on *me*."

She smiled. "Well, when you put it that way." She got up slowly and embraced me tightly. I wouldn't have expected her to be strong enough, which was silly. After all, Irene Epstein wouldn't have married some wallflower.

"C'mon, Windsor," Irene called. "Time to go home."

The car was parked in the alley behind the house. I held Windsor's leash as Irene helped Jean down the stairs. Irene always hated these stairs. She thought they were too steep, and she never left my house without some vague reference to *The Exorcist*.

I watched them descend slowly, hand in hand. It struck me I could get cancer someday, and no one would be there to help me down the stairs. I would be left to grip the banister all alone and hope for the best. And I'll admit I felt a little sorry for myself.

LOYALTY, LOVE & VERMOUTH

Once Jean was comfortable in the passenger seat, I fastened Windsor to his back seat harness and then moved around the car to say a quick good-bye to Irene.

"Thanks for coming," I said. "You didn't have to."

"Of course we did," Irene said, placing a hand on my cheek. It was warm. "You're our boy. You know that."

Jean turned to us. "In case Mamie doesn't come back until tomorrow, you make those boys take good care of you tonight."

"I will. Drive safe."

"I'm a perfectly wonderful driver," Irene said, which raised a whoop of protest from Jean. "Oh shush. I got you here in one piece, didn't I?"

In an attempt to prove it, Irene executed a near perfect twenty-seven point turn to free her enormous Subaru from my tiny alley, which greatly amused Jean. I could hear her lilting laugh the entire time. Even Windsor yipped once or twice to cheer her on. When they were finally free, they waved good-bye and I waved back, watching them disappear before I turned back to the house.

Immediately after I entered, Tucker called out excitedly. "Charlie!"

"What?"

He ran to me, holding his phone. "We've got a lead. A good one."

CHAPTER NINE

Friday, 2:21 p.m.

While I was saying good-bye to the rhyming lesbians, someone replied to one of Tucker's Facebook posts. His name was Willard Bixby, and he said he had found Mamie earlier that morning. After an exchange of numbers, Tucker and Mr. Bixby began texting back and forth before I came back to the house.

"He says he went online to see if anyone was missing a dog, and he saw a copy of our flyer."

My stomach jumped. "Ask about a collar."

Tucker typed, then waited for a response.

"No collar."

"Did he give you a description?"

"Small dog, about twenty pounds, yellow," he read aloud. "Answers to Mamie."

"Has to be her."

"Oh, gracias, Santa Maria," Lee said. "Do you have an address?"

Tucker scrolled up on his phone. "He's about three blocks away."

I inhaled fully for the first time since the night before. I was relieved and filled with pride. My brave girl had somehow evaded her captors and was probably headed home when Mr. Bixby found her. She might have made it had he not scooped her up and brought her inside. Of course, I was grateful to him. Smart and stubborn though she was, the science of traffic lights and walk signals was elusive to her, and this way she was safe.

"Angela Woolsey said she had a good feeling about this," I said. "Oh, shit—Angela Woolsey."

Tucker looked up from his phone. "What about her?"

"We have to tell her to axe the story."

"Don't be stupid," Lee said. "Let's get your dog back first. And hey, if you send her video of the reunion to include in the report, she won't even be mad."

We all agreed this was a good plan.

"We'd better drive," I said. "It's only three blocks, but it sounds like she doesn't have a collar. And I don't have a leash."

"Why don't you two go," Tucker said. "I hate to miss the happy reunion, but my boss is sending me a million texts. I don't think he's happy I took a surprise day off. I'd better go in and put out some fires."

"Totally," I said. "We shouldn't all lose our jobs over this."

Monday, I thought—this time with joy and anticipation. I couldn't wait to go back to work on Monday. A perfectly normal working day, with a fetching satchel in one hand and a triple grande hazelnut latte in the other, asking people how their weekend was and answering their polite repetition of the question with something vague like, "Pretty quiet actually." I'd be just another gay man with a good job, good friends, and a loving, loyal dog in an extra-large crate waiting for me to come home and disarm the security system, which I would activate every time I left the house for the rest of my life, forever and ever, amen.

"Thanks," Tucker said, packing his laptop away. "I feel like a shitty friend."

"Shut up," I said, full of affection. "You made the flyer. You put it on Facebook. You basically found her for me. Thank you." I gave him a hug, which he returned.

"Oh, I love my little babies," Lee crooned, embracing our embrace until we all started to giggle.

Friday, 2:48 p.m.

After saying good-bye to both Tucker and Russell, who seemed genuinely upset to be leaving us and whined when Tucker put his leash on, Lee and I got into my car and drove three blocks west and one block north to the address Mr. Bixby had given us. Knowing I'd be carrying Mamie back to the car, I tried to find a parking space nearby, but there weren't any. The best I could do was just around the corner, which was manageable, although Mamie hated to be carried as a rule and would surely squirm uncontrollably in my arms the entire way.

"This will have to do."

"It's fine," Lee said. "Let's go get her."

We got out of the car and began to walk the length of the block to Mr. Bixby's home.

"If he saw the flyer, do you suppose he's going to ask you for the reward?"

"Oh, shit. Probably."

"What are you going to do about it?"

"Kill myself?" I said. "Kidding! What the hell, I'm good for it. I don't know how, but I'll figure it out. I'll eat ramen noodles every night and he can have five hundred a month, for what—the next twenty months if necessary."

There was a moment of quiet as we considered this new reality. Why had I let Irene talk me into this? He was going to ask me for ten thousand dollars, and I couldn't refuse. But I'd have Mamie back, which was all that mattered.

"You know, ramen noodles can be surprisingly versatile."

"Yeah, Claude told me the same thing about you."

"That's valid."

I gave him a smile as we faced Bixby's house. "This is it," I said, walking up the steps. I opened the screen door and knocked.

I was a little taken aback by the silence that followed. Mamie always raised holy hell when she heard a knock at the door.

"It's quiet," I said.

Lee shrugged. "She doesn't have anyone in there to protect. She barely knows this guy." And that sounded right.

I knocked again, and the door opened soon after.

Willard Bixby was one of those men probably in his forties, but who looks much, much older. Short and slight, with male pattern baldness and an enormous sand-colored mustache, he was no one's idea of a valiant hero. He wore a plain white T-shirt in the middle of January and a pair of jeans a size too big. His skin was uniformly pink, except for the nose and the tops of his ears, which were red and shiny. Honestly, I was surprised he was white—or, in this case, pink. Most people in this neighborhood were either Black baby boomers or white hipster millennials. I was and remain the oldest white person I know within a three-block radius with the exception of the Klinkoffs, an old Russian couple who'd been here forever, but no one was sure how long because they never spoke to anyone.

Apparently, we weren't who Mr. Bixby was expecting either, judging from his frown and furrowed brow. "Can I help you?" he mumbled.

"Are you Mr. Bixby?" I said.

"Do I know you?"

"We're here about Mamie. You found my dog?"

We could see the light bulb flicker once or twice inside his foggy brain before finally illuminating. "Yes, yes, right, okay," he said quietly, going back inside the house.

Lee and I looked at each other, both trying to suspend judgment and to maintain a feeling of gratitude, but it was difficult. We were, after all, well-groomed homosexuals who had been fending off society's shame with witty barbs ever since we could talk. And he was, after all, this vacant bag of bones who seemed unable to look people in the eye, speak in complete sentences, or remember anything since that morning. Still, we held our tongues.

When he walked back into his house, he left the door open, which was as good as an invitation, so I gingerly opened the screen door. It squeaked loud enough to warn anyone inside I was coming, so I didn't feel the need to announce myself. Lee followed behind cautiously, closing the door behind him.

Stepping into his living room, we immediately noted the smell. The odor was vaguely medicinal with a hint of beef, like a meatloaf smothered in VapoRub. We entered just as Mr. Bixby was ambling back into his kitchen. So, we stood for a moment, breathing through our mouths, waiting to be once again received.

The walls were decorated with unframed posters of a religious bent, mostly Jesus interacting with peasants, signified by a halo around his head and the curious hand gesture he always seems to make when talking down to people. Above the door that led to the kitchen was a crucifix of the Catholic variety with an emaciated Messiah breathing his last nailed to it. There was an old television and a single piece of furniture: a faded ivory couch, which looked to be as old as Mr. Bixby, sporting several holes in the upholstery and bits of yellowish foam rubber sticking out.

"Holy shit. Look," said Lee, pointing to the far end of the couch. There, a little white dog sat perfectly still. It was about twelve pounds and, well, "white" was a relative term. It was a dingy animal, about the same color as the couch, which was probably why we hadn't noticed it.

"That is a creepy little dog," I said.

Lee nodded, eyes wide. "Where's Mamie, do you suppose?"

"I don't know."

The creepy little dog began to growl. The fur on top of its head was matted down, and one tiny sharp tooth jutted upward out of its mouth. Its nose was pinkish, resembling the man of the house.

And just then Mr. Bixby reappeared. He carried a mug of what looked like beige, cloudy coffee with a large black speck floating in it.

"Mr. Bixby, I—"

I was interrupted by a loud slurping. When he brought his mug down, the large black speck was still there, consuming my attention. Lee nudged me.

"Can I see my dog? Where is she?"

"It was very nice of you to come over so quickly," Bixby said, never quite making eye contact.

"I live close by."

"What are your names?"

"Um, I'm Charlie, and this is my friend, Lee. I'd like to see my dog, if you don't—"

"Hello, Charlie. Hello, Lee. I'm Willard," he said before taking another slurp from his coffee mug. "It's very nice to meet you."

"It's nice to meet you too?" Lee said, looking at me the entire time.

"Please," Bixby said. "Have a seat." He motioned to the worn and dusty couch, which still held a growling little dog.

"No, thank you," Lee said, unwilling to abandon good manners but equally unwilling to put his body on anything that might be home to thousands of fleas.

Bixby shuffled to the front window, eyes fixed on his coffee mug. How he could have missed the flotsam in his coffee was beyond me. I wondered if it was there on purpose. "Have you lived in the neighborhood long?"

I hadn't come to make small talk, and I was growing impatient, but didn't want to seem ungrateful. "Mr. Bixby—"

"Oh, please. Call me Willard."

"All right, Willard. Do you have my dog? I'd really like to see her."

"Oh, yes," Bixby said, now staring out the window. "I found your dog this morning when I was walking home from breakfast. It's a very nice dog."

"Thank you," I said. "Where is she?"

"Well, the dog's right over there," Bixby said, pointing to the growling little varmint on the edge of his couch.

I regarded this thoroughly unpleasant animal, and I felt my heart breaking. Bixby didn't have Mamie. Mamie was still gone, and I didn't have the faintest idea where she was.

"That's not my dog."

"Oh, I'm sure it is," Bixby said, digging for something in his pocket. "What's its name again?"

"Mr. Bixby. Willard. That isn't my dog. I'm sorry for any misunderstanding, and thank you for contacting us, but—"

"No, wait wait wait!" Bixby pulled his phone from his front pocket, and was furiously scrolling through it as he stumbled toward the front door. Lee and I stared at each other, overwhelmed with sadness but unsure what to do with this potentially insane man who was now blocking our exit.

"Found it," he mumbled, showing us his phone. It was a copy of the flyer Tucker made earlier that morning, the new one with the words "$10,000 REWARD" in bold print right in the center. "Watch this," he said, facing the dog, who was still growling at me. "Mamie," he said, and the growling stopped. There was a sudden silence, as if someone had taken the needle off a spinning record. Bixby chuckled. "See?"

I was unmoved. "No, Willard. Mr. Bixby. I'm sorry, but that's not my dog."

"Mamie, come." Sure enough, the dog jumped down from the couch and approached. Bixby. "Sit," he commanded, and the dog sat down, looking up expectantly, perhaps awaiting a treat.

"Um, Charlie? It's a boy," Lee said. "Look."

Not only did this dog have a penis, it presently had an erection, like an angry pink lipstick bobbing up and down. This detail mattered little to Bixby.

"Your dog is very friendly," he said, putting his hand in front of the dog's nose. The dog took a sniff and then licked his knuckles, causing Bixby to giggle for a moment. "Now you," he said, to me.

"I don't think you understand, Willard. That's just not my d—"

"But you're not even trying," he said. Either he was out of his mind, or he thought I was the stupidest man on earth.

Not knowing what else to do, I bent down and offered my downturned hand to this dog, who sniffed it, but did not reward me with a kiss. I was never so happy to be rejected.

"Well, that doesn't prove anything," Bixby insisted.

I turned to Lee. "Come on. Let's go."

"You can't go yet," Bixby said. "We haven't even talked about the reward money."

And there it was. Bixby wasn't crazy. He was a grifter, a con man. And not a very bright one.

"Mr. Bixby, I—"

"Call me Willard."

"Mr. Bixby. I'm not taking this dog, and I'm not giving you any money."

"But I found your dog for y—"

"Stop," I said, angry and finally not caring if it showed. "Just stop it. You didn't find my dog. That is not my dog. That dog is smaller, dirtier, and uglier than my dog, and that dog has a dick. Okay? I offered a reward to anyone who could give me my dog back. You are not that person."

"But we had a deal." He was calm and not at all threatening. He looked pathetic and sad, but he was insistent. "We had a deal."

"No. No, we don't. This is not how deals work."

"We had a deal," he said again, "and you're not leaving this house until you give me my money." He reached behind him and turned the deadbolt on his door. "It's my money."

"We're going to go now," Lee said.

"Please, let's talk about this. It's been a rough couple of years, you know? I could really use a break."

"Mr. Bixby," I said, "you really do have to let us go."

"You've got lots of money. I mean, look at you two. If you've got all that money to spend on one lost dog...look, I've got nothing. And I've got this heart condition, and the medicine costs a lot, and—"

"I'm sorry you're having a rough time of it, Willard. But I'm not giving you any money, and you don't have my dog," I said, not without sadness. "So, I don't think we can help each other."

"Now just hold on—" But his next tactic was interrupted by a knock on the door. It was the quick, efficient knock of someone familiar to the place.

"Willard!" A woman was on the front porch, clearly expecting the door to be open.

And then a child's voice chimed in. "Daddy, let us in!"

"Now, you go away for a minute," Bixby called out. "I'm busy in here!"

But a key was already forcing the deadbolt back into the door.

"Busy doing what?" The door opened, and a tall, casually but fashionably dressed Black woman stood behind it. "You got a girlfriend in there or something?" She was easily a head taller than Willard. She noticed Lee and me standing in her living room, and her brow furrowed as she returned her keys to her purse. "Who the hell are you?"

"We were just leaving," Lee answered.

"Hold up," she said. "Willard, who are these people?"

We noticed the little girl, simultaneously hiding behind her mother and wanting to be seen, peek her head around to get a good look at us. "I'm Glory," she said, shyly. She looked to be around five or six years old. She had big spiral curls all over her head and wore a pink winter coat.

"Hi, Glory. My name is Lee." They shared a smile between them.

"And I'm Charlie," I extended my hand. "You are...his wife?"

"Ex-wife," she said, giving my hand a firm shake. "I'm Roz. What's happening in here?"

At this point, the mangy little white dog hopped back up on the couch, perhaps to get a better view of the ensuing drama.

"I'm afraid it's all been a big misunderstanding," I said.

"They owe us money," Mr. Bixby said.

"Willard, hush," said Roz. "Charlie, is it? Why don't you tell me what's going on?"

"Well, my dog was stolen from my house, and I'm trying to find her. I've offered a reward for her return. Your husband thought he found her and called us over here, but this is not her." I pointed to the little dog, who was turning in circles on the couch, preparing for a lie-down.

Little Glory stepped into the center of the room and dramatically stomped her foot. "Daddy!" she yelled. "You were trying to sell Dudley?!"

Roz rolled her eyes. "Jesus Christ, Willard."

"Dudley's not his name anymore, sweetie," Mr. Bixby said, before turning to his woman by his side. "And don't take the Lord's name in vain in my house."

Glory pounced on her dog, to protect him from us, I suppose, and the three of them began yelling over each other so loudly we couldn't hear much of what was being said, only that Roz was continuing to take the Lord's name in vain at every available opportunity.

"We're gonna go now," I said, to no one in particular, and Lee and I circled around the mêlée and escaped without much notice.

Once Lee closed the door behind him, we sprinted away until we were ten or twelve houses down.

"That was fucking weird," Lee said.

"Yeah," I replied, gasping.

"Hey, I'm sorry. I thought we had her back."

"Yeah. Me too. And now it probably won't happen."

"What are you talking about? Of course it'll happen. One crazy asshole doesn't mean anything."

I nodded but kept going.

"Hey, listen to me," Lee said. "She's going to be on the news tonight, and a lot of people are going to see that. And even though this fucking guy was loco en la cabeza, we know people are seeing the flyer, so that's good. Right?"

I nodded again, but Lee could tell I wasn't convinced. "It's been twenty-four hours," I said sadly. "Time's up."

"You didn't get home last night until after dark."

"But she was taken between 2:47 and 3:05," I said. "Lt. Herman said if we don't get her back within twenty-four hours, we probably won't find her."

"Well, he never met Mamie," said Lee. "Has he?"

I kept walking, but Lee stopped. He efficiently stomped his foot, which was my clue to return to him where he stood.

"Has he?"

"No."

"No, he hasn't. C'mon. Let's get you home."

We got back into my car and drove three blocks east and one block south back to my place. Lee offered to send Tucker a text message with the disappointing news. The two of them were having quite the conversation with their thumbs, which left me alone with my thoughts.

At least we hadn't said anything to Angela Woolsey, and Mamie's story was still being edited together across town. I tried to channel Angela's optimism and reminded myself Lee was right. Mamie was an extraordinary little dog, and most burglaries didn't get covered on the evening news. We had to get her back, and I knew we would, based on one piece of circumstantial evidence: I refused to imagine another ending to the story.

Because of the one-way streets in my neighborhood, we had to drive in front of my house to get to the alley. Approaching the house, Lee suddenly piped up. "Charlie, look," he said. "There's somebody on your porch."

There was a car about to pass, so I couldn't take my eyes off the road. "Who is it?"

"Holy shit. It's Freddie fucking Babcock."

CHAPTER TEN

The same week Freddie and I officially parted ways, Tucker announced plans to throw Jack a big party for his thirty-fifth birthday. It was adamantly not a surprise party, as Jack hated surprises almost as much as he hated parties.

But Tucker was determined not to let the occasion pass without celebration. He wanted something perfect: the food classy but not pretentious, with just enough booze to keep things lively, but he didn't want a room full of falling-down drunks. Also, he needed enough people to let Jack know how much he was loved, but not so many it became more about the party and less about the birthday boy. Most importantly, he wanted the right people there, people who were invested in celebrating his husband, not in looking for their next hookup or creating any kind of drama.

Sadly, his plans were not to be.

About a week before the party, he called with some delicate news, too delicate for a text it would seem.

"What's up, buttercup?"

"You tell me," I said.

"Well, it's about the party on Sunday." This was not surprising news. Everything in the past two weeks had been about Jack's party. From the vantage point of a newly single man in the midst of a bad breakup, it was both sweet and terribly annoying.

"What about it?" I asked, forcing a smile into my voice, secretly hoping he noticed the effort.

"Well…Freddie's coming. To the party." This was also not a surprise. When we had announced our split to our friends, we insisted on civility and promised they would not have to choose between us.

"That's fine, Tucker. I don't mind. Really." Of course I minded, but I was determined to keep my word.

"Okay, sugar. It's just that…"

"What aren't you telling me?"

"Freddie's not coming alone. He's bringing someone."

"Probably Carol from his office. It's okay. She's cool."

"His name is Edwin. And Freddie mentioned he was excited for us to meet his new…um…"

"Boyfriend," I said.

"That was the word," Tucker said. "Sugar, I'm so sorry."

"Fuck." It was the only word that sprang to mind, I'm afraid. Freddie had moved out of my house less than three weeks before, and had already found my replacement. "Fuck fuck fuck fuck fuck."

"I can talk to Freddie. Tell him to bring Edwin over some other time when it's just the four of us?"

"No," I said, "don't do that. Might as well rip the bandage off while the wound is fresh, right?" My metaphor made no sense, I realized. Probably because this was a really bad idea, but I was going to take the high road, and I would still get to Scotland first, goddammit.

"Are you sure?"

"Yes, it's fine. Really."

"Listen, sugar, don't take this personally." I exhaled in a huff, creating an audible roll of the eyes. "I know that's a tall order, but I've known Freddie since BC—Before Charlie. He doesn't do 'single.' It's a wonder he lasted this long. It's not about you, honestly."

"Tucker," I said, processing everything I was hearing. "Was Freddie single when he met me? Tell me the truth."

"Shit," Tucker said. Truthfully it was the only answer I needed. "Not exactly?"

"Tell me."

"Shit fuck in a garbage truck," Tucker replied, and then the line went temporarily dead. He was probably waiting for me to change the subject, but I was determined to wait him out. "Do you remember Roger Lindsey?"

"He was supposed to be my chorus buddy. The one who hated me?"

"That would be he."

"Well, that makes some sense now anyway. Why didn't anyone tell me?"

"Because Roger Lindsey is an asshole, and Freddie was clearly just marking time until he met someone decent."

"Like me."

"Exactly," said Tucker. "If it makes you feel any better, I'm sure Edwin will be perfectly awful."

"Yeah, well here's hoping."

"Listen, Charlie, thanks for being so great about this. Come Sunday, I won't leave your side for a minute, and it'll be fun. I promise. Dogs are invited, so bring Mamie if you like."

❖

I don't remember the exact moment when things went south between Freddie and me, but I knew we were in trouble when we experienced the Iris Incident.

Iris Clifton was a friend of mine from college. We were theater kids together who spent every night at rehearsal and every day daydreaming about the parts we'd play and the Tony Awards we'd win someday. Had it not been for Facebook, Iris and I probably would have drifted apart after college. Neither of us was very disciplined about writing long letters to each other, particularly missives detailing how we each learned a life in the theater was not all it was cracked up to be, and how we eventually settled for a corporate training gig in my place and a husband and two kids in hers.

But thanks to social media, we were fairly in tune with each other's lives. When her son was born, and then her daughter, I was part of the congratulatory voices cooing and fawning over the baby pictures. When I made my big coming out announcement the same year, she skipped the platitudes about how brave I was and went straight for "Aha! I knew it" with a heart emoji.

After Freddie and I had been together for almost two years, Iris texted to let me know she and her now teenage son and middle-school daughter would be playing tourist in Washington, and chief among her must-see destinations was me. She wanted to take me to a fabulous brunch and was excited for me to meet her kids, especially the younger one, who was already showing some enthusiasm for school plays. And, of course, she wanted to meet Freddie.

When I told Freddie about Iris's plans, he seemed amenable enough. "Sounds fun," he said, and I put the brunch on both our calendars.

But the night before the big reunion, Freddie wanted to go out with Tucker and Jack for a good old-fashioned gay bar crawl, which usually meant getting home at around three a.m. and not quite knowing how you accomplished it.

"We can do that," I said, "but we shouldn't stay out too late or get too wasted. We're meeting Iris and her kids tomorrow."

"Who?"

"Iris, my best friend from college. Remember? She wrote to me about a month ago, and we're meeting her for brunch. She's taking us to Sequoia."

"Oh. Yeah, I think I'll skip brunch."

I was stunned. "What? No! Freddie, she went to a lot of trouble, and we've had this date on our calendar for weeks."

"But I don't even know her. You go. I'd rather hang out tonight with Jack."

"I'm not saying we can't go out tonight. Just that we should take it easy."

"Don't tell me what to do," he said, curtly. And I dropped it.

That night, we did go out with Tucker and Jack, but around eleven thirty, Tucker made his perfunctory exit, and I decided I'd better do the same. Jack, predictably, wasn't going home anytime soon, and Freddie decided he wasn't ready to call it a night either.

"Don't do anything I wouldn't do," I said as I hopped into a cab, hoping Freddie would receive it with all the lightness and humor I was desperately trying to convey. But he just rolled his eyes.

When the sun peeked through my window at six the next morning, Freddie still wasn't home. It was an hour later as Mamie and I returned from our morning walk around the block that I saw him fumbling with his keys, still drunk from last night's intemperance.

"Morning," I called out, not able to hide my pique and honestly not caring. Mamie strained at the leash to get closer to him, tail wagging, determined not to help me in my campaign to shame him.

"Hey, girl," he said, giving her a little scratch behind the ears, ignoring me altogether.

"Did you have fun?" I asked, but he was giving me the silent treatment, once again fumbling with his keys. "Here, let me." He moved out of my way, proving he *could* hear me when it suited him. I unlocked the door while he stared at his shoes.

Mamie entered first, followed by Freddie, followed by me, still tethered to Mamie on the other end of her leash.

"Mamie, c'mere." And she did, nearly tripping Freddie in the process. As I turned our little dog loose, I asked, "Did you have fun?"

"Look," he said, massaging his temples, "I don't want to fight."

"Who's fighting?" I asked, although it was clear to both of us *I* was fighting. "I'm just glad you made it home. And it's not even seven thirty. You have time to take a nap if you want. We don't need to leave for another three hours."

"I'm not going," Freddie said, so quietly it barely registered.

"Freddie, you have to go."

And suddenly he was so loud it scared even Mamie. "Don't tell me what I have to do! You're not Yoda!"

"Lower your voice, please. Look, Iris is one of my closest friends—"

"Who I've never even heard of! You've never mentioned her once in two years. How important could she be?"

"It was twenty years ago, but I've told you those stories. It's not my fault if you don't listen."

"I told you I wasn't going to your stupid goddamn brunch yesterday. Which one of us doesn't listen?"

"Look," I said, adopting a more conciliatory tone, "this is important to me. Back in college, Iris and I used to—"

"Oh, Jesus, that word again!"

"What word? Iris?"

"College. You're not a better person than I am because you have a fucking theater degree, you know."

"If you think I'm so ashamed of you, why do you suppose it's so important to me you show up today?"

"God knows," he said. "Maybe it's more fun to relive your glory days with someone who was too stupid to get into—"

"You *got* into college! You're taking college courses right now! You'll have a degree in a year! And I'm very proud of you, Freddie, of us. When you're not stumbling around drunk after being out for twelve hours doing heaven knows what."

"Then you'll be glad to know," he said, "I won't be there to embarrass you at your fancy brunch with your fancy friends. I'm going to bed, Charlie. Don't wake me up when you leave." And he walked upstairs.

"What am I supposed to tell Iris? That you couldn't give a shit about meeting one of my oldest friends?"

"Sounds about right," he answered from the landing, slamming the bedroom door behind him.

I did go to brunch with Iris by myself. I made up some bullshit about Freddie not feeling well, and I think she knew I was lying, but was too polite to say so. We had a nice time, despite my being embarrassed about showing up alone. When I got home four hours later, Freddie was gone. He wouldn't reappear until after dark. A text he'd sent said he needed to get out, to think. I'm fairly sure I believed him, which makes me an idiot. Also a kind person who gives people the benefit of the doubt, but mostly an idiot.

He returned as the sun was setting. I told him we had to talk. He didn't want to, but I insisted. As I poured myself a cup of coffee, he told me I was too controlling, too judgmental, and he was feeling constrained. He suggested "opening up the relationship" might give him the space he needed away from my condescension and snobbery. I told him I wasn't sure about an open relationship, but I apologized for making him feel disrespected. See "idiot," above.

The next three months were awful. We fought a lot, and I went to bed angry most nights, exactly the way you're not supposed to. On several occasions, Freddie wouldn't come home from work until almost midnight, and if I should dare inquire where he'd been, it was merely one more jot of evidence that I was a psychologically abusive mother hen. And then we'd either scream at each other or climb in bed, each facing opposite sides of the room, silently fuming.

We fought so much toward the end, the eventual breakup seemed almost serene by comparison. It happened on a Friday evening. It was a short conversation, as I recall. Freddie announced he was leaving, and nothing I could say would change his mind. I asked him to reconsider, but he was firm in his convictions and, weirdly, not angry. He had simply made up his mind.

That night, Freddie slept in the guest room. He called Mamie into the room with him, but being a creature of routine, she preferred to sleep in her usual spot, under my—formerly our—bed. I counted that as a small win on what I thought was the worst night of my life, but she wasn't happy in our room, either. She wouldn't hop up on the bed when it was time to turn out the light. She just sat, stubbornly, by the bedroom door, clearly unhappy with the new sleeping arrangements. I told her I understood and I was sorry, and I turned out the light.

The next day, Freddie composed an email to Lee, Claude, Tucker, and Jack to announce our separation. He asked me to read it before he sent it out, and I hated it. It read as though it was cobbled together by a lawyer or a press agent. I asked if I could rewrite it. He said no. "Fine," I said, "then take my name off it, and I'll write my own."

"Fuck you," he said, hitting the Send button.

"Very nice," I replied and immediately called Lee.

"Hey, chica," Lee said. "What's happenin', hot stuff?"

"Freddie's leaving me," I said rather nonchalantly, going into the bedroom and closing the door behind me.

After Lee stopped crying, I explained it was probably for the best, although I was yet to be convinced on that point. I wasn't a willing participant in this breakup, but it was happening despite my objections. And the most important thing was that we didn't want our friends to have to choose between us.

"You don't sound very upset about this," Lee said.

"Just numb. It'll hit me in a week probably. But I'll go visit the rhyming lesbians at the beach or something. I promise not to burden you with this."

"Burden away. I'm your friend."

"But you're his friend too. I don't want to suck you into any drama—"

"Have we met? I live for drama."

"We'll talk about it later. I need to call Tucker and Jack before they get Freddie's godawful email."

"Too late," Lee said. "They're already texting me about it."

"Oh, shit."

"Listen. Before you go, where is Freddie staying?"

"He was in the guest room last night."

"Oh, no. No, no, no, no, no. He can move in here."

"What?"

"This is not me taking sides, but I've seen this telenovela before. If you don't want to kill each other, he's got to get out of there."

"That's okay," I said. "I've got a business trip in a week, and I'll need someone to watch Mamie, and—"

"Stop it. Freddie can move in tonight, and Mamie can come over when you go. You both need to get away from each other right now. Trust me, I speak from experience."

I relented. I told Freddie he had been invited to stay at Lee and Claude's place "to give us some breathing room," I said. Freddie calmly agreed and packed a few bags. Leaving the house an hour later, he told me he'd be back for his other things when he found a place of his own.

The door closed behind him not with a bang, but with the quietest of clicks. My life had changed forever in the past twenty-four hours, and frankly I thought the moment deserved more drama. Some yelling, perhaps some crying, maybe something expensive being thrown against a wall and shattering into a million pieces? That would have been a nice touch. But the entire affair was surprisingly calm and adult. Freddie used to live here, and now he was gone. Simple as that. Mamie scratched at the door, requesting a simple walk, not knowing her other human had crossed the threshold for the very last time.

❖

When the Sunday of Jack's party arrived, Freddie had been gone for a month. I got up early and wanted to do what happy, well-adjusted single people did in the morning. I decided I'd go for a run. This was significant, because I had never "gone for a run" a day in my life before and haven't willingly done so since. I ran two blocks before I was completely out of breath. I walked home, figuring I'd try being a happy, well-adjusted single person the next week.

When I got back, I took a nice long shower, shaved, styled my hair, and delicately misted myself with my favorite cologne, the one I hadn't worn in years because Freddie said he was allergic. And when I looked at the clock, it was still an hour before I was supposed to leave so I would arrive fashionably tardy.

So, I sat on the couch next to Mamie. If she was having any difficulty adapting to life without Freddie, she wasn't making a big show of it. She was sleeping at the foot of the bed again and didn't seem to miss him all that much. Then again, I had stuck pretty close to home since the split, and it's possible she had more human companionship than she knew what to do with. Either way, it was nice.

I sometimes imagined she had taken my side in the breakup, although I knew in my heart if Freddie appeared at the door, she would greet him up on her hind legs, her fluffy tail happily swinging back and forth. I would hate this, naturally, but wouldn't blame her. She was wired for loyalty and couldn't know what a selfish little shit he'd been lately.

I decided to leave Mamie at home on the day of Jack's party, even though she'd been invited. I told myself seeing Freddie might confuse her, but in truth I was driven by spite. I didn't want to see a joyous reunion, and I especially did not want to witness Mamie jumping for joy and Freddie weeping and cooing in front of everyone. Being in the room with my ex and his newly minted boyfriend was going to be awkward enough.

"You'll be okay here while I go to this blasted thing?" I asked.

Mamie's doleful face gave me the answer I dreaded. Please don't leave me, she seemed to be saying. Or maybe I just didn't want to go.

Fuck it, I'd have to be unfashionably on time. I grabbed a liver-flavored cookie from the kitchen and shouted, "Kennel!" Mamie ran upstairs, and I followed. When I caught up with her, she was sitting in her crate, awaiting her reward. I fastened the latch as I fed her through the crate's bars. While she chewed as though she hadn't been fed in weeks, I took a deep breath, grabbed an expensive bottle of Rosé of Pinot Noir in lieu of the gift Jack begged us not to bring, collected my keys, and locked the door behind me.

When I got to the party, I was relieved to find I wasn't the first to arrive. Also, Freddie and his new paramour were nowhere in sight. As I set the wine on his kitchen cabinet, Tucker entered.

"Oh my God," he said. "You look great."

"Don't sound so shocked. It's bad for my brand."

"C'mere, sugar," he said, stepping forward for a warm hug. I obliged. When we separated, he noticed the wine. "You shouldn't have, but thank you. Should we open it?"

"It needs to be chilled."

Tucker obliged, grabbing the bottle and putting it the fridge. "He's not here yet."

I smiled. "I can't imagine who you mean."

"Don't be such a WASP."

"We all cope in our own ways. I WASP. And drink."

"Coming right up," he said.

As Tucker uncorked a bottle of Pinot Grigio he'd found in the fridge, Lee sailed into the room.

"Hostia puta, you look amazing," he said, hugging me tight. "You smell good too. But you should have told me you were dressing for revenge. I'd have brought my palettes. Nothing says 'I Will Survive' like a good smoky eye."

Tucker poured me a glass of wine, and I smiled, hoping I could handle whatever the day would bring.

By the time Freddie appeared two hours later, I was halfway through my second bottle of wine. At first, it appeared he had come alone after all. I noticed he was wearing the same seersucker shorts he had worn on the day we met. Sadly, Edwin could be seen just outside. He had stepped in something and was scraping whatever it was all over the uppermost porch step, much to Jack's chagrin. I'm not sure Edwin appreciated the power of this particular metaphor, but I sure did.

"Sorry we're late," Freddie said. "Church ran long."

I couldn't help myself. "Church?" I whispered, so only Lee could hear me.

Lee sighed. "Apparently, Edwin has shown him the way and the light."

"But Freddie's a bigger atheist than I am."

"Was. Besides, if anyone needs Jesus…"

When Edwin finally entered the house, he was truly everything I hoped he'd be. And by that, I mean too young for Freddie but already balding, with few if any discernible social skills. What hair he had left was the color of dishwater, and he seemed to have spilled something—ketchup, perhaps?—on his ill-fitting white button-down shirt. To be fair, he seemed nice enough. His smile was wide and bright, and he seemed genuinely happy to be here and meet everyone.

But he was either too kind or too stupid to notice the shocked looks on the faces of the people he was greeting a bit too effusively. Meanwhile, Jack was following him around the room, making sure whatever he'd stepped in wasn't being tracked all over his hand-knotted Persian rugs.

When he approached Lee, whom he had met two days before, he opted for a hug instead of a handshake. Trapped in Edwin's clumsy embrace, Lee shot me a look that was one part "I'm sorry" and two parts "Help!"

And then it was my turn. "Hi," he said, thrusting a clammy, moist hand in my direction. "I'm Edwin Gooch. I'm Freddie's boyfriend!"

The room fell deadly silent. Nearly everyone in attendance knew more about this explosive circumstance than Edwin did, poor bastard.

"Hello," I said. "I'm Charlie. I'm Freddie's ex-boyfriend." Edwin's big, dumb face fell, and I felt sorry for him despite myself. "It's very nice to meet you," I said, with a smile and what I hoped was an air of sincerity. I will admit to turning my back on him without shaking his hand, leaving him standing there to cringe in silence.

I returned to my familiar post in the kitchen where Tucker was waiting for me with a bottle of now-chilled Rosé of Pinot Noir in his hand.

"Unbelievable," he said.

"It's fine."

But it wasn't fine. Tucker uncorked the bottle and procured a new glass from the cabinet above the stove. He poured the pink wine into the glass and handed it to me, but before I could take a sip, Freddie stormed into the kitchen without so much as a hello. "What the fuck did you say to him?"

I took a sip anyway and took my time. "Trouble in paradise already?"

"He said he wants to leave."

"If he wants to leave, you should probably let him. After all, Freddie, you're not Yoda."

"What the fuck are you talking about? What did you say to him?"

"I believe my exact words were 'It's very nice to meet you.'"

"That's bullshit."

"I'd swear on the Bible, but I know how little that means to you."

"Charlie, you've got some fucking nerve—"

Tucker moved to my side. "Could you keep it down?"

"Mind your own business, Tucker."

"It's his party, and it's his business. Lower your goddamn voice or get out of here, Freddie. Nobody wants a scene but you."

Freddie looked at Tucker, then at me, and then at Lee, who I noticed hovering in the doorway. Freddie wanted an ally but was not finding one. "We're *not* leaving," he said.

"Suit yourself," I said, then added, "Go with God!" because I felt petty.

Freddie stormed out with the same force he'd stormed in with. Tucker, Lee, and I regarded each other and our new reality.

Not knowing what Emily Post would advise, I began to apologize. "Guys, I'm really sorr—"

"Cállate, Carlito. We know you're not making us choose between you."

Tucker took my hand in his. "We've already chosen."

I squeezed it and suppressed a laugh. Nothing struck me as particularly funny, but I didn't know until I'd heard those words how relieved I'd be.

Lee regarded me tenderly. "Need me to cut a bitch?"

"That won't be necessary, but keep the wine handy."

I kept my distance from both Freddie and Edwin for the next hour or so. Not so coincidentally, either Tucker or Lee was nearby every time I looked up. However, just as I was feeling as comfortable as possible under the circumstances, Lee and I ventured out onto the deck Tucker and Jack had attached to the house the year before. A few smokers were getting their nicotine fix down below as Jack held court with some mutual friends, and standing in the corner were Freddie and Edwin, making out like a couple of horny teenagers at Bible camp.

Oblivious to everyone around them, they performed their own private love scene, complete with longing gazes into each other's eyes, punctuated with slow, languorous, very wet kisses. It was nauseating.

When I met Freddie three years before, I told him I thought public displays of affection were tacky. Holding hands was one thing, and the ways well-established couples would take care of each other by wiping a crumb from the other's chin or removing a bit of lint from a shoulder were charming and sweet. But makeout sessions bordering on public sex were, to my mind, best reserved for private moments.

Freddie assured me he agreed completely, and indeed throughout our entire relationship he acted in complete accordance with his professed stance on the matter. So, it was a bit of a shock to witness him slurping at another man's open maw in broad daylight less than a month after announcing our breakup to the world. All four of their hands were clutching asscheeks, and their mouths resembled leeches sucking the life out of each other.

"Seriously?" I heard someone say, realizing seconds later that someone was me.

Edwin and Freddie broke apart. Freddie looked mad, then guilty, then mad again. There was no telling what Edwin felt, other than unmoored by the sudden absence of Freddie's tongue from his oral cavity.

Everyone on the deck became quiet. Most of them knew Freddie and me as a couple. The others were people I didn't recognize, but who certainly knew drama when it was happening in front of them as their eyes and smiles were wide.

Freddie cocked his head back in an effort to look cool. "Can I help you, Charlie?"

"Yeah, you can start by wiping your chin. You're drooling."

He looked a little less cool as he wiped Edwin's saliva off his face. "Look," he said quietly, as though all eyes and ears weren't riveted to us and every word we were saying, "you always take everything so personally. This isn't about you."

"Oh, I'm quite clear on that score," I answered, ignoring his request for quiet. "Nothing you do is about anyone but you, Freddie. I understand that perfectly."

I'm guessing Edwin Gooch was new to the role of the other woman, or else he might have known to remain silent. "What do you care anyway?" he asked me. "You guys haven't been together for, like, six months."

Lee, who'd been very quiet until now, uttered an involuntary "oh snap."

I said nothing at first, but regarded Edwin through narrowing eyes before returning my gaze to Freddie.

"Six months, Freddie? That's your story?"

"Charlie, I—"

"That's fascinating. Do you know why? The University of Maryland called the house yesterday, wondering if you'd be coming back next semester. It seems you stopped attending classes about... six months ago."

"So what?" Freddie bellowed. "I never cared about fucking college. That was all your idea anyway."

I took a deep breath. "Freddie, I have something to ask you."

As Freddie and I eyed each other, no one made a sound. We could hear the hum of traffic in front of the house. A half mile away or more, a siren wailed and dipped and wailed again. Silently, I catalogued everything Freddie had ever said to me, acknowledging for the first time that any one of those statements could have been a lie. Even Edwin seemed interested in what question I might put forth, and he took Freddie's hand, giving him a nudge.

"Wh...What is it?"

"Arthur," I said. "Let's talk about your ex-fiancé Arthur."

"What about him?" Freddie asked, nervous.

"Arthur isn't HIV-positive, is he?"

Freddie's jaw clenched with rage. I had my answer.

"Who's Arthur?" asked Edwin, and Freddie suddenly gripped his hand so tightly it caused the poor boy to squeal.

I should have enjoyed the moment more, but I was presently drowning under the weight of how much and how often I'd been lied to by a man I'd invited into my home and my bed for more than two years. Had it not been for those goddamn seersucker shorts, I might not have recognized him at all.

"We're going," Freddie announced.

"Yes," I said. "I think that's best." I moved to the side so Freddie could reenter the house through the sliding glass door, dragging Edwin behind him. I stood outside, soaking up the sunshine as

Freddie made his noisy exit. As Freddie was racing out of the house, dragging his boyfriend of six months behind him, I heard Edwin ask again, "Who's Arthur?"

And then there was silence.

Lee gave a half-hearted smile. "Another glass of wine?"

"No. I think I'll be going too. Thanks, though. Happy birthday, Jack. And...sorry."

"Are you kidding?" Jack said. "That was awesome."

Lee's lower lip curled in exaggerated disappointment. "You sure?"

I nodded. I was sure. Wine sounded lovely, but what I really wanted were my couch and my dog.

❖

The next two weeks were quiet enough. It was important to feel my feelings, I said to myself, but I honestly didn't know what my feelings were. The more I understood I couldn't believe a word Freddie had ever said, and I truly didn't know who this man was, the harder it became to miss him. I had moments of righteous anger, but they were balanced by other things. I was relieved he was gone, I wondered if he even knew himself under all those lies, and I was grateful not to be as lost as he clearly was. I kept waiting for Mamie to show signs of missing him, but either she didn't or she only let herself be sad when she was alone.

Then, on a Tuesday in the middle of the workday I received an email from Freddie.

From: Freddie
To: Charlie V.
Subj: Moving Forward

Dear Charlie,

I'm writing you instead of calling because there's a lot that I need to say and I don't want to fight with you.

I'm sorry if I hurt you in any way at Jack's party. It's

important that you know that it was never my intention to hurt you with Edwin. He actually came as a surprise after we broke up. I honestly just wanted to enjoy being single, but then something changed and we became more than that really fast. Neither of us knows what will happen in the long run, but for now we are enjoying each other's company. Also, I only told him that we had been broken up longer than we were so he wouldn't feel like a rebound. Once I explained that to him, he understood.

At Jack's party, it was hard to avoid each other, but it was never my intention to throw him in your face. I don't want to tiptoe around you with him, but I understand if it made and makes you upset or uncomfortable.

My life is changing and I'm becoming happier, less bitter, and less sarcastic than I was. One major shift during this time has been my need for inspiration, and I'm finding that through going to church again. I still don't believe all the supernatural stories, but when I think of a life filled with joy, peace, and love, all I can think about is the existence of God.

But I'm mostly writing today about Mamie. I know and you know that she is my dog as much as she is yours and I've missed her very much since I moved out. I think it is only fair that when I have a new place, we should both get to see her in equal amounts. I think that we could do a hand-off on Saturdays; you could either be home when I drop by or if you want I could let myself in (I still have my key).

I should be ready to take care of Mamie every other week, in about a month or so, once I've saved up enough for a security deposit on a new place. I'll let you know.

Sincerely,
Freddie

I sat at my desk, mouth agape. I knew the smart thing to do would be to close my email, take a walk, collect my thoughts, get back to work, go home, drink a glass of wine, sleep on it, and then respond to Freddie. That would be the intelligent course of action.

Naturally, I began typing immediately.

From: Charlie V.
To: Freddie
Subj: Re: Moving Forward

Dear Freddie,

I received your note. And I thought you deserved a response, and so I'm responding by telling you that you are a fucking liar and a cheating asshole. Fuck you, fuck your stupid fucking boyfriend OF SIX MONTHS. So I suppose that every Tuesday and Thursday of the past six months when you told me you were in class you were with Edwin Gooch—which is not only gross and cruel, but also totally fucking insulting. Do you know what it's like to be replaced by someone who looks like he eats his own toenails during recess? Anyway, fuck you both. If he believes anything that comes out of your mouth, he's as dumb as he looks. Also, please stick your goddamn Bible so far up your ass that it takes a team of proctologists to retrieve it.

You will never see Mamie again as long as you fucking live if I have anything to do with it. I'm sorry if this hurts you, except you know what? I'm not sorry. I'm glad if it hurts. I hope it hurts. Cry about it to Edwin, you goddamn fucking fuckwad.

I, too, am happier since we parted ways. I sleep well, probably because I'm not fuming with anger due to all the ways you found to be small and cruel and selfish and petty during the past year of my life with you. I don't miss you.

As the vitriol poured forth, I could hear the voice of a woman calling out to me, as if from a long distance. "Hey."

I don't miss your sullen attitude. I don't miss the way that all your stupid fucking insecurities became my character flaws (hint: I don't care that you don't have a degree. YOU care you don't have a degree. That's your shit and you need to own it).

The strange, disembodied voice was a little closer now, but I paid no heed. I was on a roll. "Charlie?"

One thing I definitely don't miss is doing your goddamn laundry, particularly the tighty-whities that you didn't even have the decency to put in the hamper. You know, the ones with the skid marks in the crotch? Honestly, Freddie, what kind of grown-ass adult man has never learned to wipe his ass after he takes a sh—

"Charlie!"

I looked up. Someone was hovering over my desk. When she came into focus, I could see it was Agnes Roche. Agnes, my friend, but also my boss.

"Charlie, you weren't at the three o'clock. Are you okay?"

The way she asked the question, it was clear she knew I wasn't. I fished my phone out of my pocket. I found Freddie's email, sent two hours before. I handed the phone to Agnes and watched as she read it.

Agnes and I had gone out for drinks the Friday before, and she had been thoroughly briefed on the breakup, the new boyfriend, Jack's party, the pathological lying, all of it. Therefore, nothing in Freddie's note prompted a question or required an explanation. Watching her face as it registered shock, then disbelief, on to indignation, and finally settling on a quiet, murderous calm was equivalent to a month's worth of therapy. Yes, I might be out of my mind with rage, but it was justified, and I wasn't crazy.

"I've been working on a response," I said.

"Good. Get it all out. But don't send it." I was about to protest, but she quieted me with a shake of her head. "You know I'm right."

She began typing something on my phone.

"What are you doing?" I asked. She said nothing, but her thumbs were racing. "Agnes, seriously, what are you wr—"

"Shh, hold on. I won't send it."

She jabbed my phone with her thumbs for another fifteen seconds. "Here," she said, admiring her handiwork for another moment before handing the phone back to me.

From: Charlie V.
To: Freddie
Subj: RE: Moving Forward

Dear Freddie,
    Don't worry about Mamie. I'll take very good care of her.
    Sincerely,
    Charlie
P.S. I've changed the locks.

"That's perfect," I said, hitting the send button without giving it another moment's thought.

When Freddie wrote back within minutes threatening to sue me if I didn't allow him to see Mamie again, I forwarded the entire email chain to Lee and Claude. I asked Claude if he'd like to represent me on the off chance Freddie took me to court. I received a call from Lee about two minutes later.

"Oooh, I could just wring his cuello flaco."

I took a deep breath. "I can't believe he fucking threatened to sue me."

"Claude says not to worry. One, people threaten lawsuits all the time just because they're pissed off, and two, Freddie doesn't have the money for a lawyer. Also three, no one would take his case."

"Still, I was hoping I could refer any future messages to Claude to shut him up. I don't suppose he would do me the honor?"

"Oh, you bet your ass he will. That bitch is not getting near Mamie. He doesn't deserve her. I didn't tell you this before, but when you took that business trip a week after Freddie moved in here? He was barely home. Claude had to walk her twice a day, and I fed her all her meals because Freddie was practically living with that hijo de puta."

So, before leaving the office on an otherwise uneventful Tuesday, I informed Freddie it would be unwise for us to communicate directly for the time being and his attorney could speak to my attorney if necessary.

Also, my attorney was Claude Williams.

Boom.

I never saw or heard from Freddie again.

I would hear *about* him occasionally, mostly from Jack, who would sometimes see him at Pansy's or Town, but less frequently over time. By the time I learned he and Edwin had moved to New York City, they'd already been gone for three months. I had not personally heard Freddie's voice or laid eyes on him since Jack's birthday party, and that was fine with me.

That is, until he showed up at my front door, a year and a half later.

CHAPTER ELEVEN

Friday, 3:24 p.m.

There was a strange man on my porch. He was tall, white, and slender, with black hair. It could have been him, but I wasn't sure.

"Keep driving, keep driving," Lee said. "I don't think he saw us."

I kept driving, making the two consecutive right-hand turns onto the cross street and then into my alley, and then the third into the driveway behind my house.

"It wasn't him," I said. "It couldn't have been him, right? I mean, he's in New York now."

"New York is only five hours away. Less if you take the train."

"Okay, let's say it's him. What do you think he wants?"

"A ransom?"

"If Freddie stole my dog, it wouldn't be for money."

"Por qué más?"

"I don't know, just to hurt me. If he stole Mamie yesterday afternoon, he's already in New York with her, and this guy is, I don't know, someone else."

"I'm telling you it was him."

"Okay. Let's see what he wants, then."

We climbed the stairs from *The Exorcist*, unlocked the back door, and entered through the kitchen. For a moment, I strategized how I might speak to Freddie without allowing him to see Mamie. Then I remembered for the tenth time that day she was gone and I didn't know where she was.

From the kitchen, we could see through the front windows. The wooden blinds were drawn, but we saw the shadow of a man trying to peer in.

"Stay here," I said.

"What if he has a gun?"

"Those true crime podcasts have gone to your head. I slept next to Freddie Babcock for more than two years. If he wanted to murder me, he had ample opportunity."

I motioned to the corner of the kitchen where Lee could stand and not be noticed by Freddie or whoever was out there. He silently moved into position, as did I. If it was Freddie, I was grateful to have a witness. I wasn't sure what was about to happen, but attempted gaslighting was always a possibility with Freddie.

I put my hand on the doorknob, took a deep breath, and silently unlocked the deadbolt. In one fluid motion I opened the door, and there he stood.

Lee was right. Holy shit. Freddie Babcock was on my front porch. He seemed as surprised as I was, and we regarded each other in silence for a moment. His hair had grown out a little since I'd seen him last, but it suited him. He still looked a little like Superman. Goddammit.

"Can I help you?" I finally said.

Freddie stood on the other side of the storm door, his hands buried in his coat pockets. "Hi, Charlie."

"Hello, Freddie."

"You look good."

"Really? I feel like shit."

"Can I come in?"

"That depends," I said. "What do you want?"

"I, um…I heard about Mamie."

"Really? How?"

"What?"

"Who told you about Mamie?"

"It's all over Facebook. I do have some DC friends left, you know. Not everyone dropped me like a hot rock on your command."

So he was hurting. And he was nervous. Good.

"Are you going to let me inside?"

I wasn't going to let him stand there in the cold, but I didn't want to say it out loud, so I just walked away from the open door, allowing him access. I was already seated in the armchair by the time he walked in and shut the door behind him. I opted for the armchair instead of the couch because I didn't want to share a piece of furniture with him, and I didn't want him to touch me. I either loathed him that much or I was falling in love with him again. I'm almost certain it was the former, but I couldn't rule out the latter. It was best to keep as much distance as my little room would allow.

"Place looks the same," he said.

"Yeah. You didn't bring much with you, so you didn't take much when you left."

Freddie removed his coat and sat down on the couch. It occurred to me if he would just avoid my gaze and stare out the window, and we could replay the entire scene where he told me all about Arthur's diagnosis. It had all been a lie, of course. Arthur, I had since confirmed, was in fine health and had never cheated on Freddie. No, Freddie was the cheater. And a liar. With perfect eyebrows. Fuck.

"So," I said, "you want to talk to me about Mamie. What about her?"

"I thought maybe I could help."

"Do you know where she is?"

It took Freddie a moment to realize he was being accused of something.

"No," he said innocently, then again "No!" angrily.

"It's a fair question."

"No, it's not! You think I stole our dog?"

"My dog," I said. "She's been my dog for over a year."

"That's because you cut me off."

"You didn't put up much of a fight for her."

"You got a lawyer!"

"Because you threatened to sue me, Freddie. When someone says 'I'm taking you to court,' it's not unreasonable to get a lawyer."

"Listen, Charlie, I didn't come here to fight."

"Besides which, you didn't even want Mamie. You just wanted to convince yourself you were the victim in this whole situation. The victim. After cheating on me, lying to me, potentially getting me sick. And you couldn't even leave poor Arthur out of it."

"You don't even know Arthur," Freddie said calmly. "He wasn't a saint."

"Anyone who lives with you is a saint in my book. If Arthur does have any fatal flaws, I'll need more than your word for it."

"Wow, you really hate me." I couldn't tell whether this was an observation or an accusation.

"Believe it or not, I don't think about you much when you're not here. But honestly, Freddie, you can't blame me for not believing a word you say. Can you?"

Freddie was struck dumb for a moment. He got up and then sat back down again.

"No, Charlie. You don't trust me. And I certainly wouldn't expect you to shoulder any of the responsibility about what happened to us. Nothing's ever your fault, is it?"

And then he stared out the window for a time, as was his habit. Feeling very put upon, I supposed, or perhaps concocting his next deception. I wondered what my faults were in his eyes. He thought I was a snob, that was clear, but I put it down to his own insecurities. Still, maybe he was right. Perhaps neither of us were the pure victims we imagined ourselves to be.

"I never lied to you," I said. "Not ever."

"Have it your own way." He turned to look at me. "Did you really think I stole Mamie?"

"I did. I couldn't think of anyone who'd want her specifically. And who might want to hurt me. I don't anymore."

And I didn't. I always doubted it was Freddie, but if it hurt his feelings to think he was my number one suspect, I was okay with that. I always had an image of myself as a nice, caring person who didn't want to hurt anyone, but suddenly I wanted Freddie to hurt. It didn't feel like revenge, though. I wanted him to see what happens when you tell a million lies and just walk away. That felt more like justice.

"Who did, then?"

"I don't know, Freddie. Probably some random burglar, someone who wanted a TV, maybe a laptop, and oh look, here's this cute dog."

"But she's fixed. They can't get any money for her."

"I know that, Freddie, and you know that. The people who took her might not know that. They might not have given her a full veterinary exam before deciding to take her. They were probably just kids."

"What makes you say that?"

"Because that's who robs houses around here. Apparently. I don't know. I have no fucking idea."

"I only wanted to help. It's why I came here."

"Help find her?"

"I mean, yeah."

"How? Are you a cop now? A reporter? Private detective?"

"No, I mean, just go look for her."

"Well, go ahead. Roam the streets and best of luck to you. If you find her, let me know."

"I have friends here, people you don't know. Folks I used to work with. I can spread the word, have them keep an eye out."

"You could've done that from New York," I said.

"So, what? Are you just going to sit here and hope for the best? She's out there, Charlie."

"I hope so. And no, I'm not just sitting here. The cops are involved."

"They'll be a lot of help, I'm sure."

His sarcasm was not lost on me. It occurred to me they never showed up to dust the basement for fingerprints and probably wouldn't at this point.

"And Mamie's going to be on the news tonight."

"The news? Really?"

I nodded. "Channel Two. You remember Angela Woolsey?"

"Black lady," he said. "Pretty."

"She was here earlier. You just missed her." I made my eyes go wide for effect. "Very dramatic, but it'll get the word out. I hope."

"That's great, Charlie."

"But she's been gone for over a day. That's bad. And there's not much else to do."

"So, you don't want my help," he said, defeated.

"I want everyone's help. Freddie. I'm going out of my mind. I'm worried all the time, and I've had a knot in my stomach since I got home last night. If you can think of something we haven't already done, then sincerely, with all my heart, do it. Just go do it."

I looked at him. Six foot two, black hair, pale skin, blue eyes. He may have resembled Superman, but he couldn't see through walls or leap tall buildings. He couldn't help me. But he wanted to, or he said he did. I still couldn't trust him an inch.

"In the meantime," I said, "do you want a cup of coffee?"

"Sure."

"Stay there," I said, trying to make it sound like an offer and not a command.

I walked to the kitchen, where there was still some coffee left in the pot from before, and Lee was still hovering by the refrigerator. I could tell he wanted to say something but was afraid to.

"Alexa," I said, "play songs by Tchaikovsky."

I'm not sure why I picked Tchaikovsky. The only other options that sprang to mind were Stephen Sondheim and Lady Gaga, both of which seemed wildly inappropriate. I didn't want to listen to music at all, but I did want to check in with Lee. And if a little bit of classical music solidified my persona in Freddie's mind as an overeducated aesthete, that was okay.

As the finale of *Swan Lake* filled the kitchen, I made myself busy with the coffee machine, careful not to look Lee's way.

"You're doing great," he whispered.

I opened the cupboard and retrieved two yellow packets of artificial sweetener. How apt, I thought. "Thanks," I said, not looking his way.

"I still think he did it," Lee said, as he took two coffee mugs from the cabinet above the sink and set them down on the granite island, still out of Freddie's line of sight. "After he leaves, don't touch his mug. We can have the cops dust it for fingerprints too."

"Sure."

Freddie was looking my way and gave me a sheepish smile.

"When did you get the piano?" he called out.

"Tucker and Jack," I yelled back. "They upgraded to a baby grand and let me have this one."

"Cool."

Having delivered the mugs, Lee went back by the refrigerator.

"Are you okay?" he asked.

"Of course."

"No, you're not. You want to strangle him, admit it."

"No, that would be too quick."

I deposited a packet of sweetener into each mug, then filled them with hot, bitter coffee.

"I can't say I blame you. It's better than feeling dead inside."

I smiled and marched back into the living room with two mugs of coffee. Freddie was sitting at the piano. Suddenly we were quite the picture of domesticity, except he didn't live here anymore and I hated his guts.

Freddie didn't play the piano, but he sat staring at the keys, sometimes touching them, never making a sound. I set his coffee on top of the piano and sat on the couch. I thought he might turn around, but he didn't. When I took my first sip, it was a loud slurp, anything to break the awkward silence.

Finally, he spoke. "I always wanted a piano."

"You don't play."

"Maybe I could learn."

"Easy as that," I said.

"Why not? You don't think I'm smart enough?"

"I don't think you're disciplined enough. I don't think you know what you want. Freddie, I don't think you know who you are."

"What's that supposed to mean?"

"Why are you here?"

He put his hands on the piano keys and tried playing a chord. It sounded dissonant and confused. He tried again, this time with better luck. He was about to try a third time, but I interrupted him.

"Why are you here, Freddie?"

"I told you. I wanted to help find Mamie."

"That's just not true. Even if you think it is, it's not."

"I felt bad."

"Bad for who? For me?"

"Yeah. And Mamie, obviously. She must be scared."

"If she's still alive," I said.

"You don't think—"

"I don't know. I'm hoping for the best, preparing for the worst." I took another sip of coffee and then put the mug down.

"That's harsh."

"Yeah, Freddie, life can be harsh sometimes. So, you felt bad, thought you'd come on down here and do a good deed."

"What's wrong with that?"

"You figured maybe we'd all realize you're not such a bad guy after all. Maybe we'd see another side of you."

"So?"

As *Swan Lake* concluded in the kitchen, it was replaced by silence. Lee must have wanted to listen in. I picked up my coffee again and held it in my hands for warmth. Freddie stared at the piano, still refusing to look at me. "I always wondered why you picked me, Freddie."

"Picked you for what?"

"The day we met. Your little boyfriend didn't show, and you picked me out of a literal crowd of men. You put your hand on the small of my back, you flirted, and you ignored pretty much everyone else in the room when it was your job not to. You sat next to me at rehearsal. You singled me out. I guess I was an easy mark, but I wonder how you knew that."

"I don't know what you mean," Freddie said. "I liked you. You were cute, and you were funny. And you had your shit together." He faced me. "But mostly, I just liked you. Pretty soon I loved you. You can be a very lovable guy. I wish you knew that."

I searched his face for another lie. I wanted to believe him. I could have simply chosen to believe him. But nothing explained why he twisted himself into a pretzel to become my ideal boyfriend, only to leave me three years later and become someone completely different for Edwin Gooch. I realized I might never know the answer.

I got up and collected Freddie's coat. "I think you'd better go." I held the coat out for Freddie to take.

He didn't move. "You're never going to forgive me, are you?"

"For what?"

"For whatever you think I did wrong."

Unbelievable. After all the deception, he still couldn't put a name to any of his sins. The correct response would have been to throttle him, but as he sat there looking sad and defeated, I realized he truly believed himself to be the wronged party. Perhaps the simplest answer was the correct one. He was a narcissist and believed whatever he wanted to, no matter how much damage he left in his wake.

"Do you even know what you did wrong?" I gently set his coat on the bench next to him. He just sat there, avoiding eye contact and silent. "Then no, Freddie, I don't forgive you. First truth, then reconciliation."

I went to the door and opened it. Freddie got up and put his coat on.

"We probably won't see each other again," he said.

"Probably not."

"I hope you're happy again. Someday."

"I hope so too. And I wish the same for you, honestly." And I did. Maybe then, I thought, you'll stop hurting people.

As Freddie approached the door, he nodded toward the kitchen. "Say good-bye to Lee for me." He was proud of himself and not afraid to show it. "I saw you two drive around the house together. I'm not an idiot. Take care, Charlie." And then he was gone.

I watched him walk to the street, take a left, and walk in the direction of Union Station. Only when he was out of sight did I close the door behind him.

By this time, Lee was standing behind me with open arms. "Oh,

Carlito," he said, standing on his tiptoes to give me a hug. With his arms still around me and his chin resting on my shoulder, he asked, "Did he touch the mug?"

"Negative," I said.

"Shit."

He patted my back and broke the embrace, taking a moment to pinch my cheeks as though I were a toddler. Then he went into the living room, retrieving Freddie's untouched coffee mug and bringing it to the kitchen. I grabbed my own mug and followed, taking another sip along the way. While making my way through the dining room I monitored my feet in case Mamie was underfoot, remembering for the eleventh time that day she was gone and I didn't know where she was.

When I reached the kitchen, Lee had already poured the contents of the mug down the drain and set it in the sink. He gestured toward mine. "You done with that?"

"I got it," I said, taking his place at the sink, emptying the rest of my coffee down the drain and placing the mug in the dishwasher. Lee sat by the island.

"It's not your fault, you know."

I pretended not to hear. "Hm?"

"I heard what he said. He wants you to feel bad in some way for how things went down. But you did nothing wrong, you hear me?"

"Nothing's ever just one person's fault."

"Look. Freddie is loco. That's not on you."

"And no one is perfect, either. I didn't listen to you when you tried to tell me about him. Remember?"

"I was too late. You were already in love by then."

He was right, of course. But then it occurred to me, maybe that's what I did wrong.

"I need a glass of wine," Lee said. "Take me home."

CHAPTER TWELVE

Friday, 6:17 p.m.

Angela Woolsey was wrapping up her report on Mamie. I didn't want to watch, so I sat on Claude's luxurious blue couch nursing a glass of dark red wine while Lee and Claude watched in their kitchen. Soon after I heard the television go silent, I felt Claude patting me on the shoulder with his enormous hand.

"Well done, kid," he said. I smiled in return.

Lee floated into the room. "She did a great job," he said. "Everyone is going to be looking for little Mamita now. We'll get her back by tomorrow at the latest."

"I hope so."

"So," he said. "What are you going to do now?"

"Not much."

"Well, you can't mope around here all night by yourself." Lee was worried about me. It's possible he was right to be.

"I won't be by myself," I countered. "Claude will be here."

"Claude will be in bed by eight with his HGTV, and he'll fall asleep in the middle of someone flipping one of those goddamn McMansions by eight thirty."

"Do you have any more wine?" I asked.

"Not for you I don't."

Claude had already sauntered into the other room, but decided to be unhelpfully helpful. "There's a whole case in the garage."

"Look, I'm not going to allow you to sit around and drink yourself into a suicidal depression."

"I'm not depressed."

Lee gave me a look.

"I mean, of course I'm depressed, but I'm having a depressing life right now. It's nothing chemical."

"Oh, so let's just pour alcohol all over it and sit alone in a dark room all by ourselves."

"I'll leave a light on, I promise." I began to fall back on the giant blue couch. God, I loved that couch. More than anything I needed to find Mamie, but in the meantime all I wanted was Claude's fluffy cerulean velvet pillows under my head.

Before I could complete my downward glide, Lee grabbed my arm and jerked me upward. I hated Lee. "Venga. You're coming with me."

"Coming with you where?"

"I got a show tonight. You can help me get ready."

Lee had a show every other Friday at Pansy's Bar & Grill. His alter ego, Banana Daiquiri, was the principal hostess of Drag Bingo. Typically, it took him about an hour in front of a mirror to transform himself into Señorita Banana.

"No. No way. Seriously, why would you make me do this? C'mon, Lee, I've only ever been good to you."

He took me by the hand and led me like an unwilling toddler past Claude in his recliner and down the hall to the master bath, where he'd already laid out his powders and paints in front of a backlit magnifying mirror.

"Let's make some magic, papi."

Friday, 8:02 p.m.

"Drive faster. We're late. Shit, shit, shit."

"Relax," I said. "The first round doesn't even start for another hour."

"But you have to warm up the crowd before the game starts,"

she explained—she being the newly transformed Banana Daiquiri with red lips, wide hips, long lashes, and foam rubber tits, thanks to the sorcery of cosmetics and modern chemistry. "Otherwise you're just interrupting their hookups and they hate you."

Tonight, Señorita Banana was in full Carmen Miranda mode, including a headdress—now in her lap—featuring cherries and bananas circling around a giant pineapple in the center. Needless to say, I was behind the wheel. "Calm your tits, lady. We're almost there."

On show nights, Banana could park in the lot behind Pansy's where we could sneak in through the kitchen without being seen by the patrons. We decided to take Lee's car because it would be recognized and no one would call for a ticket or a tow truck. Before I could put the car in park, Banana was already fumbling to undo her seat belt and open the passenger door. "Vamonos, vamonos." She affixed the headdress to her head, grabbed her makeup bag, a pair of six-inch platform heels, and a bag full of bingo chips, and ran for the back entrance. Getting from the car to the door was no easy feat for a drag queen in a giant hat, a bikini top, a flowing skirt festooned with various Frida Kahlo self-portraits, and puffy winter boots.

Miraculously, I made it to the stage door before she did and opened it. "Madam."

"Gracias, señor."

Her dressing room was a small closet stacked with cases of vodka, vodka, and fruit-flavored vodka, with an end table and a barstool. I pondered for a moment why the American homosexual held brown liquor in such disdain. With a keen sense of urgency, Banana began to unpack.

I loitered in the hallway outside for a while. "Do you need me?"

"No, you're fine. Here, take a seat."

"I think I'm going to go inside and get a drink."

She tut-tutted. "Do you think that's wise?"

"Look, I'm having the shittiest weekend of my life, okay? I'm upset."

"Lo sé, honey. But I don't know that you should get so drunk two nights in a row."

"You brought me to a *bar*."

"So? You're staff tonight. You don't have to do the two-drink minimum."

"Besides, Jack just texted me. He and Tucker will be here soon, so they can look after me in case I have a sudden desire to slit my wrists. Unless, of course, you need me here."

She sighed. "Okay. Go."

"You look beautiful."

She leaned forward and puckered. We gave each other air kisses on each cheek so as not to smudge the delicate masterpiece that was her face, and I headed for the bar.

As I opened the door from the kitchen to the main bar, I was assaulted by the noise of the place. It wasn't the usual syncopated thump of disco music. Instead, all the televisions were tuned to a Capitals game, and the crowd was groaning with disapproval at a missed goal.

Sports was always a mystery to me. I never understood how people got so despondent about this stuff. Then again, I remember how I felt when Glenn Close lost the Oscar for *Dangerous Liaisons*, so perhaps I shouldn't judge.

I noticed one empty barstool at the very end of the bar, which signaled the faint possibility I might be able to order a drink within the hour. It had a clear view to the front door, so I'd know when Tucker and Jack arrived, and I'd have an opportunity to sit, which is the best position in which to be alone and feel sorry for oneself, next to lying down.

I forced my way through the crowd of people. Later, the dance floor would be filled with hordes of shirtless men—yes, even in January—who had spent two hours in the gym before setting out for the evening, but at the moment it was all sweatshirts and backward baseball caps, and the occasional twink with a jock fetish.

I noticed Tucker and Jack entering through the front. They had already seen me and were waving. When I waved back, Jack pointed to the other end of the bar, a signal to meet them there. I nodded and began pushing my way back through the crowd again.

When I finally arrived, Jack had already secured a barkeep's attention. Somehow, being a gorgeous, chiseled specimen of unbridled masculinity made that an easier task in a place like this.

Tucker hugged me tight. "Whatcha drinkin', sugar?"

Still in Tucker's embrace, I turned to Jack. "Tanqueray martini. Dry, slightly dirty." And Jack, in turn, relayed my order to the bartender.

Tucker pulled away. "That bad, huh?"

I nodded. It was that bad. I watched as the bartender poured just a drop of vermouth into a martini glass, swirled it around, and dumped it in the trash behind him. Perfect.

"No news, then?"

"Not yet, but we'll find her."

"That's the spirit."

Friday, 9:48 p.m.

Drag Bingo was already in full swing, and the third winner of the night was a tall Asian man who looked barely old enough to drink.

Señorita Banana beckoned him onto the stage. "Come on up here, cutie pie," she said into the microphone as he ambled toward her. "Ooh, you're a big boy, aren't you?" He was appropriately embarrassed, but the crowd loved her. "What's your name, honey?"

She held the microphone to his lips, and he nervously answered, "Randall."

"Randall what?"

"Ito."

"And where are you from, Randall Ito?"

"I grew up in San Francisco," he said, which provoked a smattering of applause to Señorita Banana's left.

"Oh, look, the hippies and stoners are here," she quipped, and the crowd roared.

Winning a game of Drag Bingo at Pansy's afforded you three prizes: a free drink or appetizer of your choice, the chance to be humiliated onstage by Señorita Banana's prying questions, and the opportunity to request a song she would lip-sync before the next round of play started.

When she asked Randall what song he'd like her to perform, he smiled and said, "'Conga' by Gloria Estefan." The crowd went crazy, and even I clapped a little.

"Oh, you bastard. Go sit down. I hate you." In truth, she was grateful. This was Señorita Banana's signature number, and everyone knew it. She handed her microphone to her assistant, who also removed the bingo cage from the stage, then she struck a dramatic pose, head held high, to raucous whoops and hollers.

Three short brassy notes punctuated the club, and suddenly Banana stood flawlessly mouthing Gloria's mile-a-minute vocals, urging the crowd to shake their bodies and do the conga.

Maybe it was a good idea to get me out of the house. I wasn't having a good time per se, but it was good to be surrounded by people who were. I was still checking my phone every twenty minutes, looping through Facebook, Twitter, Nextdoor, and Instagram, searching each platform for #FindMamie to see if there was anything new. The later the hour, the angrier the comments got. Who could do this to a poor little dog, people are terrible, and you better find those sick bastards. All of which made me feel slightly better, but as usual didn't accomplish anything.

When I looked up from my phone, Jack was standing before me with yet another Tanqueray martini-dry-slightly-dirty. I didn't need a third cocktail, but I figured it would be rude to reject it. After all, he was only trying to help. I noticed some of the younger men at the bar watching me accepting an unsolicited cocktail from Jack of all people, and I imagined they wondered what someone like him could possibly see in me, an ordinary mortal.

"Hey, I'm taking off," he said. "It was good to see you. Hope you get some good news tomorrow."

"Thanks," I said, glancing over at Tucker, who avoided my gaze.

"I know you don't pray or anything," Jack said. "And I don't either, usually. But I've been, y'know, sending good thoughts up there."

"I appreciate it. At this point I'm for anything that can't hurt."

"I think you're gonna find her. I really do."

"Thanks," I said, raising my glass. "I'll drink to that."

Jack turned to Tucker. "See you at home."

"Okay," Tucker said with a cursory smile that disappeared as soon as Jack turned around.

As Jack exited, Señorita Banana danced wildly as the trumpets blared. Tucker studied his drink as I studied Tucker, ready to divert my attention back to the stage immediately should he attempt to look my way.

Eventually the song ended to raucous applause. Both Tucker and I set our glasses on the bar behind us so that we could join in, and in doing so our eyes met.

"You okay?" I asked.

"Fine," he said. But something on my face must have told him I was dubious. "What?"

"Nothing."

"I'm fine."

"Okay," I said, pretending to be interested in the next round of Drag Bingo with Banana Daiquiri.

"Look, I don't need any shit right now, okay?"

I had seen Tucker lose his temper before. He was usually the picture of calm, but occasionally Jack would trigger him, and he'd blow up, usually at whoever was around when Jack left the scene. I could sense he was spoiling for a fight and reminded myself not to take anything he might say too personally. He was mad at his husband, not me.

"Fine, okay," I said, sounding anything but fine. I knew I wasn't to blame for the coming outburst, but I wished Tucker would have the courage to direct his outrage toward its rightful target. After all, I was having a worse day than he was, and I wasn't the one who had married him and ditched him on a regular basis to hook up with other guys. God, I thought, I sound just like my mother. I didn't have anything against open relationships, I reminded myself. They weren't for me, not because I'm a prude, but because relationships were already fraught with land mines. Opening them up made everything even more explosive, but I tried my best not to be too judgmental of those who lived by different rules. And yet perhaps I was more like my mother than I wanted to admit. I chuckled at the thought.

But Tucker wasn't in on my joke. "What's so funny?"

"Nothing."

"Come on, Charlie. If you have something to say to me, why don't you just say it?"

I should have apologized and let it go. Instead, I said, "I don't think that's a good idea, do you?"

"God, you're so passive-aggressive." The pot was about to boil over. Tucker typically couldn't conjure anger even when it was necessary, but tonight was not going to be typical. I reminded myself again he wasn't angry with me. He's mad at Jack, I thought, and he's taking it out on me, so don't take any of this personally. I attempted a smile while trying to think of the perfect sentence to defuse this suddenly tense exchange.

But I never got the chance. "Oh, just fuck off," he said, heading for the same exit Jack had used two minutes ago.

"Tucker. Dammit, wait up." I took a giant swig of Tanqueray-martini-dry-slightly-dirty, deposited my glass on the bar, and followed him out.

Señorita Banana shot me a what-the-hell-is-going-on look, but I could only shrug and hurry out after Tucker. Her curiosity would have to be satisfied later. "G-52," she announced.

When I reached the pavement, I remembered it was January and I'd left my coat inside. I looked to my left, then right, and saw Tucker huffing and puffing away.

"Tucker Pickett, don't you dare take another step." And he stopped. He didn't turn around, though. I was going to have to come to him. I folded my arms for warmth and walked in his direction until I was closer than shouting distance. "Okay, what on earth is wrong with you?"

"You tell me."

"I have no idea! I'm not the one who picked a fight with you."

"Oh, that is such horseshit."

"Okay, would you please tell me what the hell I did to you, then."

"You've been picking this fight for the last three years, Charlie. I finally had it up to here. All your condescending looks, the passive-aggressive asides. If you want to be a little bitch, have the balls to do it because I am so sick of your shit."

"Seriously? You're going to do this today? Right now? Because I asked if you were okay?"

"You know it's not just that."

"If you hadn't noticed, Tucker, I'm having a pretty fucking awful weekend myself. I'm really not trying to make it any worse."

"If I haven't noticed?" Tucker was now red in the face. "Charlie, I've done more to help get Mamie back than you have. If I'd left it up to you, you'd still be at Lee and Claude's moping. Honestly, it's like you don't even want her back."

Suddenly, it wasn't cold outside any longer, or I no longer felt it. Whatever was happening here, I was no longer worried about coming out of this looking like the good guy.

"Oh, is that right?"

"Look, Charlie, I didn't mean that exactly. I'm just—"

"No, no, no," I replied coolly. "It's fine." I yell when I'm angry, but when I'm furious I'm extraordinarily calm. "I suppose I have been at a loss today. Mamie's been taken, and I have no idea where she is or who could have taken her, so I'm not quite sure how to get her back. At least I'm honest about the fact that I'd like her to come home. And when people express concern for my well-being, I'm not biting their fucking heads off because I'm too invested in a goddamn illusion to admit I'm miserable."

"And here we go," he said. "Life must be pretty goddamn peachy up on that mountaintop, looking down on everyone else here on the ground."

His voice was cracking. He was either so mad he was about to cry, or his marriage was in more trouble than I thought.

"So, I guess it would be better if I didn't notice when Jack drops everything to hook up with some trick who he's been texting for all of two seconds, and I should just look the other way when you wallow in self-pity every single time it happens."

"Yes, you goddamn well should look the other way. My marriage, Charlie, is none of your business. You're not my mom, you're not my shrink, and you're not my husband."

"No, I'm the one who's still around after your husband leaves. Again and again and again! Face it, Tucker. You're not mad because I'm sticking my nose where it doesn't belong. Because if you were happy it wouldn't matter, and you wouldn't care. You're mad because I'm right. Your heart gets broken every day, but you don't have the stones to take it out on Jack, so you take it out on me."

"I love my husband."

"You're a doormat."

"Oh, and I suppose I should take after you instead. Charlie, let me tell you something. You're going to die alone and lonely, and it'll be your own goddamn fault. When Freddie left, we all expected you to lick your wounds for a while and recover, and no one was mad at you when you did. But it's been over a year, and you're still locking yourself in your room with no sign of ever coming back out. If a guy so much as looks at you or, heaven forbid, flirts with you, you act like he's a piece of shit on the bottom of your shoe. Okay, maybe Freddie was an asshole—"

"*Maybe* Freddie was an asshole?"

"But get over it, Charlie. You pick yourself up and move on. Find someone new."

"And what if I don't want anyone new? What if I'm fine on my own?"

"That is such bullshit," he screamed. "You're *not* fine. You're scared out of your mind."

"I'm not Jerry Maguire, Tucker. I don't need to be completed. I'm not so scared of being alone I'm going to tie myself to another Freddie Babcock who can rip my heart out of my chest for a daily stomping."

"You think you're brave because you live like a hermit? You're the biggest chickenshit I know. You're too scared of your own shadow to even leave the house. Courage is letting someone in, Charlie, not locking them out. And you can look down on me all you want, but at the end of the day I've got someone to share my life with. You've got yourself a dog. And right now, you don't even have that."

"Yeah, well, when you get home, be sure to say hello to your life partner for me. Oh, wait—he won't be there."

I didn't wait for a response. I simply turned and walked. I really wanted to have the last word, and besides, the initial flush of anger was over and the cold was starting to get to me. How long he stood and watched me go, I have no idea. Just in case he was waiting for me to turn around, I wasn't about to give him the satisfaction. I opened the door and walked straight through it.

Having snuck in the back way earlier with the featured entertainment, I hadn't paid a cover or received one of those flimsy paper bracelets that always rip out a couple of tiny hairs on your wrist when you remove them, no matter how careful you are to fasten them precisely. So the first thing I had to do upon entering Pansy's again was to pay up and be tagged like a big gay cow entering the herd.

"Here all alone?" asked the bearded blond bear behind the glass.

"That's correct," I said rather cheerlessly. Mercifully, the hint was received and no more conversation ensued.

Upon reentry, I was once again assaulted by the noise and the crowd and the smell of the sweaty male musk and the futile efforts to conceal it. This was the place where I was having such a good time moments ago. Well, good in the relative sense. I returned to my former post, not knowing where else to go, and found my coat draped over a still-empty barstool, and half of a gin martini, slightly dirty, undisturbed on the bar. Turns out I hadn't been gone that long.

I reclaimed my seat, finished off my drink in one gulp, and looked at the stage. Señorita Banana noticed my return, but the game was still in progress. "N-37, darlings," she intoned into the microphone.

My phone buzzed in my pocket. It was a text from Agnes at

work. *OMG just saw you on the news! Why didn't you tell me why you were out today? Take as long as you need, honey. I'll handle the odious Muriel.*

Agnes was a good person. I was lucky to have her in my corner. I wanted to tell her how grateful I was, but I didn't trust myself not to be impossibly gooey in my current state of drunkenness, so I settled on a simple *Thanks.* I was about to put my phone back when it buzzed again.

This time the text was from Tucker Pickett. *Fuck you.*

I inhaled deeply through my nose, jaws clenched. *That's quite a comeback. How much time did it take you to conjure that? It's devastating.*

But as I exhaled, I decided not to send it. Delete, delete, delete, and the phone went back into my pocket. I didn't feel like fighting any more.

"You want another?" asked the barkeep behind me. I knew I shouldn't, but I also knew I was going to, so I turned around to place my order. "Tanqueray martini, dry, slightly dirt—oh, fuck me."

Staring back at me was the vacant, stupid face of Bunny Montebank.

"Bingo!" somebody yelled.

CHAPTER THIRTEEN

About two months after Jack's wretched birthday party, I met Bunny Montebank.

Just as the air cooled and the sweaters emerged from the bottom drawers of our dressers, but before the leaves had quite begun to turn, Lee decided I should try dating again. I insisted I wasn't ready, but he was equally insistent that I was and it was time.

Mostly, I think he wanted to set up my Tinder profile.

"Isn't that a hookup app?"

"It can be," he said wryly. "And don't give me that look. You eventually want a boyfriend, naturally."

"Do I?"

"But a little hanky-panky in the meantime wouldn't kill you, and of course you do. Don't be silly."

I was in Lee's kitchen on a Sunday afternoon, making us some grilled cheese sandwiches while he was scrolling through my photos trying to find a sexy picture of me. I doubted such a thing existed, but Lee remembered one and described it in perfect detail. He had taken the picture with my phone. It was taken in Rehoboth, he said, at Aqua Grill the summer before last, and I was wearing a tank top. Freddie was in the picture, but Lee was certain we could crop him out.

"Here it is!" He handed me my phone. Yes, I was wearing a tank I'd purchased in Provincetown the month before. I had been facing Freddie but had turned my head to face the camera. I was smiling. Freddie was smiling too. It looked as if he'd said something funny, but I couldn't remember what. The adaptive lenses of my glasses had darkened in the sun, but it was obviously me to anyone who knew me. I held what appeared to be a vodka and cranberry in my hand. As Lee had predicted, Freddie was standing at some distance and could be easily removed. Just like life, I thought.

"I look fat here."

"You look hot."

"Hot and sweaty. Look at my belly. Don't you have any photos of me taken from the front?"

"Your belly is sexy," he said, and I made another face. "And if someone doesn't think so, then they can swipe left and keep moving. Confía en mi, cariño. You're going to get a lot of attention with this."

He raised his fingers to my lips before I could object and uploaded the picture to my new profile. I returned my attention to my grilled cheese sandwiches and attaining that perfect shade of toasty goodness on both sides. Better than a lover, I told myself, almost believing it.

It wasn't until I delivered a perfectly toasted grilled cheese sandwich, the bread both crispy and buttery, the cheese both gooey and plentiful, to the kitchen counter that I realized Lee was typing, on my behalf, a message from me to my potential suitors.

"Let me see that," I said, but Lee swiveled away before I could reach my phone. "Leonardo García Dorsett. Give me the phone."

"I'm almost finished. You're going to get so much dick with this."

"But I—"

"So. Much. Dick."

"I really think I've had enough dicks for the year," I said. "Just let me see it. I don't want you to—"

"Hush," he said. "Besides, your grilled cheese sandwich is burning."

It wasn't, but it was toasted more than it should have been. I should have given the slightly charred sandwich to Lee, but I was afraid he'd retaliate by telling every gay man in Washington, DC I was chomping at the bit to chomp at their bits.

Half of my sandwich was gone before Lee had even taken a bite of his, and frankly it annoyed me. I worked hard on that sandwich. That was a goddamn perfect sandwich.

"Your cheese is congealing," I said.

"Your mom's cheese is congealing."

"You're disgusting."

"I know, papi, I know. You'll thank me later."

When he was finally done, he handed me my phone and bit into his sandwich, for which he was appropriately full of praise. And yes, I was forced to admit he had done a good job of capturing my personality in the profile he created. Both Freddie and my protruding stomach were cropped out of the photo he'd chosen, and he described my situation accurately—recently single and okay with it—without making me sound like a hermit or a whore.

"Okay, where do I hit send?"

"Oh, sorry. I sent it. It's already out there." I wanted to be upset, but he was enjoying his grilled cheese sandwich too much. I'll be honest. That was a fucking good sandwich, and the version of me he'd broadcast to the world wasn't half bad, either.

On Monday evening, when Lee called, he was upset to learn I'd received only two responses, both from men we agreed were not for me.

"I don't get it," he said. "Fresh meat always gets noticed."

"Sorry to disappoint." Mamie hopped up on the couch next to me to get closer to the speakerphone, tail wagging. She found Lee irresistible.

"Are you sure you're swiping right? You don't get matched unless you both like each other."

"Yes, I—"

"And don't be too picky."

"Not being picky is how I ended up with such a winner the last time."

"Swipe right some more, and I'll call you tomorrow. You'll get more responses tomorrow, okay?"

But to be honest, I didn't much care. While my ego might have appreciated lots of fawning attention from an army of chiseled homosexuals, it would have meant going on a first date and wondering if I was too fat or too gay or trying too hard or playing it too cool, and hoping he'd text me the next day, and fretting if he didn't while being slightly weirded out if he did, and wondering all the time if I should be texting him. I was much happier sitting on the couch, watching old movies with Mamie curled up beside me.

True to his word, Lee checked up on me on Tuesday evening and was happier with the response rate. I had been furiously swiping right per his instructions, and this time there were seventeen gentlemen callers vying for my affections. Tennessee Williams would have been proud. I sent screenshots to Lee so he could look them over.

"You could send me your password, and I could look them up with you."

"Not a chance," I said. "You'd spend the next three days swiping right on every man within a thousand mile radius."

He huffed and puffed a bit, but didn't deny it.

Already in my pajamas at eight p.m., I sat down on my couch. Mamie jumped up and moved to the other end, curling up in a little ball, oblivious to Lee's attempts to find her another daddy.

"Oooh. Victor's cute."

I scrolled down to find Victor, a skinny man who couldn't have been more than twenty-five years old with blond hair and blue eyes. "Meh. He's awfully young."

"What's wrong with young? Look at how white his teeth are."

"So other than tips on dental hygiene, what are we supposed to talk about?"

"If you can't find anything to say, Charlie, just put something in your mouth."

There was a time in my life I would have gleefully accepted

that advice. In fact, I'd taken it many, many times. I'm neither proud nor ashamed that I couldn't begin to number the men I've fellated in my life. It's probably not information I'd share with my mother, but it's typical for anyone who's ever been thirty, gay, and sexually active at the same time. It struck me as strange I rejected this advice now. Was I becoming a prude in my old age? Did a sudden surge of puritanism happen to everyone when they got older? Was I just sad?

"Next," I said.

I didn't feel sad. Or if I was, maybe I was in denial. I was fairly certain I didn't miss Freddie. With each passing day, it was clearer and clearer how much I didn't really know him. The lies he told were hard to fathom, and I began to wonder how much he'd lied to himself. It dawned on me that perhaps I knew Freddie as well as Freddie knew Freddie. If I missed anything at all, it was my life with Freddie in it—or rather, my identity as someone who was with someone—the access it gave you, the feeling of *hello, look, someone chose me and, therefore, I am worthy of being loved.*

All I knew with certainty was the rest of my suitors were either too fat, too thin, too young, too old, too into video games, too religious, or just too much. Honestly, who wears a ball gag in a dating profile photo?

"Charlie," Lee said, exasperated, "these are all men that you liked."

"I never claimed to like them."

"You swiped right!"

"That's because you told me to! And in my defense, the ball gag photo wasn't his primary picture. I didn't notice it last night. But c'mon, you can't unsee that."

"Okay, the gimp is out, but you liked something about each of these boys. You can't reject them all the next day."

And yet that's exactly what I was doing. I didn't know why, but my entire being recoiled at the idea of writing any of these men back and asking if they'd like to have a drink sometime. That would entail picking out clothes in which I looked approachable but not too eager, sexy but not slutty, young but not trying to look young; applying just a drop of cologne; scanning my face for middle-aged acne; arriving at the restaurant exactly on time and killing time at a nearby Starbucks in case I was too early, because being too early makes you look desperate; greeting a total stranger as though I were happy to see him, but happy in a casual way, not overjoyed or anything too psychotic; laughing at all of his jokes while monitoring every word to make sure the jokes were intentional, or else risk laughing *at* him when he was being deadly serious; telling jokes yourself but also being appropriately sincere at least half the time; talking about Freddie without a trace of bitterness, and talking about Mamie without sounding like a weird, dog-obsessed recluse; looking for signs he liked what I just said or didn't, and editing everything I said or did in response to these imprecise clues; slowly learning to hate him; and when it's all over, desperately hoping he called me back. The whole process was infuriating. The idea that anyone enjoyed this arcane and abusive ritual seemed to me both ludicrous and sad.

"What about Bunny?" Lee asked. "What was wrong with him?"

"For starters, his name is Bunny."

"I'm sure that's just a name he uses for the app. He's cute, admit it."

Bunny was thirty-five years old. Younger than me, but within a decade, which seemed reasonable. His asymmetrical smile was goofy but endearing. His eyes twinkled, undeniably. Yes, he was cute.

"Drop him a line," Lee said. "You don't have to say much. Just ask him a question about something in his profile or say hello. You're probably going to chat for a couple of days before anyone asks anyone out anyway."

"Maybe." Mamie lifted her head and looked at me quizzically. Perhaps she could tell I was annoyed and was preparing to come to my defense.

"No maybe, Charlie, just do it—"

"Look, if you want to go on a date with a dude named Bunny so badly, then *you* write him back. I'll be honest, Lee. Nothing about this sounds fun to me. Maybe in another few months or so."

"Or maybe you'll wake up tomorrow, look in the mirror, decide you're too cute to deny the world your fabulousness any longer, and you'll decide to write him back then."

"Maybe that."

"Te quiero, you big ol' chicken." And then he hung up the phone.

I could hear an ambulance in the distance. Mamie could hear it too, and as it got closer she pointed her little snout to the sky and began to howl along.

The next morning, I didn't see an overwhelming amount of fabulousness in the bathroom mirror. However, when I meandered back to the bedroom, I did see three notifications on my phone. Bunny had taken the bull by the horns.

BUNNY: Hi, cutie.
BUNNY: Wanna hang out?
BUNNY: Doing anything on Friday?

I wasn't, in point of fact, doing anything on Friday. And I knew Lee and Claude had theater tickets, as I'd already asked if I could show up at their place on Friday with Mamie and a bottle of wine. I could tell Lee felt guilty as he declined my intrusive offer. He kept apologizing, and I told him not to be ridiculous. I felt a little guilty myself, constantly imposing myself on them like a wayward orphan in need of shelter.

I planned to spend Friday night at home with Mamie and something in black and white featuring Ginger Rogers or Katharine Hepburn, something featuring dialogue racing by at lightning speed, too fast to allow me to wallow in my nobody-loves-me blues.

I should say yes to Bunny, I thought. It'll solve everything.

On the other hand, what if one date leads to another? I can't marry someone named Bunny.

I heard a scolding voice inside my head, belonging either to Agnes Roche, Banana Daiquiri, or Nancy Pelosi, saying, "It's one date. You're not marrying anyone."

On the other hand...

No. Agnes or Banana or Nancy was right. I had no good reason to turn him down and I knew it. I typed my reply.

CHARLIE: It's a date.

I hit send as Mamie hopped up on the bed to let me know that while she had been looking forward to *Kitty Foyle* or *The Philadelphia Story*, she understood my decision and would support it. I thanked her with a scratch behind the ears and got dressed for work. As I was slipping a sweater over my head, I heard the faint ding of a bell.

BUNNY: Your place or mine?

Maybe, I thought, but you'll have to at least buy me a cocktail first. I offered the name of a little pub on H Street where we could meet and size each other up before committing to anything else, and he seemed amenable.

I decided I wouldn't tell Lee just yet. I'd tell him eventually, but not until afterward. I knew he'd cluck like a proud mother hen, and I didn't feel like being congratulated just yet. Most of all I didn't want any advice. Whatever happened, I'd call him on Saturday and tell him all about it.

❖

That Friday, Agnes left work a little early, and I followed her out the door almost immediately. These were the days before the insufferable Muriel Ball, and no one minded when someone's work was done and they wanted a head start to their weekend.

The drive home was accompanied by National Public Radio, and there just so happened to be a story about what to wear on a first date, specifically about the gender-based double standards existing in the straight world. Women, according to NPR, were expected to look like they just stepped out of a magazine, whereas men could pull a T-shirt over their unshaven faces and hop into a pair of jeans, accessorize with a blazer and dress shoes, and run a comb through their hair, and this was completely acceptable. I smiled as I listened, mostly because I was thankfully not a straight woman, but also because I no longer had to worry about what to wear or whether to shave. If a scruffy face was deemed acceptable by NPR, it was good enough for a Tinder profile named Bunny.

After walking Mamie around the block, I showered, spending a little extra time on those hard-to-reach areas just in case, and donned my T-shirt, jeans, blazer, and dress shoes. To gay it up a little, I picked a tee featuring the Golden Girls carved into the side of a mountain like Mount Rushmore. I dried my hair with a little bit of product, but not too much, in case someone might be running his fingers through my hair before the night was out. I sprayed my cologne into my hair and on my *Golden Girls* T-shirt in case someone might be kissing my neck at some point. I will admit hoping for a little nooky was exciting. The end of my relationship and my life after its demise had been entirely celibate, and I had almost forgotten about sex. It was nice to be reminded.

When I was satisfied with my reflection in the mirror, I glanced at my phone. True to my nature, I had more than an hour to kill before Bunny and I were scheduled to meet, so I took Mamie for a second walk around the block, mostly to kill time. Also, I felt a little guilty about leaving her at home inside a crate while I was out trying to convince a cute boy to like me.

When we returned, I unfastened her leash and said, "Kennel!" This was her cue to jump into her crate and await a treat, which she joyfully consumed as I fastened the latch. I was now only forty minutes early, but if I walked to H Street instead of driving, I'd arrive right on time. Besides, that way we'd only have to worry about one car if we decided not to end the evening at the pub.

The air was pleasantly cool that early autumn night, but after ten minutes I was a little chilled, and before long I was doing a sort of walk-jog just to keep warm. So, despite all my stalling tactics, I was still early. I didn't want to stand outside, so I walked in, grabbed a barstool, and sat.

The barkeep, a young woman with wild blond curls, approached me immediately. "I'm Coral," she said. "Can I get you something to drink?"

"Maker's Manhattan," I said, hoping it would seem more rugged and masculine than the cosmopolitan I truly wanted. "Up."

"Coming right up," Coral said with a smile. "Are you stopping by for a drink, or can I get you a menu?"

"I'm, um...meeting someone. We'll probably have dinner, but I'll wait until he gets here."

Coral smiled. "First date?"

"How could you tell?"

"You look a little nervous," she said, and my face must have fallen. "But not in a bad way. It's adorable."

Bunny arrived about twenty minutes late, but I was inclined to forgive him. They call lateness "gay time" for a reason. Besides, he was even more attractive in person. Shorter than I expected, but definitely cute. He had those sad eyes which made him look permanently in need of a hug, and a little cleft in his chin reminiscent of Dudley Do-Right.

"Are you Charlie?" he asked. I smiled and nodded. "Cool," he said, sidling up next to me at the bar.

"Oh, we can get a table if you want," I said. "I was just waiting here. I was early, until you, um, y'know?"

Shit. I was nervous. I didn't think I would be. I told myself not to be. But I hadn't done this in years, and I wasn't very good at it then.

"No, this is better," he said, placing his hand on my inner thigh. "I have easy access this way." And he proceeded to slide his hand all the way up to my crotch and give it a little squeeze.

I mentally objected to this brazen action taken without my full and informed consent. But the longer his hand remained there, the less either of us could deny a physical reaction that told a different story. "Nice," he said, smiling.

Okay, so Bunny would probably never attend feminist lectures with me or march by my side down Pennsylvania Avenue, holding signs reading "Crush the Patriarchy" or "Feminism Is My Second

Favorite F-Word." We would probably not marry, move to the suburbs, and quibble over the kitchen backsplash. But I was probably going to get laid.

"You keep that up, and I'm not going to be able to walk home," I said.

He removed his hand from my groin as Coral reappeared and handed him a cocktail menu list. "Don't worry. I brought my car."

Coral smiled and gave me a wink. She approved of Bunny, it seemed. "Ready for those menus?"

"Sure," I answered, and she walked away, beaming. "So, I have to ask. Who named you Bunny?"

"Oh, that's a name I picked up in college," he said. "Sometimes I'd keep my roommates up all night."

"But what does it mean?"

Just as Coral reappeared with the requested menus, Bunny answered, and not quietly. "It's how I fuck."

Coral's eyes widened. She set the menus on the bar and walked away. I wondered for a moment if she was offended, but while Bunny and I were perusing our menus, she caught my eye and began fanning herself dramatically.

Yeah, I was definitely going to get laid.

Our conversation over dinner was terrible, honestly. We had no cultural touchpoints in common. Bunny had no idea who either Bette Davis or Ella Fitzgerald were, but in fairness neither could I name a single Real Housewife from anywhere. I did learn that Bunny came from a wealthy family who happily paid his rent and utilities while he discovered himself as either an aspiring actor or lead singer of a rock band that did not yet exist.

He had no interest in my career, and without much in common, our conversation frequently hit a dead end. But we found we could always salvage the moment by letting our hands do the talking. I typically opted for a hand on the knee, but Bunny wasn't the only one who scaled the mountains in search of a peak before the evening was out.

So, while it was painfully obvious after an hour of awkward

conversation and roaming hands we were not headed for boyfriend status, it was just as clear the evening was not going to end at a little pub on H Street. I found I was no longer nervous. Nothing I could say to this horny little elf was going to dissuade him from coming home with me after our meal, but nothing I could say would induce him to call me the next day, either. In fact, a call or text from Bunny the next day was about the last thing I wanted.

Eventually, I asked for the check and paid it, rewarding Coral's theatrics with a thirty percent tip. As I got up and put my blazer on, Bunny slipped his hand into my back pocket, and he squeezed my left butt cheek all the way back to his car.

Neither of us were all that interested in any more strained chatter, so we quickly opted for my place, which was only four minutes away by car. He found a parking spot right in front of the house, and I was already fumbling with my keys as I opened the car door and stepped into the street. We could see our breath as we sped to my front door. Before letting us in, I kissed him.

"Hurry up," he said.

I opened the storm door, and it squeaked a little. The sound caused Mamie to begin barking furiously from her crate in my bedroom.

Bunny's eyes grew wide. "What the hell is that?"

"Oh, that's just Mamie. She's smaller than she sounds from out here." In my haste to get inside and rip Bunny's clothes off, I was attempting to insert the key to my front door upside down. "And don't worry if you're allergic or anything. She doesn't shed, so— aha!" I finally managed to unlock the latch. As I opened the door, Bunny took a barely perceptible step back. Perhaps he was afraid of dogs.

"And she's very friendly," I said. "She barks like this whenever someone's at the door." I stepped inside. "Mamie, hush! C'mon in."

He peered inside the house from where he stood. "Where is it?"

"She's upstairs in her crate."

At the sound of my voice, the barking was quickly replaced by an excited whine.

"You lock it up?"

"It sounds awful, but apparently they like it. Here, I'll go get her." I dashed upstairs to free the maiden from her cell.

"Wait, where are you—"

"Just close the door behind you!" I yelled.

When I appeared in the bedroom, Mamie was sitting up, wagging her tail furiously. As I opened the door to her crate, she met my face with a barrage of kisses until she heard the front door latch. Realizing we weren't alone, she began to bark again in earnest, going to the top of the stairs to get a view of the intruder.

"Mamie, stop," I commanded. "We like him, I promise." But the barking continued. Bunny stood like a statue, both still and silent.

Wanting to get this part over with as soon as possible, I scooped Mamie up in my arms and carried her downstairs. Bunny didn't look happy to meet her and, based on her growling, the feeling seemed mutual.

"She won't bite you. Promise. Just let her sniff your hand, and we should be good to go." He obeyed warily. Mamie got a good sniff and seemed satisfied with the results. "You going to be a good girl?" I set her down on the floor, and she took in the scent of Bunny's ankles. When the tail started to wag, I smiled at Bunny. He looked calmer. "Now," I said, "where were we?"

I positioned myself in front of him and gently rested my thumb in the little cleft of his chin. When his lips parted, I began to kiss him. The first kiss involved only the lips. The second was deeper, but brief. I pulled away until he opened his eyes, and once I'd established a deep kind of eye contact, I opened my mouth a little wider to kiss him again.

Apparently, this was Bunny's cue to use his tongue to try to find every nook and cranny within my mouth in twenty seconds or less. There wasn't anything remotely sensual about his technique. It was less like an arousing exploration and more like the world's fastest dental exam.

Okay, so kissing wasn't his strong suit. I have a theory about bad kissers. As Bunny poked and prodded, it occurred to me that he wasn't enjoying himself in the slightest. He was probably only kissing me because the movie industry taught us that it was a necessary step between flirtation and penetration. Given his druthers, he would have probably skipped the kissing altogether, the way one might skip the shrimp cocktail and head straight for the prime rib, so to speak.

"Shall we go upstairs?" I asked.

"Fuck, yeah."

I took him by the hand and led him upstairs. Mamie, who had been gathering data on Bunny since he arrived through the various aromas contained in his ankles, happily trotted after us, passing us on the stairs and waiting for us on the landing. When I was eye level with her, I gave her a little scratch under the chin. "Hey, sweetie, who's my good girl?"

"Are you gonna put it back in its cage?"

I pretended not to hear the question, hoping he'd drop it. I wasn't averse to crating Mamie for the hour or less I was guessing Bunny would be here, and I wondered about his obvious aversion to her. Bitten as a kid? Allergies? Random antisocial tendencies that manifested in a hatred of nature's most perfect and loyal animal? Still, I was hoping she'd just quietly crawl under the bed as she used to do whenever Freddie and I got a little frisky.

But when we reached the bedroom to find Mamie making herself comfortable among the pillows at the head of the bed, he spoke up again.

"I really think it needs to go back in the cage."

"It's a crate. Um, okay. Mamie! Kennel!"

Happy to receive another treat, Mamie bounded off the bed and into her crate. I placed a doggie biscuit between the bars for her while I closed the latch behind her. For a moment she chewed happily.

"Wow, it's really well-trained," Bunny said.

"I can be very commanding. You. Take your clothes off." And just as happily Bunny obeyed.

Once naked, Bunny jumped on the bed and lay on his back, his erection standing at a perfect ninety-degree angle, like a weather vane waiting for a breeze. Trying to be seductive and alluring, I was removing my clothing much more slowly, giving Bunny a bit of a show, which he seemed to appreciate. Once I was stripped myself, I slowly climbed on top of him. Before I kissed him again, I grabbed a fistful of his hair. I figured he'd like it, and he did, but mostly I did it for control to avoid another cavity search like the one downstairs. Letting go of his hair, I kissed his neck. Foraging through his hairy chest, I found a nipple and teased it with my tongue, which elicited a moan.

Wow, I'm better at this than I remembered, I thought. I moved lower, past his belly button. I teased him a little, showering his inner thighs with little kisses until the anticipation made him groan. Then, quickly, so he wouldn't quite expect it, I swallowed him whole.

Taken by surprise, he cried out in what I hoped was ecstasy. About a split second later, Mamie began whining in her crate. She was done with her biscuit, and we clearly weren't going anywhere. Her continued imprisonment was a violation of precedent, and she wasn't having it.

I tried to disregard it, focusing intently on the task at hand, but after about twenty seconds of her plaintive cries, Bunny couldn't ignore it either.

"Can you make it stop?"

I took his dick out of my mouth just long enough to holler out, "Mamie! No!" and then I went right back to work. My authoritarian tone bought us another five seconds of uninterrupted fellatio, but then the whimpers began again. Undaunted, I scolded her one more time, and again received the same five-second reprieve.

"Dude, you have to make it shut up."

I knew I couldn't make Mamie stop protesting, so I got up and let her out of her crate.

"Hey, what are you doing?"

"Under the bed," I commanded, and miraculously Mamie obeyed. I noticed her favorite antler in her crate, and I gingerly placed it under the bed in case she needed a distraction, and a moment later heard a familiar scraping sound. She was happy. I was happy. Bunny was horny, and that was good enough for now.

But he was also nervous. "Can't you put it downstairs?"

"She wouldn't stay there," I said. "She's fine. She won't bother you."

He raised himself up and walked on his knees to the edge of my bed. We kissed again, in his usual enthusiastic and thorough manner, but he resisted when I tried to coax him onto his back again. Instead, he started kissing my neck. Apparently, it was his turn, and he was taking it.

Like the way he kissed me, his approach seemed to boil down to as much as possible, as quickly as possible. Like a starving beggar who hadn't eaten in weeks, he devoured me. Still, apart from one moment involving teeth, it wasn't unpleasant—particularly after my prolonged dry spell.

"Okay, let's get to the good stuff," he said as he turned around, buried his face in my pillows, and presented me with his posterior. At the pub, I had wondered whether Bunny was going to top or bottom, and this sudden move was my answer. I was relieved. Based on his performance thus far, I imagined being fucked by Bunny Montebank would be something akin to being gently explored by a jackhammer, and it wasn't an experience I longed for. I went to the nightstand, opened the drawer, and removed a small bottle of lube and a condom sealed in foil.

"Aren't you on PrEP?" he asked, half of his face hidden in pillows.

"No. Like I said, I just got out of something, and we were monogom—"

"Okay, whatever, just hurry up."

I hurried. Once I was wrapped in safety and bathed in lubrication, I stood behind him and slipped my thumb between his cheeks. I moved in a clockwise circle, then counterclockwise, just like I learned in my now worn copy of *The New Joy of Gay Sex*. Jack always called this move the wax-on-wax-off.

"I'm not a fucking virgin," Bunny said. "You can skip the formalities. Just get in there."

So, without so much as a hello-how-are-you, get in there I did.

He moaned a little too loudly for my taste, but I was determined to enjoy the present moment before the time came to bid Bunny adieu and never see him again. I closed my eyes as he began to buck wildly against me. I wondered if his nickname was offered in the same congratulatory vein as Bunny had received it, or perhaps it was a commentary about style rather than frequency or endurance. I held on for dear life as if I was riding a mechanical bull, wondering if this was what hate sex felt like. I'd never experienced hate sex myself because my last three months with Freddie was more like hate celibacy.

With my eyes shut tight, and the guttural sounds Bunny was making, I hadn't noticed Mamie crawling out from her hiding place. She probably felt unsafe under a bed that was shaking back and forth like a seven on the Richter scale. I noticed her out of the corner of my eye right before she jumped up on the bed to see what the hell was going on.

She landed right next to Bunny's head. His eyes grew wide as his moans morphed into a loud scream, and before I could stop him, he lifted himself up and pushed Mamie off the bed, hard.

She let out a piercing yelp, probably more surprise than pain, but she cried out again, and louder, when she landed on the wood floor on her back.

"What the fuck!" Bunny yelled.

"Mamie!" I immediately dislodged myself from Bunny and ran to my little dog, who was lying down, staring at the floor and then trying to stand but unable to, either from shock or pain. "Are you okay? Mamie, are you all right?"

Finally, she stood up, and I began to examine her, gently squeezing her joints to see if she flinched or yelped. She seemed fine, just a little shaken. Eventually, she met my gaze with a look that communicated both sadness and confusion.

"I told you to put that fucking dog downstairs," Bunny said.

"Get out."

"Excuse me?"

"I said get the fuck out of my house. Now."

"What for?"

"You're a bad kisser, a lousy lay, and you threw my dog across the goddamn room. Get out."

"That's not my fault. Your stupid dog jumped up here and scared the f—"

I picked up Bunny's windbreaker from the floor, and pitched it directly into his face.

"Ow!"

"Out. Now." I found my underwear on the floor next to Bunny's shoes, and put them on.

"Let me look at her. I'm sure she's fine."

"You don't touch her." I threw his shirt, then a sock, at him.

"You're being an asshole."

"I'm crushed you think so." I took his jeans, boxers, shoes, and his remaining sock and walked down the stairs with them.

"Where the fuck are you going?" He pulled his shirt over his head and followed me.

As he reached the bottom of the stairs, jacket and lone sock in hand and naked from the waist down, I was tossing the remainder of his clothes onto my front porch.

"Give those back!"

"Go get them," I said. "Or do you want me to toss you out in much the same way? Because I'm mad enough to do it."

Once he was gone and the door locked behind him, I walked back upstairs to check on Mamie, who had managed to jump up on the bed a second time. She sat at the edge, her head raised ever so slightly and her tail wagging, happy the loathsome stranger had been removed. Downstairs, I heard a man screaming expletives at the house from the sidewalk. A moment later, I heard him start his car and drive away into the night.

"And don't come back," I muttered.

I retrieved my blazer from the floor and fished out my phone from the inside pocket. I draped the blazer over the desk chair as I moved back to the bed, Mamie at my feet.

I felt her rest her chin against my foot as I opened my phone and promptly deleted the Tinder app. Once that was done, I picked up the remote and regarded my brave little dog.

"Well, Mamie, what's it to be? *Kitty Foyle* or *The Philadelphia Story*?" Mamie gave me a dissatisfied little sneeze. "All right. *Stage Door* it is."

Chapter Fourteen

Friday, 10:02 p.m.

"Bingo!" Someone else was a winner, with the predictable cheers and groans that followed.

Señorita Banana beckoned the lucky champion. "Well, come on up here, baby."

Bunny Montebank didn't recognize me at first, but I could see the light flickering, flickering...and then it turned on.

"Never mind," I said, turning back around to the stage.

"Hey!" Bunny slammed a fist on the bar behind me. "Hey, fuck you, you fucking fuck!"

We were the people who produced Noël Coward and Cole Porter? I thought. How did we also yield this Neanderthal specimen? Dorothy Parker would weep.

Left to my own devices, I would have just collected my coat and gone home, but the drag queen onstage was depending on me for a ride, and the bingo game was slated to last at least another two hours.

I resigned myself to stay in one place and enjoy the show as best I could, despite the crowd, the stink, the noise, despite an angry bartender I once threw half-naked into the street, despite one of my best friends spontaneously combusting in my face, despite the fact he might have been absolutely correct about me, and shit, despite the fact Mamie was still out there scared and alone.

"Hey. I was talking to you."

And suddenly Bunny was in front of me, his simian jaw jutting forth.

"And with such wit and charm, how could I ever resist you?"

"What are you doing here?"

"Just watching the show."

"Why'd you kick me out that night?"

A couple of young boys canoodling on the barstool next to mine suddenly perked up, giving us an audience of two.

I sighed. "Let's just say I didn't see a future between us."

"It was a dick thing to do."

"Then I sincerely apologize."

"God, you can't even say you're sorry like a normal person," he said. "You're an arrogant prick. Why are you really here?"

"I told you, I'm here to see the sh—"

"Oh, bullshit. No one comes here to see this lame-ass show."

The boys at the next barstool reacted. I think one of them might have gasped. They were clearly part of Señorita Banana's devoted fan base.

"The only reason people come here is to get drunk or get laid, or both."

And then I regarded him more closely. One foot was positioned slightly in front of the other, allowing him to lean in my direction. His hands were balled into fists, but at his sides. He wasn't trying to fight me. He was…flexing. His biceps pulsed at a regular rhythm in perfect time with his grip.

"Y-you're not flirting with me, are you?"

"What? I mean, no." But the way he puffed up his chest told a different story. He'd been working out since I'd seen him last, and he wanted me to notice.

"You look good," I said, hoping a quick compliment would send him on his way. It didn't.

He scrunched his forehead as if doing so might allow his few brain cells to better communicate with one another. "I do?"

"Yeah. But I'm not having such a great night, so why don't you just—"

"Why don't I just what?"

"Look, Bunny, I'm sorry, okay? I'm sorry I kicked you out that night. I was hasty."

Now he was approaching the barstool, and his hands pounced on my knees, forcibly spreading my legs so he could get even closer. "Hey, I get off at two thirty. I think we should go back to my place." Now his mouth was hovering close, the stale beer on his breath impossible to ignore. His crotch was on top of mine, grinding and stiffening.

I should have gently pushed him to the side. In my defense, I was having a terrible day and had probably consumed a fifth of gin in the past two hours. I was angry. I was angry at whoever took Mamie, I was angry at Tucker for yelling at me, I was angry at myself for maybe deserving all of it, and I was angry at this dim-witted sex gnome for putting his hands on me.

"Not if you were the last power bottom on the Eastern Seaboard," I said.

"Wait. What?" He cocked his head back slightly, but his hands remained planted on my thighs.

"I've met coin-operated massaging recliners that fuck better than you."

"Hey, fuck you, man," he said, a little too loudly, garnering a response from more than just the boys next door.

"Not bloody likely," I said. "Get out of here and leave me alone."

One of the boys beside me gave a little snort-laugh, which made Bunny turn pink in the face and red about the ears.

"Fuck you, goddammit. I hope you go home alone tonight."

"Jesus, so do I."

"And I hope that creepy little dog of yours gets run over by a car."

And then my hands were on him. It was an action without any conscious thought. I grabbed the official Pansy's tank top he wore and pulled him to me. I only remember the whites of his eyes getting closer and closer as his head rapidly approached mine, and his gaping mouth retreating as I pushed him away just as suddenly, sending him falling toward a table littered with bingo detritus and martini glasses, all of which ended up on the floor beside him. It wasn't until I heard glass breaking against the concrete floor that I realized what I'd done.

When I looked around, all eyes in the place seemed to be on me. Bunny was on the ground, shell-shocked, and even Banana Daiquiri was stunned into silence—which, if you knew her like I did, was a significant accomplishment.

I've never been in a fistfight, I thought, but this might be the moment. If Bunny wanted to meet violence with violence, I couldn't blame him. I had started it, and due to some ancient masculine code even I, an urbanite of the homosexual persuasion, could not violate, I would have to see it through. But as a couple of patrons helped him to his feet, careful to avoid any shards of glass in the rescue attempt, the look on his face told me he was genuinely frightened of me.

"What the hell is going on?" Another official Pansy's tank top stood behind me, bringing order to the gay chaos that had just descended upon Drag Bingo.

"Byron, he…he pushed me!" Bunny's finger was pointed at me. I noticed it was trembling and will admit to feeling somewhat satisfied at the sight of it.

"Montebank," said blond, broad-shouldered Byron. "Should've known."

"He threw me into that table!"

"What's this, the third customer you've sexually assaulted this week?"

"What?! No, it's not like th—"

"Well, consider yourself caught in the act this time," Byron said. "Also, you're fired."

"No! You can't do that. There were witnesses!" And he looked at the crowd around him, most of whom had no idea anything was amiss until he flew across the room and landed among pieces of broken stemware. It's an eerie feeling when a crowded room is as quiet as this one was. I looked toward the stage for moral support, but Señorita Banana was too busy enjoying the drama of the moment to cast a sympathetic glance my way.

I suppose I'll need to tell the truth, I thought. And I pictured the rest of the night unfolding before me. The arrest, the booking, and my first visit to a jail cell, being bailed out by a drag queen with cherries and bananas on her head.

"It's true," said one of the boys next to me, before I could fess up. "This one," he said, motioning towards Bunny, "was totally grabby. Went straight for the crotch. It was self-defense."

"That's a lie!"

"Get the hell out of here, Bunny," Byron said. "Now. Unless you want me to call the cops."

But Bunny Montebank only rooted himself to his post, standing as tall as nature would allow.

"Okay," said Byron, "you asked for it." He walked away, presumably to call the police.

Defiantly, Bunny pulled his official Pansy's tank top off and threw it behind the bar. He approached me with more swagger than the moment deserved. "Fuck you," he said, greeted only by a shake of my head and roll of my eyes. "And that goes double for you, asshole," he said to the young boy who had spoken in my defense.

"Get bent, you little turd," the young man replied. "We heard what you said about his dog. That's fucked up."

"And besides," said his boyfriend, "nobody calls a performance by the legendary Señorita Banana Daiquiri a 'lame-ass show.'"

Saturday, 12:42 a.m.

I was in no state to drive, so Lee sat behind the wheel of his car, a modest beige wig cap where his elaborate headdress used to be, but his face still flawless.

He was silent and stoic, and I figured he had a right to be angry. He had heard the official version of events, that I'd been groped and had acted in self-defense. And he knew Bunny Montebank well enough to know this was a plausible story. But he also knew my history with Bunny and my current state of mind enough to be wary.

We weren't speaking much. He was concentrating on the road,

and I was concentrating on keeping the contents of my stomach in place every time the car hit a bump.

"You okay?" he'd say.

"Fine," I'd answer.

We repeated this scintillating dialogue about four times before I finally said, "I'm sorry."

"For what?"

"For getting drunk. For ruining your show."

"You didn't ruin my show," he said. "Bunny Montebank being tossed across the room in the middle of Drag Bingo is the best publicity I've had in years."

We drove a little while longer in silence. Crossing New York Avenue was always a bit tricky. While Lee was a good driver and stone cold sober, I think he was nervous about being pulled over in sequins and a full face of makeup.

"Did he really feel you up?"

"No. No, he didn't. He just made me mad."

"Charlie, should I be worried about you?"

"Yes, please. Worry about me. It's nice to know someone is."

"I mean, drunk off your ass two nights in a row isn't that weird, given the circumstances. I'm not calling Betty Ford or anything, but I've never seen you be violent with anyone, ever. Not even Freddie, not even when he very much deserved it. That's unlike you."

"I know. I'm sorry."

"And I don't even want to say this, but it's been more than twenty-four hours. If we don't get Mamie back, are you going to be okay?"

"No. No, I won't."

I stared out the window at the houses rushing by in the dark. When I was a kid, I wanted nothing more than to live in a big, bustling city. And Washington is an important city, but it was barely past midnight on a Friday, and it looked like nearly everyone was asleep. It wasn't the urban jungle I'd once dreamed of, and yet it could still be dangerous, as I now knew.

I looked at Lee, whose eyes were fixed on the road ahead while the rest of his face looked concerned. He thinks I'm losing it, I thought. He thinks I'm a badass motherfucker, I thought happily for a moment. But the happiness was short-lived. It was one thing for Bunny Montebank to have a completely distorted picture of me, but lying to Lee made me sad.

"Bunny said he hoped Mamie got run over by a car."

"What?"

"Swear to Liza Minnelli," I said. "He doesn't know she's missing. He was still pissed off at the way she ruined his big moment a year and a half ago, but still…Timing is everything."

"That little fucker. Now I regret trying to get the brass to give him his job back."

"You did what now?"

"Don't worry, it didn't work. Apparently, he's a real shitty bartender. Byron has been looking for an excuse to fire him for weeks."

We drove in silence a while longer. Perhaps one day, I'd be able to enjoy a little schadenfreude at Bunny's expense, but I was currently too occupied with what I'd lost. Mamie, and who knows, maybe Tucker as well.

When we got to the stop sign at Constitution and Fifteenth Street, Lee gently slowed the car to a full stop. I couldn't see any traffic in either direction. We stayed motionless for a good ten seconds even though no one was coming. It took a moment for me to notice.

"What are you doing?" I asked.

"I don't know. Where are we going?"

I didn't understand the question at first. It seemed awfully philosophical in nature, or perhaps I'm just philosophical after five extra-large Tanqueray martinis, slightly dirty. I had been given free beverages for the rest of the night after Bunny cleared off, and I didn't refuse them.

"You're welcome to stay at our place again," Lee said. "Your car is still there, but I didn't know if…You don't have to stay there if you don't want to, but…you know what, just forget it. You're staying with us. I don't know why I even brought it up."

"No," I said. "Take me home. It's okay."

"You sure? What about your car?"

"We'll figure it out tomorrow," I said, and Lee eased off the brake and took a left. "It's going to be really quiet. Too quiet."

"Just spend another night at our house, cariño."

"No, no. I'm not packed or anything. And I *have* to go back eventually."

"You don't have to be brave, Charlie. No one will think any less of you."

"I will. Think less of me, I mean. Besides, this is better. I still think I'm going to get her back." Lee looked like he might start to cry. Please don't, I thought. There's nothing more pathetic than a drag queen with rivers of charcoal eyeliner running down her cheeks. "I want to go home now while I still think she's coming back, not because we lost. You know?"

"Okay," he said.

As he pulled up to my front door, he checked again to be sure I was doing the right thing. I asked if he felt okay to drive.

"I'm sober as can be. Nothing but Diet Cokes all night. Here, don't forget your house key."

"Thanks," I replied, taking it. "Just be careful. You'll have a hard time explaining this getup to whoever pulls you over."

"You'll be my first phone call from the pokey."

"Not Claude?"

"Claude would snore right through the whole thing and wouldn't get up until noon if I didn't push him out of bed," he said. "Sorry, bitch. You're it."

"Love you."

"Love you more."

I closed the door and watched him drive away. He was nearly out of view entirely before I noticed a silent figure standing on my front porch, waiting for me.

I jumped a bit. I might have squealed like Jamie Lee Curtis in the first *Halloween* before she became a vengeful badass. Perhaps in response to my damsel-in-distress routine, the mystery man lumbered from the porch to the steps, where the streetlight in front of my house illuminated his fiery red curls.

"Tucker?"

He didn't say anything. He just stood there. Had an eerie score kicked in, it would have been my cue our Tucker was some kind of mute zombie about to eat the flesh from my bones, but there was no music, just complete silence except for the neighbor's cat meowing in the window. And Tucker didn't look scary. Merely sad.

"Tucker, what are you doing here?" I approached him, and he slowly, silently wrapped his arms around me, pinning my arms to my side and making it impossible for me to return the gesture.

"Tucker? Tucker, I...I can't feel my thumbs." He didn't let go. "Is this a peace offering or are you trying to kill me?"

"Sorry," he said, although he didn't let go immediately. "I'm sorry."

"If I forgive you, will you let go?"

"Sorry," he repeated, loosening his grip, then stepping back. "Sorry," he said again.

"How long have you been standing there?"

"A couple of hours."

"God, you must be freezing. Come inside, and we'll put something warm inside you."

"How you talk," he said, with a barely perceptible grin.

"You're a pervert and a whore," I said, prompting a giggle—a sad and pathetic giggle, but a giggle nonetheless—and I knew we had already forgiven each other.

After I put the kettle on and convinced Tucker to remove his shoes and swap them out for my fuzzy slippers, we went through the formal motions of forgiveness anyway.

"Can I blame it on the alcohol?" he asked. "I never should have said any of that. I didn't mean it."

"Sure you did," I said, sitting on the couch next to him. "But it's okay. You were right about most of it."

"No, no. I mean, I *do* want you to find somebody."

"Why?" I asked. "Sick of dragging a fifth wheel around?" I smiled so he knew I wasn't fighting.

"No, of course not. I just want you to be happy."

"Happy sounds great. I'd like that too."

"So?" Tucker looked up at me. "We're not built to be alone, Charlie."

"I'm not alone. Look at me. It's past midnight, and I'm sitting up talking to a man who stood outside my door waiting for me. For hours."

"You know what I mean."

"Yeah, I do. But history has not shown me a boyfriend is any kind of happiness guarantee."

"Freddie was an asshole. You got unlucky, that's all."

"He showed up here today, you know."

"What?"

I nodded, and the kettle started to whistle. I hopped up and moved to the kitchen with Tucker right behind me.

"When?"

I took some mugs down from the shelf. "Today, around three."

"What happened?"

"He didn't take Mamie. Herbal decaf, I presume?"

"Yeah, perfect. What did he say?"

I selected a few Lemon Zingers and dropped them into the mugs, letting the strings dangle delicately over the sides. "He said he was worried about her. That he wanted to help."

"Anything else?"

"Not really." I poured the boiling water into the mugs and watched the tea steep.

"He came all the way to New York to say he wanted to help?"

"Apparently. I think he's mad that I kept the house, the dog, and all our friends in the divorce. Maybe he thought he could just show up and do a good deed, and everyone would forget all the other stuff. I think he had good intentions, and—typical Freddie— he thinks his good intentions are all that matter."

"What did *you* say?"

"There wasn't any kind of grand reconciliation, if that's what you're asking. Not that I would have believed him, so it's just as well."

Tucker gratefully accepted his mug of steaming hot tea and sat at the kitchen counter. "How did you leave it?"

"I don't know. Good-bye, I guess." I sat down next to him and took a sip. "Don't get me wrong, I was glad he came. At the very least, it's nice to know for sure I don't feel anything about him one way or the other. I used to be scared that if I saw him again, I'd stare into his big blue eyes and, I don't know, fall under his spell maybe. I hoped I'd be filled with rage instead, which he deserves. But neither thing happened. He was just somebody I used to know, like the song."

"That's good, I guess."

"Yeah, I think so."

"Time to get out there, then," he said.

I rolled my eyes and threatened to stand until Tucker caught my hand in his.

"Said with love. Honest."

"Can I find my dog first?" Yes, I played the missing dog card, and I'm not ashamed.

"Of course," he said, but he didn't let go of my hand. "But don't be alone for the rest of your life to get even with Freddie."

"Is that what I'm doing?" It was an honest question.

"Isn't it?"

"Honestly, I have zero desire to get out there. I've always hated dating. I used to joke if I could skip the butterflies and insecurity and move right into old boring married couple, that'd be great."

"It doesn't work that way, Charlie. And besides, the butterflies can be fun if you let them be."

"Pass." I took another sip of tea. "And more importantly, I'm not even sure I want old married couple anymore. Don't take offense at what I'm about to say, okay?"

"I think I know what it is, but go ahead."

"I just look at the marriages around me, and I don't know that I'd want any of them for myself."

Tucker nodded, drinking his tea in silence for a moment.

"Be honest," I said. "It makes you sad when Jack runs off like that. Doesn't it?"

"It used to. When I met Jack, I thought for sure we wouldn't last long. I mean, look at him."

"He *is* pretty."

"And once things got serious, I thought maybe I could convince him not to play around, at least not as much. When I asked him to move in with me, I tried to set some limits there, but it was a nonstarter. And I wanted to be mad about it, but Charlie, he never lied to me. He's not Freddie, you know? And I stepped into this willingly, eyes wide open."

"It's none of my business," I said. "But do you guys have any, you know, rules?"

"We have to have sex at least once a week. And no fucking around on birthdays or anniversaries."

"And that's it?"

"That's it. And he keeps reminding me I'm as free as he is."

He said he was happy, but he looked sad. We sat in the quiet for a moment, taking sips and warming our hands against the mugs.

"I actually admire that in a way," I said. "But again, no offense, that's not what I want. I'm happier alone than I would be in your situation. I'm certainly happier alone than I was with Freddie."

"So find your own thing. Be like Lee and Claude. They're monogamous, as far as I know."

"Jesus, I couldn't live with Claude." My eyes flared in mock exasperation, and Tucker giggled in response. "I mean, he's family, but let's face it, Lee is a fucking saint."

"That's fair. So be like Jean and Irene."

"They're lesbians. They don't count."

"Now you're just making excuses."

"Maybe. But in the meantime, I'm also okay. Okay? Don't worry about me so much."

"I'm an old Southern woman. It's what we do."

Tucker put his mug down, stood up, and walked around the kitchen counter to where I was sitting. Then he hugged me. And it wasn't a simple friendly hug. It was another Tucker Pickett hug, weighed down with meaning. Had I been prepared, I would have stood as well, as my seated position grew increasingly awkward as the seconds passed, as Tucker refused to let go.

"I love you," he said. "You're my sister."

"I love you too, but let go already."

Before he did, he gave an extra squeeze.

"Thanks for all you've done today," I said. "You didn't have to."

"Hush," he said. "Of course I had to. Mamie is family too. And it'll all be worth it when we get her back."

I noticed Tucker's mug was nearly empty. "You should get home. Jack will worry."

"Jack will be thrilled if he thinks I'm getting laid."

"I won't tell him you were here," I said, marking my heart with an *X*.

He smiled. "I'm ever so grateful." He kicked off my slippers and went into the living room to put his shoes back on. I opened the door once he had his jacket on and was ready to go.

"Love you," he said.

"Love you more."

"Hey, Charlie. I have an idea."

"Oh yeah?"

"Tomorrow. We should find your dog."

And this time I hugged him.

CHAPTER FIFTEEN

Saturday, 7:19 a.m.

I woke up early for a Saturday, desperately hung over from two consecutive nights of alcohol and anxiety. I wondered what could have led me to drink so much, and then I opened my eyes to see Mamie's crate still on its side. Of course, I thought. She's still gone. And the worry returned to my gut, where it had been making itself at home since Thursday evening. Oh well, I thought, at least it's a distraction from how much my head hurts.

As I gingerly placed my feet on the floor, it felt like a ball-peen hammer right between the eyes. Oh well, I thought, at least it's a distraction from my stomachache.

I walked over to the crate. On its side, it came up to the middle of my chest. When Mamie comes back, I thought, I want the house to look like it did before. She shouldn't have to see her crate upended like this. So, even though I wanted to vomit but was afraid to because I knew it would make the pounding in my skull even worse, I picked up the crate up, turned it ninety degrees, and gently set it back down on the floor. I opened the door and arranged her favorite blanket so it bunched around the edges and created a safe warm cocoon for her to sleep in, with enough space to turn around three times before plopping herself down in the center.

Satisfied with my work, I looked for my fuzzy slippers but

couldn't find them. I unplugged the phone from its charger and walked downstairs. I began to sweep my social media accounts the way Tucker had taught me.

Tucker. Oh, shit. We had a fight. But then we made up. It was all slowly coming back. I needed fuel. I went to the kitchen and fired up the coffee machine. My slippers were on the kitchen floor where Tucker had left them the night before. I put them on.

It dawned on me that a regularly occurring sweep of Facebook, Twitter, Nextdoor, and Instagram might be a new routine for me, at least until she was found. If she was...no. When. *When* she was found.

My interview with Angela Woolsey was on Tucker's Facebook page. There were lots of comments on his post, many from our mutual friends in the chorus, but nothing helpful: *omg how cute, that's terrible, hope you find her*, stuff like that.

I found my #FindMamie post on Nextdoor, but no new leads there, either. I took a moment to browse around in case there was something about a little yellow dog spotted by a neighbor or, even better, taken in for the night.

> *Randall Hudson, Eastern Market North:* **ISO Plumbing Help.** *Pipes burst again, ugh. Are there any cheap, reliable plumbers in this town?*
>
> *Tawanna Berkeley, Trinidad East:* **Found iPhone off H Street NE.** *It's a larger phone, pink with a black case. It died so I'm charging it now. Describe the lock screen photo and I'll get it back to you.*
>
> *Joanna Gutterman, Hill SE:* **Gross.** *There's a dead dog behind my house, in the alley (north side of Independence Avenue on the 1300 block). Who do you call to pick up roadkill? This is disgusting.*

I noted the time stamp. This had been up since last evening. No description, no time of death. This could be anybody's dog, I told myself.

There were many comments below Joanna Gutterman's post. I quickly scanned them to see if there was any description of the dog, or any helpful details, but they were mostly dog people like myself informing Ms. Gutterman *she* was the disgusting one. I wasn't going to argue the point. I didn't disagree and besides, I didn't have time. I raced upstairs to collect my keys, replace my fuzzy slippers with adult shoes, and put on a warm coat. Despite my trembling hands, I managed to lock the door behind me.

It would take roughly three minutes to drive to Thirteenth and Independence if I even trusted myself to drive. Then I remembered my car was at Lee's house in Silver Spring. I could call for a ride, but I wanted to move. It would be a fifteen-minute walk. A kind of morbid logic was already taking shape: *if she's dead, hurrying won't change anything.* Even so, as I turned south on Fifteenth Street, my pace was brisk, eventually turning into a jog.

Exhale for three beats, inhale on one. The cold winter air was stinging my lungs, but I kept up the pace. If I focused on how painful it was to breathe, or that I hadn't tried to jog in over a year, perhaps it would help me picture anything but Mamie's lifeless body lying in the middle of a concrete alley. It didn't work.

I couldn't have slowed down if I wanted to, but part of me did want to. If the dog was anyone but Mamie, of course, I wanted to know right away. If my worst fears were realized, I didn't know which was worse—knowing or not knowing. It didn't matter because both were objectively awful.

Less than two blocks later, I was already short of breath. Why was I so out of shape? I hoped I could teach Mamie to jog as a puppy, but she was too insistent on smelling every little thing. Smart and stubborn. But she loved slow, leisurely walks more than anything. I imagined her walking at the end of the leash, inspecting all the wonderful aromas the world had to offer and only occasionally checking in with me to see if I was still tethered. I couldn't remember the last time I'd given her a substantial walk. I failed to appreciate that moment. I hadn't realized it would be the last time. I tried to picture her dying in a lonesome alley, but I couldn't do it. When I tried, my mind conjured a picture of her face, happily panting. Still, it was no comfort. The more I thought about my happy, obstinate companion, the more I knew memories were all I had. It was cold. Exhale for three beats, inhale on one.

I turned right on North Carolina Avenue.

I thought about everyone telling me how brave I've been since Mamie was taken, and how wrong they were. My optimism wasn't bravery. It was its opposite. Facing the fact she might die would be brave, and up until this point I'd said the words but hadn't genuinely entertained the possibility, the finality, of losing her.

If Mamie is dead, I thought, I'll have to go to work on Monday and not melt into a puddle whenever someone asks about my weekend. And after a day of willing myself upright, I'll have to drive back home and face the dreaded quiet. If Mamie is dead, the rhyming lesbians will eventually encourage me to get another dog. I will resist. I'll say I need more time, but there will never be enough time. If Mamie is dead, I might never find the courage to fall in love with another man or beast ever again. I'll be nice to people, but I'll build myself an invisible suit of armor, heavy at first, but wearable, and soon enough unnoticeable. I'll be able to see out, but no one will be able to get in. And then I'll die alone. Everything Tucker had accused me of last night at Pansy's would be true. And maybe it already was.

By the time I reached Lincoln Park, my body could go no farther. I braced myself against a tree, staring at the ground, desperately trying to slow my breathing. But the more I tried, the more panicked I felt, and the harder it became. If Mamie was alive and here now, she'd be pulling me on. But nothing propelled me forward. I was alone. She was less than a block away, I knew it, but she was also gone.

I thought about how she could have died. Had her kidnapper, once he figured out no one was going to pay thousands of dollars for a spayed dog of mixed breed, taken her into the alley and shot her? Did she die instantly or did he leave her there to bleed out until her breathing and heartbeat slowly, painfully, came to a stop? Or had she escaped her captors only to be hit by a car and crushed beneath someone's front tire? She was in the middle of an alley, but

I'd seen drivers in my own alley almost hit me when I was putting the trash out. It could happen that way.

So, she was gone. Still, I had to see it for myself. I had to squeeze her little paws and say good-bye. When I could breathe again, I started the slow walk to Independence Avenue.

The alley I was looking for was on a triangular block, defined by Thirteenth Street and Independence on the sides, and Massachusetts Avenue on the diagonal. Entering the alley, it curved to the right, obscuring the view. I stopped. Sorely out of breath, I was still panting.

I took just a few seconds more to steel myself and catch my breath before going any farther. A dog, either mine or someone else's, lay dead just around the corner. I felt a little light-headed. I had to do this.

In three more steps, I'd know. Now two, and then just one.

I looked. And I saw nothing. The alley was empty.

This was the alley on the north side of the 1300 block of Independence Avenue. I was sure of it. A dead dog was supposed to be lying in the middle of it, but perhaps not. I began peering down individual driveways, checking under cars, walking, walking.

And there it was. Not a body, but a dark dried bloodstain on the concrete. Whatever had died here was gone, and only a bloodstain remained. Whose blood? Was it Mamie's?

Goddammit, this was torture. What was I supposed to do now?

I examined the backs of these houses, looking for some clue that any of these homes would welcome the knock of a hysterical homosexual at their back door, asking for details about the dead dog recently lying in their alley. Was she small, was she yellow, was she dear to me, could you please verify for me that my heart is irreparably broken? But I saw no sign of life.

"Hello?" I asked. Not a shout, but something you might hear if you were outside or very close to the window. A bit louder the second time: "Hello?"

Aside from the noise of faraway traffic there was no sound, not even a breeze.

I fished my phone out of my pocket and opened the Nextdoor

app again, looking for the original post and any comments I might have missed in my earlier search. Toward the bottom, I saw Joanna Gutterman's name again.

Jim Cronin: Hill SE: Call Animal Control, (202) 535-2323.
Joanna Gutterman, Hill SE: Thanks. Calling now.

The comments were from the evening before, but in my haste to leave the house, I'd missed them. I decided to call Animal Control myself. Perhaps they could provide me with a description or search for the microchip or something. I repeated the number as I closed the app and prepared to dial.

Two...Oh...Two...Five...Three...Five...Two—

And then my phone began to vibrate; a call was coming in. I knew this number. It was Lt. Herman. They'd already scanned the microchip. The death was so violent the police needed to be called. The dog's body matched my description, and he was calling me to tell me Mamie was dead. I took a deep breath and accepted the call.

"Hello?"

"Mr. Vernon, good morning." He was trying to sound cheerful, as if it could soften the blow somehow. It couldn't. This was not a good morning.

"Hello, Lieutenant."

"So, yeah, um...I'm looking at this dog."

There was a maddening silence.

"How did she die?"

"What?" he asked, laughing. "No, this dog is very much alive."

"Well, what does the dog look like? Can you describe her to m—"

"Naw," he said. "Let's do this another way. What's your dog's name again?"

"Mamie."

I heard his now muffled voice calling, "Hey! Mamie!" And then he returned to me, loud and clear as the morning itself. "Yeah," he said, chuckling. "We got your dog."

CHAPTER SIXTEEN

Saturday, 9:41 a.m.

The police station was on Bladensburg Road. After Lt. Herman answered my endless questions, I opened the app on my phone and called for a ride directly there. While in the back seat, I sent a text to Lee, Claude, Tucker, and Jack: *She's been found. Headed to the police station now.* I called Irene directly, who began to cry when I told her Mamie was found and, as far as I knew, healthy. I could hear Jean cheering in the background. My driver didn't make a big show of listening in, but he gave me a big smile as he pulled up to the station. In turn, I gave him a big tip.

Lt. Herman told me the stolen goods taken by the newly apprehended thief would be taken in a van to the police station and kept in a closet for months while the case against him was prepared. However, he assured me he would make an exception in Mamie's case, and she would not have to live in a closet. I could collect her at ten o'clock, he told me. Naturally, I had arrived forty minutes early and was not-so-patiently waiting.

At eleven thirty on Friday night, DCPS received a tip. A woman who lived in a public housing unit with her daughter and sister had an apartment next door to a single mother and her teenage son. Earlier that night, she and her sister were walking back to their building from their car and spotted the boy walking a dog who looked exactly like the dog they'd seen on the local six o'clock news.

Early the next morning, around six thirty, Lt. Herman arrived at the apartment with a uniformed officer and knocked on the door. He had to knock several times, each series of raps meeting with stony silence before the boy's mother, obviously roused from sleep, answered. She was not happy to be awake so early, and probably less happy when Lt. Herman flashed his badge.

"May I come in?"

She opened the door only enough to reveal a sliver of her face. She stood about five-two, extremely thin, African American, dressed in sweatpants. "What for?"

"Ma'am, by any chance do you have a little dog in there that does not belong to you?"

"No."

"Mind if I look around?"

"You got a warrant? 'Cause if you ain't got a warrant, you can just—"

The officer in uniform produced a piece of paper. The muscles around her mouth tightened. She made her decision. She opened the door.

As Lt. Herman made his way through each room, the boy's mother followed along, and the uniformed officer stood close by. As she trailed him through the apartment, she took great effort to clear her throat, and—to hear Lt. Herman tell it—make as much noise as she possibly could. And so he started listening for little noises between the coughs and harrumphs. What was this woman trying to hide? He peered into what had to have been the boy's room. The bed was unmade and empty, and he placed his hand on the pillow.

"What you doin'?"

"It's warm," he replied.

The mother exhaled with a little huff. Lt. Herman went to the boy's closet and noticed that although the woman behind him wasn't trying to stop him, she was fidgety and nervous. He opened the door. Behind it was a gangly seventeen-year-old boy, dressed in a T-shirt and briefs, holding a small yellow dog who was shaking in his grip.

"You want to give that animal to me, son."

In between finding Mamie and contacting me, four officers

were called to the scene, where contraband from seven area robberies was found around the apartment. They didn't find anything valuable, as all the computers, televisions, smartphones, and jewelry had been fenced right away. But little trophies from each break-in—candlesticks, a throw blanket, even a cast iron skillet—were tagged as evidence. These, said Lt. Herman, were likely gifts for his mother, enticements to look the other way and not ask any questions when the household experienced an unexplained influx of cash. No souvenirs had been taken from my house, which led Lt. Herman to believe the trophy in this case was Mamie herself. Upon further questioning, he learned the boy's mother had lost a dog of her own a few months before.

In fact, the mother initially tried to pass off Mamie as her own dog, but her story fell apart when Mamie refused to come when she was called. Norah from Knickerbocker Farms had warned me. Smart and stubborn.

Once the police finished all the necessary work and filled out all the forms, the first phone call Lt. Herman made was to me.

Three hours later, I sat in the waiting area of the police station, seemingly alone. I was so focused on Sgt. Hernandez, the woman in uniform behind the safety glass, I didn't hear Tucker and Jack enter behind me.

"Hey," Jack said, flashing that handsome grin of his. Startled, I got up and faced him. "Told ya."

"Yeah," I said. "You sure did."

"We got your text," Tucker said. "Have you seen her yet?"

"No. I've been sitting here. I'm early."

"Is Angela Woolsey coming?"

"I sent a text and left a voicemail, but I haven't heard back yet."

Then, Hernandez stood up. "Mr. Vernon? Lt. Herman would like a word." I gave Tucker and Jack a slight nod, then walked up to the counter.

Lt. Herman walked out of the door to the right of the counter. It dawned on me we'd not physically met until now. He was taller than I expected, probably about six-four. He was a handsome African American man with kind hazel eyes only slightly darker than his skin. I hadn't counted on the pencil mustache, but it suited him somehow. "You must be Charlie," he said, and his deep baritone was unmistakable. He extended a hand to me, and I shook it.

"Hello, sir," I said. "Thank you. It's good to meet you."

"It's good to meet you, Mr. Vernon. I won't make this long. I know you're excited to get your dog back," he said. "But I wanted to come down and say hello. In fact, the whole crew wanted to be here for *this*," he said, pointing to the door behind Sgt. Hernandez. "If you don't mind."

I looked at the glass but saw nothing. Then it opened. Toward the floor, a little black nose appeared. And then there was Mamie on a leash, leading a parade of eight or nine uniformed cops toward the waiting room. "We don't get many really good days," Herman said. "When we do, we like to celebrate."

For a moment, Mamie and the crowd disappeared from view. Seconds later, the door to my right opened, and then there she was, this tiny furry creature who'd made me the most miserable man on earth for the past day and a half.

My voice cracked a little. "Mamie?"

She approached me slowly, as if I were a stranger. I'd been imagining this reunion every minute for the last thirty-six hours, and in each reenactment, Mamie stood tall and leaned against me, as was her habit. But today Mamie kept all four of her little paws on the floor. She stretched her neck forward and her nose twitched a little. I knew she was satisfied it was me when her tail began to wag back and forth, but slowly. Gently.

"Hey girl. It's okay, baby. You're home. You came home."

If she wasn't going to jump up to me, I was going to have to bend down to her level, so I unbuttoned my winter coat and sat cross-legged on the ground in front of her. She approached me slowly, her tail still floating to and fro. With her front paw, she stepped onto my calves and looked down at my lap. I lowered my head toward her, trying to get her to at least look at me. She wouldn't look up, but her head touched my shoulder and she leaned forward, pressing into me, burrowing back and forth until her face was buried in the crook of my neck. She whimpered a little, softly.

"You're home, Mamie. You came home."

For the first time since she had disappeared two days before, indeed for the first time in years, my cheek was wet with tears. When I realized I'd been holding my breath, I opened my mouth and inhaled sharply, which was all it took for the sobs to take over. To keep my balance, I placed my hands on either side of Mamie's neck and held on.

The bridge of her nose was warm against my neck but the nose itself was cold, as it should be. I didn't mind. Occasionally, she looked up at me and attempted to clean away the tears and the snot from my face, but soon after returned to her original posture, her head pressed against me. There we sat for what felt like an hour on the floor of the Bladensburg police station, under the gaze of one plainclothes lieutenant and eight or nine uniformed cops, one of us shaking and bawling, the other perfectly still except for a long tail still somberly gliding back and forth, back and forth.

Saturday, 10:53 a.m.

Jack was very pleased with himself. "I got video of the whole thing."

I rolled my bloodshot eyes. "Seriously? I hate you so much right now."

"I want to see," said Tucker as Jack handed him his phone.

We were seated in the waiting area at the Beekman Animal Hospital. Tucker thought we should come in for a checkup, just in case, and Lt. Herman concurred. It was a typical crowded Saturday, and I obviously hadn't made an appointment, but Dr. Paige said she'd be happy to squeeze her in. Her happiness notwithstanding, it would have been hard to refuse after Bea led the entire staff in a standing ovation upon our arrival. I had finished taking down all the flyers we'd hung up here yesterday and was holding them in my hand.

"This is really good," Tucker said. "This could go viral."

"Ugh, no thank you. We already got her back. I do not need to achieve ten thousand hits of me heaving and blubbering."

"Laughter through tears is my favorite emotion," Jack said.

"I'm not laughing in that video."

"Yeah, but I am." And Jack chuckled, as if to prove it. "You should send it to Angela Woolsey, though. I mean, those mystery women wouldn't have called without her."

"You totally owe her," said Tucker. "And if she happens to put it on the air as a follow-up piece and twenty thousand people happen to see it, well…"

"Yeah, I'm going to decline your kind offer, but thanks."

"Technically," said Jack, "it's my video. And it was a public place. What's that called? Citizen journalism."

"You wouldn't."

"Actually, I would." And he proceeded to do just that.

Once or twice I made a half-hearted attempt to pilfer his phone as he was typing, but Tucker prevented me. Once the email was sent, I sighed. "You're not my friend."

"Whatever. I'm going to be famous."

And Tucker was beaming. I think he even giggled.

"She's ready, Charlie." Dr. Paige stood behind me with Mamie, whose mood was a little lighter, having escaped her captors, left the police station, and survived a visit to the vet with no shots or plastic-gloved fingers. "Everything checks out. No fleas, no ticks, nothing out of the ordinary from what I can tell."

She handed me the leash, and Mamie was mine again. I looked down and gave her a smile. She returned my gaze with a look that seemed to say, *it's been grand, but can we go home now?*

"Thanks, Doc," I said.

"Bea can help you."

I handed the leash to Tucker and went to the counter to pay the bill. While my credit card was being approved, I glanced back to see Mamie sniffing Tucker's ankles and wagging her tail with a little more energy now, probably wondering why the Pickett-Forrester humans were here but her old pal Russell was not.

I signed the credit card slip, and Bea handed me a receipt. Tucker, crouching down to scratch Mamie's neck beneath her ears, looked up at me. "Headed home?"

"I think so." But then I felt my phone vibrating. Someone was calling. It was a local number I didn't recognize, so I declined the call. "I'll be back at the office on Monday, so I think I'd like to spend tonight and tomorrow just crashing," I said. "Keep it low key."

And the phone vibrated again. Same number. "I don't know who this is, but they're persistent."

"You should pick it up," said Jack. "It's probably Angela Woolsey, calling about my video."

I shot him a withering glance, but it made sense. I accepted the call and lifted the phone to my ear. "Hello?"

"Mr. Vernon," said a strange voice, a woman, on the other end.

"Hello? Ms. Woolsey?"

"No, Mr. Vernon. You don't know me. I'm calling about the ten thousand dollar reward you offered."

Oh. Oh, shit.

"Who is this?"

"We haven't met. But I called the police last night. About your dog? And the police took her away this morning. I trust you have her back now?"

"Yes, she's right here."

"I'm glad for that."

Tucker and Jack listened intently, brows furrowed. I held up a finger to let them know I'd be with them in a moment.

"Listen, could I call you back?"

"Is this a bad time?"

"Um, a little. We're at the vet."

"Is your dog all right?"

"She's fine as far as we know." I looked down, and Mamie was looking back at me. Even she seemed curious about this mystery caller. "But we're leaving now. I'll call as soon as I'm home, I promise." And I read her the number displayed on my phone to confirm.

"I'll be here," she said. I hung up.

Back out on the street, I walked with Tucker and Jack toward their car.

"You need a ride home?" Jack asked.

"No, I think Mamie wants to walk."

Tucker was thinking about my recent phone call. "How do you know she called in the tip?"

"Well," I said, "it sounds as if she saw the cops take Mamie away this morning. Your video isn't viral yet. Also, she called me Mr. Vernon."

Jack bent down and gave Mamie a little head scratch. "Charlie, everyone who saw you on the news yesterday knows your name."

"That's true."

"This is us," Tucker said, stopping alongside their SUV. "What are you going to do?"

"I'm going to call her back, I guess. I don't really have a plan after that."

"I'd call the cops first if I were you," Jack said, and Tucker nodded in agreement.

CHAPTER SEVENTEEN

Saturday, 12:17 p.m.

"See, this is why I don't like rewards," said Lt. Herman, who probably assumed this case was closed and he'd heard the last from me.

"I know. And I'm sorry for being such a pain in the ass, but she might not have called in the tip if not for the reward, so—"

"And I get that. I just want you to know before we say anything else here. You are under no legal obligation to pay this woman."

"I'm not?"

I went to the kitchen to make myself a cup of coffee.

"A number on a flyer posted to a telephone pole is not a legally binding contract. Of course, you can pay her if you want. Do you want to?"

"Maybe?"

"Okay, tell me what's on your mind."

"I mean, if she called it in, I guess I owe her even if I'm not bound by law. But how do I know she's the one who called it in? I'd just be taking her word for it. How do I know she didn't help steal the dog and figured this was a way to maximize her profits?"

"Those are some good questions. Did I tell you I hated it when people offer rewards?"

"You did, but—"

"But you got your dog back. Look. I am going to do this for you one time and one time only. If you want to pay this woman"—and here he sighed deeply—"ten thousand dollars, then you can tell her to meet you at the police station. I will meet you there and verify that one, she was the one who called us up, and two, to the best of my knowledge she had nothing to do with your home being violated and your property stolen. But tell her if she wants her money, that's the deal."

"Sounds good. Thanks."

"But talk to her first. And if you get a weird feeling in your gut, trust it. You don't have to pay this." I could hear Mamie in the living room, rubbing her scent all over the couch. I wondered if she caught Freddie's scent and how she felt about it.

"Okay."

"Call me back if you want to arrange a time."

"I will."

"How's the dog?"

"Hungry," I said, hearing intermittent growling in the next room.

"That's good," he said chuckling. "That's good."

I thanked him again and hung up the phone.

I knew I had to call the woman back, but I did need to put some food in Mamie's bowl. "Didn't those people feed you?" I opened the bin, took out a healthy scoop, and delivered it to the bowl. She sniffed it, seemed satisfied she would still be fed upon command, as was her habit, and happily sauntered into the living room and hopped up on the couch.

I followed her and sat. "Silly," I said. She regarded me haughtily, very pleased with herself. I picked up my phone and looked at my previously received calls. I pressed the call received at exactly eleven a.m. I lifted the phone to my ear. After one ring, my mystery caller picked up.

"Hello?"

"Hi. This is Charlie Vernon."

"We've been waiting for your call."

"I know. I'm sorry. I've been monitoring the dog a bit. I want to make sure she…anyway. I'm sorry it took me so long to call you back. You're calling about the reward."

"That's right."

"Can you tell me exactly what happened?"

"How do you mean?"

"You know, when you saw the dog, how did you know she was mine?"

"What does that have to do with anything?" She spoke with an accent I couldn't quite place. She was clearly fluent in English, but the way she spoke so deliberately made me wonder if it was a second language.

"Please."

And she proceeded to tell me the story. She lived with her sister and her daughter in an apartment complex on Benning Road on the same floor as the boy who took Mamie. The night before, she and her sister had called for some takeout and were returning home with the food when she saw the boy approaching. He was taking Mamie for a walk.

Now, if there's anything Mamie loves in life, it's a walk outside, but the way this woman described it, Mamie was being dragged along the road, doing everything she could to get away from him.

"Very pretty, though," she said.

"Thanks."

She told me they asked the boy about the dog. They knew his mother had a little dog, but they had never seen the boy take him for a walk. He said this was his mother's new dog. They asked for the dog's name. He simply said he bought this dog for his mother as if to suggest he was a model son.

After he and Mamie reentered the building, not without some struggle, the woman turned to her sister and asked if that wasn't the same dog they'd seen on the news earlier in the day. They returned to their apartment, and with some help from her young daughter, logged on to the internet to see if they could find the story. Once they watched it again, they were sure. They discussed the matter as a family and decided to call the police.

"When did you make the call?"

"About ten thirty," she answered. This squared with the story Lt. Herman had told me.

"Okay. So, I need to be honest with you right now. I don't have ten thousand dollars just lying around."

"But you said—"

"I know what I said, on the news, on all the flyers I posted around town."

"Are you a man of your word, Mr. Vernon?"

Ouch. "I want to pay you this money, and I will. I'm going to need some time is all."

"Mr. Vernon, I need you to understand something. When my sister and I recognized your dog, we didn't immediately call the police. In point of fact, my sister was urging me to call, but I did not want to do it. I understood you missed this animal very much, but Mr. Vernon, I have a daughter. And I am raising her, with my sister's help, in a building full of criminals. I knew the moment I called the police about one of my neighbors, I was putting her life in danger. If they ever find out what we did, anything could happen."

"Look, I empathize, I really do, but—"

"Now, with ten thousand dollars my daughter can live somewhere else, somewhere safe." She spoke coolly and evenly. "Without it, she has a target on her back. I have been honest with you, Mr. Vernon. And now I wonder how honest will you be?"

"I want to be, but it's not that easy."

"I'm not asking you to do the easy thing, Mr. Vernon. I'm asking you to do the right thing."

I took a seat on the couch and looked down at Mamie, who met my gaze. Her casual presence, curled up on the sofa like it was any other Saturday, still seemed like some kind of miracle. Her ears fell slightly. Perhaps I was imagining it, but she looked disappointed in me. I gave her a little scratch behind the ears, as I took a deep breath, sure of what I was about to say, but scared to say it.

"Can you give me a week?"

"Yes. We can wait a week."

I told her about my plan to meet at the police station where Lt.

Herman could verify she was the one who made the call and had nothing to do with Mamie's capture.

She didn't hesitate. "That would be fine. Next Saturday, then?"

How the hell was I going to get my hands on ten thousand dollars before Saturday? "Okay, just give me your name, and I'll bring a cashier's check with me."

"No, I'd rather not say. Keep the check blank, and I'll share my name with the policeman when I get there."

"But—"

"You may believe I am paranoid, Mr. Vernon. But living in this place, I have learned to be careful. We will both be safer if you do not know who I am. Keep the check blank, and I will cooperate with the police. Please."

"All right."

"Thank you, Mr. Vernon. Before you go—"

"Yes?"

"I have another request, if you don't mind."

Beyond ten thousand dollars? "Yes, what is it?"

"Well, could you bring your dog with you? My daughter would very much like to meet her."

And suddenly I knew I'd move heaven and earth to get my hands on that money. All of it. "She'll be there."

Saturday, 3:09 p.m.

Lee had his own key to my place, and burst through the door without even knocking. "Dios mío, Dios mío, Dios mío!"

I was down in the kitchen, pouring a rare but necessary afternoon cup of coffee. Mamie was upstairs sleeping on her favorite pillow, but she woke with a start and immediately broke into a howl that eventually settled into furious barking.

"Señorita Mamita! Dónde está mi pequeña magdalena? C'mere, you little fucker."

Halfway down the staircase, as soon as she recognized Lee's voice, the barking transformed seamlessly into a whimper, which was all it took for Lee to begin crying himself. Claude, following behind him, shut the door as Lee gathered Mamie in his arms. The sight of his husband and his friend's dog loudly weeping into each other's faces prompted him to roll his eyes in mock cynicism, but I could tell he found the scene to be touching, if slightly ridiculous. As did I.

"We were so worried about you," he chided her, causing her to whimper even more loudly. "So worried!"

Claude eyed my mug. "Is that coffee?"

"Want some?"

"Throw some Baileys in it," Lee said, his eyes suddenly dry, "and I'm down."

I returned to the kitchen to prepare some more coffee and spike my own, and Claude followed.

"So, what do you know about the kid who did this?"

"Well," I said, "apparently he committed seven or eight burglaries in the neighborhood. And Mamie brought him down. I am the owner of one badass cockapoo."

"What did he look like?"

"Oh, I didn't see him. I probably won't unless there's a trial, and Lt. Herman says there might not be. All the same he wants me to write some sort of victim statement so they can use it somehow. I'll do that tomorrow, I guess."

"You didn't get any kind of a description?"

"No, Claude, I didn't. Why?"

"Cállate, Claudine," said Lee, striding into the kitchen, still holding on to Mamie. "Just because you married Latina Spice, it don't mean that shit ain't racist."

"I never said race," Claude said, turning back to me. "Did I?"

"Not going there," I said. "Colombian or French Roast?"

"He likes the Colombian," Lee said, gently returning Mamie to the floor. "Obviously."

I motioned to Claude. "You. Go back in there. Have a seat."

Claude grabbed a treat from Mamie's jar on the counter and sauntered back into the living room, which ensured Mamie would follow.

"Here," Lee said, handing me my car keys. I looked out the window, and the car was in my driveway. I hadn't even heard them drive up.

I took the keys. "Thank you."

"You're welcome." Lee, not moving, stared at me as I worked on the coffee. "What's wrong with you?"

"Nothing. This is a great day." And I flashed him a smile. "Obviously."

"Hi, my name is Leonardo. We've met," he said. "What's going on? You should be over the moon."

"I am, truly I am."

"But?" He raised his eyebrows, waiting for the rest of the sentence he knew was coming.

For a once-aspiring actor, I'm apparently a terrible liar. "Congratulate me," I finally said. "I have a ten thousand dollar dog."

"Someone called about the reward," he said.

I nodded, and rolled my eyes.

"What's your plan?"

"I'll go to the bank tomorrow," I said. "Take out a loan."

"Or you could just visit the Bank of Claude in there."

"No. This is why I didn't even want to tell you about it."

"Listen, chica. Everyone thinks I'm a trampy little gold digger," he said. "I either get no respect, or I get a phone call every week from a different cousin I never heard of asking if I can help pay their rent. The three things I get are a husband who loves me, a giant house in the suburbs—"

"Your house is pretty great."

"—and the ability to spend his money however I want."

"I heard that!" Claude bellowed from the next room.

Lee ignored him. "You can borrow the money from us." Sensing a protest about to burst forth, he shushed me. "Borrow, I said. Pay us back whenever you can, no interest."

"I don't need you to do that," I said. "I can get a loan. My credit rating is pretty good these days."

"You realize this is why we hate you."

I poured a dollop of Baileys into a hot cup of coffee and handed it to Lee. "I'm sure nobody hates me."

"You're right. Nobody hates you. In fact, we love you a whole lot and you're too dumb to get it. Charlie, you're not my best friend because you make me laugh or because you pretend to understand my Spanish or because you can name five movies starring Bette Davis, including some of the shitty ones. I don't want you around to amuse me when times are good, okay? I also want to *be* around when life is fucking terrible. I want to, not because I have to, but because that's what love is, you stupid cabrón."

I wasn't sure what to say. I was embarrassed, but the longer I remained silent, the prouder Lee would be of his little speech. "So, wait," I finally said. "I'm your *best* friend?"

"Don't tell Tucker."

I met his gaze, and gave him a wink. It would be our little secret.

Saturday, 11:07 p.m.

That night I climbed into bed—sober, if you can believe it—to watch the video Jack had taken, which was broadcast throughout Washington on the evening news. Mamie's return wasn't the lead story, obviously, but after a story about a planned protest outside the Capitol Building by an anti-abortion group featuring gruesome signs held by women with tears streaming down their cheeks, and a report on an especially contentious City Council meeting regarding zoning for new luxury condominiums in a rapidly gentrifying neighborhood, Angela Woolsey appeared behind the anchor desk to give a special update on yesterday's case of the purloined pooch.

After she greeted her colleagues behind the news desk, she faced the camera to tell her audience about the miraculous reunion.

"Tonight," she said, "I'm happy to share a real life happy ending." As she spoke, Mamie's photo appeared to the right of her head. Angela seemed genuinely thrilled by this turn of events, either because she took the credit for it or because she's a genuinely nice person. Or a little from Column A and a little from Column B. I was too happy myself to care and was perfectly willing to give her all the credit she desired.

Mamie, who usually preferred to sleep underneath the bed, was curled up at my feet. I wondered if she was as unwilling to let me out of her sight as I was to let her out of mine. Physically, she was as perfect as she'd been two days before, but I suspected she somehow blamed me for her dognapping. And, I thought, maybe she has a point. As we listened to Angela Woolsey detail the break-in and burglary for those who hadn't heard the story, I thought, I'm the human. It's my job to keep her safe and sound, and I failed. In any event, she didn't seem to be holding a grudge, aside from choosing the far corner of the bed to perch. But that wasn't unusual for Mamie, who preferred to be in control whenever possible and who would naturally choose a spot allowing for a quick exit should one become desirable or necessary.

"Let's take a look at the emotional reunion," Angela said, and then we quickly cut to Jack's cinema verité masterwork.

"Mamie?" said the television in my shaking voice.

At the sound of her name Mamie looked at me. I wondered if she was confused, but she didn't appear to be. Just content to be home.

"Hey girl," I said through the television. "It's okay, baby. You're home. You came home."

Mamie's tail began to wag. And I'll admit I started to cry again. That was twice in one day, but at least these weren't the wracking sobs I was about to relive on my television screen, merely a quiet tear forming on each eyeball and a slight constriction of the throat. It was manageable.

"You're home, Mamie," said the television. "You came home." And the sobs began.

Luckily, Angela Woolsey soon began a voiceover before I really started moaning and wailing. "Mr. Vernon was reunited with Mamie at ten a.m. today," she said, "after the police received a tip from an unidentified woman who saw our story last night on News Two. Because Mamie's kidnapper is a minor, the police were not able to give us any details, but we have learned the young man has been implicated in seven other burglaries in the neighborhood. There's no word yet on whether Mr. Vernon has paid the $10,000 reward."

When the scene cut back to the anchor desk, Angela's colleagues were full of praise and she was full of pride. "Seven burglaries!" exclaimed the sixty-ish white man to her right with a face full of pleasant wrinkles and a head full of Grecian Formula. "We should put that dog on the force!" And everyone laughed.

I lifted the remote and pushed a button to turn the television off. I regarded my little yellow dog.

"You're a hero," I said. And she sat up, as if to assume a posture more befitting her heroic stature. She did not approach me but sat proudly on her corner of the bed, head erect. In response, I sat up cross-legged and faced her.

Had I a sword in my hand, I would have knighted her. Lady Mame Dennis Vernon, nemesis of squirrels and thieves, slayer of soft plushy toys, and protector of the hearth. Instead, I looked into her eyes and spoke. "Don't ever do that again," I said, but kinder than it might sound. "You scared me, Mamie. You weren't supposed to put me through something like that. We had a deal."

In response, Mamie hopped onto the floor. I could hear her scurrying to her usual spot under the bed, directly below my feet.

"I haven't finished speaking to you, young lady," I said. But no matter, she was done speaking with me. I stretched out on the bed and placed my head on the pillow, when it struck me. Mamie never made me a deal, never promised not to hurt me, worry me, or break my heart. I struck that deal on her behalf. And had she understood the terms of such a contract, she never would have agreed. She would have called it unreasonable. Smart and stubborn, she was. I had been warned. But of course she was right.

"Hey, Mamie," I called out. "You still there?" A moment later I heard her tail thumping against my wood floor.

I reached for the lamp next to my bed and turned out the light.

Sunday, 3:42 a.m.

I was awakened by a slow and steady growling in my ear.

It was the middle of the night, and Mamie needed to pee.

I usually took her water dish up at eight p.m., but she had seemed unusually thirsty and I didn't know if her captors had given her enough food or water. So I made an exception. I filled her water bowl to the brim last night in case she needed it, and now I was paying the price for my generosity.

I opened my left eye and peered in the direction of the water bowl. It was empty. And Mamie's little bladder was full. The low, rolling growl continued.

"Okay, okay," I said, rousing myself. "Need to go outside?"

Taking her cue, Mamie bolted from the room, running to the top of the stairs.

I moved with considerably less speed while Mamie waited impatiently. As I fumbled for my robe and slippers in the dark I could feel her disapproval from the hallway. I was tying the robe around my waist when a shrill bark announced her displeasure. "I'll be right there, madam."

As soon as I appeared, she ran to the bottom of the stairs and sat, watching me lumber downward. She whined a little. She was using every trick in her limited vocal repertoire, but I couldn't fault her because, to be fair, it was working.

I freed the deadbolt from its casing and opened the door. By the time I got the storm door open, Mamie ran outside and down the porch steps toward the tiny fenced yard, and into…the snow.

It was snowing. That is, snow was falling from the sky. Barely any of it was sticking to the ground, and tomorrow morning there'd be no way of knowing a snowfall had even occurred. I stepped onto the porch, and it was lovely to see the flakes perform their tiny arabesques in the sky as they descended to earth. The street was quiet, and the snow made everything even quieter somehow.

Mamie hadn't even bothered to step on the grass and was relieving herself on the concrete sidewalk. "Very classy," I said. She paid me no mind. When she stood up, I beckoned her back inside.

"Come on, girl." But she apparently wasn't done with her late-night duties. She sauntered into the yard and sniffed her way around the perimeter.

And so I regarded the snowfall once more, overwhelmed with a feeling of peace, of order restored to my little world. Just twenty-four hours before, I'd been tossing and turning in my bed, sick with worry, already suffering the hangover that would have typically waited until morning. A day ago, I'd have given anything to be standing on my porch, in the cold, in the middle of the night, watching snow fall from the sky, waiting for a dog to decide where within a thirty-square-foot patch of ground to take a shit as seriously and intently as if she were deciding where to go to grad school. And now here I was, roused from sleep and deeply inconvenienced, and smiling. Grinning like a happy infant. I'd have laughed out loud, but I didn't want to spoil the tranquil mood.

Eventually, Mamie's circle grew smaller and smaller. She found the perfect spot, twirling like a ballerina before assuming the crouch. She looked at me in the way dogs often locate their alphas at moments such as this. It wasn't weird or gross on this snowy night, and I returned her gaze. There are no predators waiting to pounce, I told her. Go ahead and do what you gotta do.

When she was finished, she trotted up the stairs, clearly experiencing a physical relief that matched my emotional state. Her coat was dusted with a few random snowflakes, and she was ready to go back inside. "All done?" I asked, and her wagging tail answered.

I opened the door, and she scurried back upstairs. By the time I returned to the bedroom, she was already under the bed, returning to her slumber. Was she as happy as I was, I wondered. Did she know how much danger she'd been in? Did she know how sick with worry I'd been? I wanted to believe the answer to all these questions was yes. But as I climbed back into bed and returned my head to its pillow, I admitted to myself I didn't know. Mamie's prefrontal neocortex was probably only twenty percent as big as mine and might not be able to process the trauma I couldn't help from obsessing over. She was, after all, only a dog.

But she was my best girl, and she was home. When I

remembered to be happy again, she was already asleep. I could tell from her breathing.

The following Saturday, 12:52 p.m.

A million years ago, when I was an undergraduate at a university run by the Jesuits, the priest who taught my Religion 101 class had an interesting take on the miracle of the loaves and the fishes. According to all four gospels, Jesus fed over five thousand people with five loaves of bread and two fish, for no real reason, other than the fact that he was Jesus and he was showing off. But this particular priest theorized the people had plenty of food. They were just scared and selfish and unwilling to share. So, when they saw Jesus give up all that he possessed so willingly, they secretly put some of their own loaves and fishes in the mix when the food was passed around. As it turned out, he suggested, the miracle wasn't a magic trick. The innate generosity of people just needed a little nudge, and Jesus gave it to them.

I was already a budding atheist when I heard this alternate version of events, and I liked it, mostly because it didn't rely on a completely unbelievable act of sorcery to make sense, but also because, in my experience, that's how miracles typically happen.

So there I stood, back at the Bladensburg police station, with a cashier's check for $10,000. And I was reminded of my professor's revisionist theology every time I checked my pocket to make sure the check was still there.

In this version of the story, Lee plays the role of Jesus. His Catholic mother would be so proud. After we spoke, Lee casually let it slip among our little circle that I was paying the reward and he was going to lend us the money, but that I was very upset about it. I told Lee I had a thousand dollars in savings I could use, so I only needed nine thousand more. Tucker and Jack pitched in an additional three thousand dollars, and the rhyming lesbians gave another two thousand. "Don't blame me," Irene said. "Jean insisted."

This left Lee and Claude with the remainder of four thousand dollars, less than half of what they initially planned to put in. Lee wanted me to know everyone gave what they could, and no one was feeling any kind of unnecessary pinch to help me out. He thought it would make me feel better. And it did.

Jesus, as played by Leonardo García Dorsett, had given them a little nudge, and there I stood holding all the money I needed to pay my debt with the understanding that I'd pay it all back when I was able. My pride had taken a hit, but I was grateful.

Mamie was with me as requested, but she didn't like the police station. Or maybe she didn't like being indoors on a leash. That's probably a more reasonable explanation than the post-traumatic stress disorder I had conjured for her. Come to think of it, I wouldn't much like being indoors on a leash either. In public, at least.

"Not much longer," I told her. She didn't believe me. I had said the same thing five minutes before.

I relentlessly minded the door, waiting for two adult women to enter, accompanied by a young girl who wanted to meet my dog. And when they finally did, I was fairly sure it was them. Still, I didn't move. I trusted they'd know who I was, having seen Angela Woolsey's story the week before, and they'd know who Mamie was as they'd actually met, briefly. Besides, when you're in a police station, I figured you don't want to assume anyone there will be happy to see you.

"Hello, Mr. Vernon," said the shorter of the two women. I recognized her voice. She was the mother, the one I'd spoken to on the phone.

"Hello," I said and then turned to her slimmer, taller sister and her young daughter. "Hello."

"Hello," said the little girl, who I guessed was about eight years old and trying to sound brave while practically hiding behind her aunt.

All three were wearing large sunglasses obscuring most of their faces, and the two adults were in full hijab, completely covering their hair and neck. Whether the garment was inspired by religious devotion or a wish to remain completely anonymous, I didn't really know.

The little girl, save for the shades, looked like any other little Black girl with Afro-puffs I might see walking to and from school in front of my house each day. As my house stood directly between their apartments and a local elementary school, it's entirely possible I had.

"It is nice to meet you," the aunt said. And for a moment we just stared at each other, neither of us knowing exactly what to do.

"Lt. Herman will be here in a moment," I finally said.

"Yes," the mother replied. "Yes, of course."

"Can I pet your dog?" the little girl asked.

"Of course you can," I said, kneeling down to Mamie's level. "She sometimes gets nervous, but she's very gentle. She won't hurt you."

Mamie typically does not enjoy young children, but something in me was hoping she'd make an exception for the young girl whose mother saved her from a kidnapper. Sadly, this was not to be the case. When the little girl raised her hand up, Mamie winced, which then caused the girl to snap her hand back for fear of being bitten.

"Here," I said. "Like this." I held my hand in front of Mamie's nose. Mamie obviously knew what her own human smelled like, and she looked at me as if I were the stupidest man on earth. Still, she couldn't resist giving me a tiny sniff. "Now you try."

The little girl offered her hand as I instructed her, like the heroine in a Jane Austen novel who had been asked to dance, and Mamie's curiosity was too much. She craned her head forward and the nose began to twitch.

"Just a little longer," I said.

Her mother placed a hand on the little girl's shoulder. "Don't be afraid."

"Okay," I said, "now touch the side of her neck and give a little scratch. She likes that."

The little girl obeyed, and Mamie licked the air in front of her face, a gesture that caused the girl to giggle.

"She's always wanted a dog," her mother said.

Her aunt nodded. "Maybe soon."

This was news to the little girl, who looked to her aunt, who smiled, and then to her mother, who pouted, and then back to her aunt, who chuckled.

"Sorry I'm late," said Lt. Herman, startling all of us slightly. "Are we all here?"

"Yes," said the mother.

"Okay then, shall we?" Lt. Herman gestured toward an unmarked door. "Did you bring some ID?"

"We both did," the mother said, pointing to her sister.

"That's fine," said Lt. Herman, giving me a nod to suggest I should stay put for the time being. "This way, ladies."

Lt. Herman led the way, followed by the shorter woman first and her taller sister after. The little girl was still scratching behind Mamie's ear and looked as if she wished to continue doing exactly that, but her aunt beckoned her. "Come along."

The girl looked up at me and sighed before running after them.

Lt. Herman closed the door behind them while I picked up the scratching where she had left off.

"Not much longer," I told Mamie. She didn't believe me.

They were only gone for a minute, two at the most, before they reappeared, the mother adjusting her hijab and the aunt donning her sunglasses.

"We're all set," Lt. Herman said. "I am happy to confirm these ladies are the ones who called in the tip that led to the discovery of your property."

"All right, great," I said.

"I apologize," he continued, "but I'm needed upstairs."

"Thank you very much," I said, offering my hand. He shook it.

"So," the mother said. "Anything else?"

"No." I fished the folded check out of my pocket. I offered it to the woman and she took it, slowly, almost solemnly. It felt somehow like a ceremony, and I wondered if there was some kind of Muslim cultural nuance regarding the paying of debts I was unaware of.

She unfolded the paper and checked the amount. Satisfied, she showed her sister, who laughed, more relieved than joyful. The little girl below them seemed oblivious and was already holding her hand out to Mamie exactly as I'd taught her only moments before.

"You'll want to write your name on that as soon as possible," I warned. The check was blank per her instructions. "Without your name on it, that check is as good as cash. I've been on edge for two days."

"I understand," said the mother. "We will. Thank you."

"It was a pleasure to meet you," I said, offering my hand for a businesslike shake. The woman didn't take it, but humbly nodded instead. I lowered my hand. "Oh, sorry."

"Not at all," she said, with a slight bow. "It was a pleasure to meet you too. And little Mamie. We're so glad she came back to you."

"Thank you." I turned to the aunt and smiled, knowing better than to offer another handshake.

"It's time to go now," said the mother to her daughter, who took her hand. The aunt took a step closer to me but kept her hands folded in front of her. She reached under her giant sunglasses to wipe something from her eye—tears, I assumed.

"*As-salaam-alaikum*," she said, her voice shaking.

"Yes," I said, having no idea what I ought to say in response. "I mean...you too."

CHAPTER EIGHTEEN

About four months later, Thursday, 11:47 a.m.

We had arrived in Provincetown the day before. When Jean was officially fired by her oncologist after no traces of cancer could be detected, Irene and I felt we needed to celebrate. Jean was okay with whatever we decided, she said, so long as it didn't involve her cooking or doing any dishes. After much back and forth, I remembered one of the partners at Claude's firm owned a bungalow in P-Town with a guesthouse on the property. I called Lee, who called Claude, and a couple of days later the plan was set.

As it turned out, Claude was unable to join us, as he was working a big case at the time. Lee and I were staying in the main house with Claude's colleague and his husband while Jean and Irene camped in the guesthouse. The best part was that the dogs were invited too.

For our first Provincetown brunch, the four of us—eight if you counted Peggy Lee, Mama Cass, Windsor, and Mamie—had decided on Bubala's by the Bay on Commercial Street. Irene swore by the lobster rolls, but Lee and I were more interested in the scenery. From our table on the front porch, we could see all the boys arriving on the ferry and going to their various lodgings.

Our tattooed waiter arrived with our drink orders, mimosas all around except for Irene, who opted for straight champagne. "At my age, I worry less about hangovers and more about heartburn," she said.

Before anyone could drink, I raised my glass, forcing everyone to follow suit. "A toast to Jean Muldoon," I said. "She's a great lady, a mean gin rummy player, and she just kicked cancer's ass."

"And the new hair looks fabulous," Lee added. After cancer, Jean had decided to stop dyeing her hair, and it was pure white. Very striking.

"To Jean," I said, raising my mimosa just a little higher.

"To Jean!" everyone repeated, and there was much clinking of glasses and sipping of cocktails.

And then, behind us, we heard a squeal. "Oh, look! How precious!"

I looked over my shoulder, and two tall men in shorts were headed straight toward us, each rolling an enormous suitcase behind him. I didn't recognize these guys and shot an inquisitive look to Lee who shrugged, also completely baffled.

Of course, they weren't approaching us but making a beeline for our dogs, who were tethered to the table with their leashes.

"Aren't you adorable?" they cooed. The bearded one was scratching the top of Windsor's head while the scruffy one with the horn-rimmed glasses was giving Mamie a scratch behind her ears. Cass and Peggy were safely ensconced in their little stroller and were frankly happy about it.

"Pardon us," the scruffy one said when he finally looked up. "We left our dogs at home for the week and were just talking about how much we already miss them. Is this a cockapoo?"

I nodded.

"What's her name?" the scruffy one asked.

"Mamie," I said.

"You named your dog after Auntie Mame? Shut up."

"Yes," I said. "I'm *that* gay."

At that, he started to sing. Cradling Mamie's head in his hands, he crooned a quiet little uptempo number about needing a widdle Chwistmas. If Mamie minded, she didn't show it.

As the scruffy one serenaded Mamie, Irene turned to the bearded one. "And this is Windsor. He's ours."

"He's very handsome," the bearded one answered.

"Peggy Lee and Mama Cass are in there," I said, motioning toward the doggie stroller. The scruffy one looked up and made an oh-how-cute face, but his hands didn't leave Mamie's head.

"What kinds of dogs do you boys have?" Lee asked.

"I have a Yorkie. His name is Rock Hudson," said the bearded one, "and he just adopted a labradoodle. Zaza."

"Well," I said, "she is what she is."

"Exactly!" said the scruffy one, turning to his bearded friend. "See? He gets it."

"Wait," said Lee, pointing to the bearded one. "You've got a dog, and he has another dog. You're not together? I mean, *together* together."

"No," they said in unison.

"I'm married, but not to him," said the bearded one.

"Really!" said Lee, pointing a finger at me. "I'm married but not to him too."

"We're best friends from college," said the scruffy one. "This one got married and moved to Chicago and left me in Washington all alone."

"You're from Washington?" shouted Lee and Irene together. Absolutely shameless.

"Washington State or DC?" I asked.

"DC," he said.

"And you're single?" Lee asked.

The scruffy one nodded. "Where are you from?"

"He's from Washington, DC!" Lee said, now pointing at me. "*And* he's single."

Honestly, Lee's desire to be a matchmaker was sweet, but even Dolly Levi was subtler in her approach. I turned to Jean and Irene for moral support, but their faces didn't register empathy. Instead, they seemed to mirror Lee's mania. It was clear the only way to save myself from humiliation at their hands was to take the reins myself.

I turned to the scruffy one and extended my hand. "I'm Charlie."

"Everett," the scruffy one said, shaking it. "And this is Tanner."

"Well, this is Lee," I said. "And Jean and Irene."

"We're his lesbian mothers," Jean said, taking Tanner's hand.

Tanner shook Lee's hand next, and then Irene. All the while Everett's hand remained in mine. I'll admit, I didn't hate it.

"How long are you boys in town?" Irene asked.

"Just through Tuesday," Tanner said. "You?"

"We head back on Wednesday," I said. "So maybe we'll run into you again while we're here."

Everett finally took his hand back. "I hope so," he said. "You'll be at the Tea Dance later?"

"Yes!" Lee said.

"We were planning on it, yeah," I said.

I looked up at Everett's face. His black hair complemented his horn-rimmed glasses. Noticing my gaze, he smiled. His teeth were very white and slightly crooked, and each cheek sported an adorable dimple. It occurred to me to flirt with him. I thought I should probably smile back, and realized immediately I was smiling already.

Face-to-face with a cute single man I'd very much like to kiss later that evening, my automatic response was to retreat into my shell, like one of the leatherback turtles swimming all around us in the Cape Cod Bay. What if he didn't like me? What if he found me physically repulsive? What if he was a lousy kisser like Bunny, or a habitual liar like Freddie, or a gambling addict, or severely incontinent? What if he broke my heart eventually? These questions swirled around my head, each representing one of the million ways this as-yet-unhatched romance could go horribly, humiliatingly wrong.

But I suddenly didn't care. I barely knew Everett, but I wanted to get to know him better. Sure, he might break my heart, but there was also the chance that knowing him, even for a short time, might be wonderful. There were no guarantees. On the off chance he might want to get to know me too, I decided to poke my head out of my shell and take a look around.

"Tea Dance can get pretty crowded," I said, handing Everett my phone. "Put your number in there, and I'll text you when we get there."

Everett didn't seem to hesitate as he recorded his digits in my phone. Tanner poked his arm playfully, but he seemed to take no notice. He handed the phone back to me and gave me another toothy grin.

I sent a text message to the number he'd provided me. *This is Charlie*, I typed, and hit Send.

"Okay, now you've got mine too," I said. "See you tonight."

"Yeah," Everett said. "Yeah, great."

Tanner and Everett each grabbed their suitcases and pulled them away from us.

"You work fast," I could hear Tanner say as they spirited away.

"Shut up," Everett said.

As I turned back to my little family, I saw nothing but wide eyes and open mouths.

"Who are you," Irene asked, "and what have you done with Charlie Vernon?"

I smiled and shrugged. "What can I tell you?" I said, scratching Mamie's head. "It's good to have a wingman."

I raised a champagne glass, prompting my friends to do the same. As we clinked and drank, I caressed Mamie's neck with my other hand. She looked up at me, panting. Her big brown eyes shone with love.

"There's a good girl," I said.

About the Author

Eric Peterson is a novelist and playwright. His plays include an adaptation of Nathaniel Hawthorne's *The House of the Seven Gables*, *Seven Strangers in a Circle* (nominee, Best Play, Washington Theatre Festival), and *Afterglow*, which has been performed throughout the US and Europe and was made into a short film. He has been a regular contributor to *Letters from CAMP Rehoboth* and *NBC Out*, and cohosts *The Rewind Project*, a podcast about old movies and modern times. For the past two decades, Eric has been an organizational Diversity, Equity, and Inclusion (DEI) practitioner. *Loyalty, Love & Vermouth* is his first novel.

facebook.com/ecp.writer
twitter.com/RedSevenEric

Books Available From Bold Strokes Books

Busy Ain't the Half of It by Frederick Smith and Chaz Lamar Cruz. Elijah and Justin seek happily-ever-afters in LA, but are they too busy to notice happiness when it's there? (978-1-63555-944-6)

Pursuit: A Victorian Entertainment by Felice Picano. An intelligent, handsome, ruthlessly ambitious young man who rose from the slums to become the right-hand man of the Lord Exchequer of England will stop at nothing as he pursues his Lord's vanished wife across Continental Europe. (978-1-63555-870-8)

Best of the Wrong Reasons by Sander Santiago. For Fin Ness and Orion Starr, it takes a funeral to remind them that love is worth living for. (978-1-63555-867-8)

Coming to Life on South High by Lee Patton. Twenty-one-year-old gay virgin Gabe Rafferty's first adult decade unfolds as an unpredictable journey into sex, love, and livelihood. (978-1-63555-906-4)

Death's Prelude by David S. Pederson. In this prequel to the Detective Heath Barrington Mystery series, Heath discovers that first love changes you forever and drives you to become the person you're destined to be. (978-1-63555-786-2)

His Brother's Viscount by Stephanie Lake. Hector Somerville wants to rekindle his illicit love affair with Viscount Wentworth, but he must overcome one problem: Wentworth still loves Hector's brother. (978-1-63555-805-0)

The Dubious Gift of Dragon Blood by J. Marshall Freeman. One day Crispin is a lonely high school student—the next he is fighting a war in a land ruled by dragons, his otherworldly boyfriend at his side. (978-1-63555-725-1)

Quake City by St John Karp. Can Andre find his best friend Amy before the night devolves into a nightmare of broken hearts, malevolent drag queens, and spontaneous human combustion? Or has it always happened this way, every night, at Aunty Bob's Quake City Club? (978-1-63555-723-7)

Death Overdue by David S. Pederson. Did Heath turn to murder in an alcohol-induced haze to solve the problem of his blackmailer, or was it someone else who brought about a death overdue? (978-1-63555-711-4)

Every Summer Day by Lee Patton. Meant to celebrate every summer day, Luke's journal instead chronicles a love affair as fast-moving and possibly as fatal as his brother's brain tumor. (978-1-63555-706-0)

Everyday People by Louis Barr. When film star Diana Danning hires private eye Clint Steele to find her son, Clint turns to his former West Point barracks mate, and ex-buddy with benefits, Mars Hauser to lend his cyber espionage and digital black ops skills to the case.(978-1-63555-698-8)

Cirque des Freaks and Other Tales of Horror by Julian Lopez. Explore the pleasure of horror in this compilation that delivers like the horror classics…good ole tales of terror. (978-1-63555-689-6)

Royal Street Reveillon by Greg Herren. In this Scotty Bradley mystery, someone is killing the stars of a reality show, and it's up to Scotty Bradley and the boys to find out who. (978-1-63555-545-5)

Death Takes a Bow by David S. Pederson. Alan Keys takes part in a local stage production, but when the leading man is murdered, his partner Detective Heath Barrington is thrust into the limelight to find the killer. (978-1-63555-472-4)

Accidental Prophet by Bud Gundy. Days after his grandmother dies, Drew Morten learns his true identity and finds himself racing against time to save civilization from the apocalypse. (978-1-63555-452-6)

Counting for Thunder by Phillip Irwin Cooper. A struggling actor returns to the Deep South to manage a family crisis but finds love and ultimately his own voice as his mother is regaining hers for possibly the last time. (978-1-63555-450-2)

Of Echoes Born by 'Nathan Burgoine. A collection of queer fantasy short stories set in Canada from Lambda Literary Award finalist 'Nathan Burgoine. (978-1-63555-096-2)